Praise for Rachel Yoder's

nightbitch

A Vulture and *Esquire* Best Book of the Year

Longlisted for the VCU Cabell First Novelist Award

Longlisted for the PEN/Hemingway Award for Debut Novel

"*Nightbitch* is fantastically rendered. Yoder's voice is razor-sharp, poignant and wry. While it's seeped in mythical qualities, the haunting premise doesn't seem that far-fetched. *Nightbitch* is a stunning modern feminist fable that shouldn't be missed." —*The Seattle Times*

"[*Nightbitch*] feels like reading a deliciously long text from your smartest friend, with a hint of Kafka, if Kafka lived in the age of mommy bloggers and designer doggy raincoats. No need to be a parent, a dog owner, or a fan of magical realism to enjoy; Yoder writes about contemporary anxieties with so much intelligence and charm that she can cause you to reflect without spiraling into deep depression. That's a feat, these days, greater than metamorphosis." —*Glamour*

"Electric." —*Entertainment Weekly*

"[*Nightbitch*] might well be the debut of the year. A feral fairy tale of maternal dissatisfaction, it's best to go into this one knowing as little [as] possible, the better to let Yoder work her devious magic on you." —*Chicago Review of Books*

"Wild and strangely hopeful, *Nightbitch*'s success lies in Yoder's controlled style . . . and its leap just beyond reality."

—Vulture

"If you're a fan of Angela Carter, Miranda July or Charlotte Perkins Gilman, you won't want to miss this." —Refinery29

"Rather than childbirth twisted into hideous shapes by the male artistic eye, in this book art crawls out of motherhood with an exhausted, sweating, blood-strewn, but joyous howl. . . . Creativity and motherhood don't need to be at each other's throats, like vampires or zombies. In *Nightbitch* they feed in the same night on the same wild prey."

—*The Boston Globe*

"A feral, unholy marriage of Tillie Olsen and Kafka—*Nightbitch* is an incredible feat." —Carmen Maria Machado, *New York Times* bestselling author of *In the Dream House*

"I could not love a novel more than Rachel Yoder's *Nightbitch*. It's such a uniquely brilliant book, one that looks at the intersection of motherhood and art, the terror of 'a thousand artless afternoons.' It is so wonderfully observant, so precise, and yet manages to expand and expand upon those initial concerns, turning magical, dark, and funny."

—Kevin Wilson, *New York Times* bestselling author of *Nothing to See Here*

"A high-wire act of a novel that expertly balances the uncanny and quotidian moments of early motherhood. Yoder's writing is graceful, funny, and unnerving as hell." —Jenny Offill, *New York Times* bestselling author of *Weather*

Rachel Yoder

nightbitch

Rachel Yoder grew up in a Mennonite community in the Appalachian foothills of eastern Ohio and now lives in Iowa City with her husband and son. She is a founding editor of *draft: the journal of process* and holds MFAs from the University of Arizona (fiction) and the University of Iowa (nonfiction), where she was an Iowa Arts fellow.

nightbitch

nightbitch

———

RACHEL YODER

ANCHOR BOOKS

A Division of Penguin Random House LLC

New York

FIRST ANCHOR BOOKS EDITION 2022

The Library of Congress has cataloged the Doubleday edition as follows:
Names: Yoder, Rachel, [date] author.
Title: Nightbitch : a novel / Rachel Yoder.
Description: First edition. | New York : Doubleday, 2021.
Identifiers: LCCN 2021933498 (print)
Subjects: LCSH: Artists—Fiction. | Mothers—Fiction. |
Housewives—Fiction. | Metamorphosis—Fiction. | Dogs—Fiction.
Classification: LCC PS3625.O3385 N54 2021 (print) | DDC 813/.6—dc23
LC record available at https://lccn.loc.gov/2021933498

Anchor Books Trade Paperback ISBN: 978-0-593-31214-8
eBook ISBN: 978-0-385-54682-9

Book design by Maria Carella

anchorbooks.com

Printed in the United States of America
10 9 8

FOR MY MOM

&

FOR ALL THE MOMS

one

When she had referred to herself as Nightbitch, she meant it as a good-natured self-deprecating joke—because that's the sort of lady she was, a good sport, able to poke fun at herself, definitely not uptight, not wound really tight, not so freakishly tight that she couldn't see the humor in a light-hearted not-meant-as-an-insult situation—but in the days following this new naming, she found the patch of coarse black hair sprouting from the base of her neck and was, like, *What the fuck.*

I think I'm turning into a dog, she said to her husband when he arrived home after a week away for work. He laughed and she didn't.

She had hoped he wouldn't laugh. She had hoped, that week as she lay in bed, wondering if she was turning into a dog, that when she said those words to her husband, he would tip his head to one side and ask for clarification. She had hoped he would take her concerns seriously. But as soon as she said the words, she saw this was impossible.

Seriously, she insisted. I have this weird hair on my neck.

She lifted her normal hair to show him the black patch. He rubbed it with his fingers and said, Yeah, you're definitely a dog.

To her credit, she did appear more hirsute than usual. Her unruly hair moved about her head and shoulders like a cloud of wasps. Her brows caterpillared across her forehead with unplucked growth. She had even witnessed two black hairs curling from her chin and, in the right light—in *any* light at all, to be honest—you could see the five o'clock shadow of her mustache as it grew back in after her laser treatments. Had she always had so much hair on her arms? Descending the edge of her jaw from her hairline? And was it normal to have patches of hair on the tops of your feet?

And look at my teeth, she said, baring her teeth and pointing to her canines. She was convinced they had grown, and the tips had narrowed to ferocious points that could cut a finger with a mere prick. Why, she had nearly cut hers during her nightly examination in the bathroom. Every night, when her husband was gone and their son was happily playing with trains in his pajamas, she stood at the mirror and pulled her lips back from her teeth, turned her head from side to side, then tilted her head back and looked at her teeth from that bottom-up angle, searched the Internet on her phone for pictures of canines to which she might compare her own, tapped her teeth with her fingernails, told herself she was being silly, then searched *humans with dog teeth* on her phone, searched *do humans and dogs share a common ancestor*, searched *human animal hybrid* and *recessive animal genes in humans* and *research human animal genes legacy*, searched *werewolves*, searched *real werewolves in history*, searched (somewhat inexplicably) *witches*, searched (somewhat relatedly) *hysteria 19th century*, and then, since she wanted to, searched *rest cures* and *The Yellow Wallpaper*, and she reread *The Yellow Wallpaper*, which she had once read in college, then stared blankly for a while at nothing in particular while sitting on the toilet, then stopped searching altogether.

Touch it, she insisted, pointing to her tooth. Her husband reached out and prodded the tip of her canine with his pointer finger.

Ow! he said, pulling his hand back and cradling it close

to his body. Just kidding, he said as he held up an unscathed finger and waggled it at her face.

Your tooth looks the same to me. You always think something's wrong with you, he said pleasantly.

Her husband was an engineer. He specialized in "quality control." What precisely this meant, the mother was not entirely sure. So he went around and looked at machines to make sure they were maximizing efficiency? Adjusted systems to keep them humming along at higher frequencies? Read output reports and made suggestions toward improvement? Sure. Whatever.

What she did know was that he had little time for feelings, a condescending patience for intuition, and scoffed openly at talk unsupported by peer-reviewed scientific studies or statistics. Still, he was a good man, a caring man, an affable man, whom she appreciated very much, despite everything. She was, after all, prone to indecision, doubling back on things she had once felt but had since come to feel differently about. She was prone to anxiety, to worry, to a sensation in her chest that her heart might explode. She ran hot. She buzzed. Either she needed to keep busy or else she needed to lie down and sleep. Her husband, on the other hand, needed nothing whatsoever.

No wonder, then, that they deferred to his judgment, his good levelheaded judgment, his engineer's evenness. Of course there was nothing wrong with her. This she told herself as they lay in bed, their child between them, asleep and wedging his toes beneath her leg.

I think I should sleep in the guest room, she whispered to her husband.

Why? he whispered back.

I get so angry now. At night, she said. He didn't respond. I think I just need a good night's sleep, she added.

Okay, he said.

She rolled from bed without a sound and felt her way down the stairs and tucked into the clean sheets of the guest bed. She rubbed the patch of coarse hair on the back of her neck to soothe herself, then ran her tongue over the sharp edges of her teeth. In this way, she fell into a thick and unbothered sleep.

ONE DAY, THE MOTHER was a mother, but then, one night, she was quite suddenly something else.

Yes, it had been June, and, yes, her husband had been gone the entire week. In fact, it was his twenty-second weeklong absence that year, a year in which only twenty-four weeks in total had passed, not that anyone was counting.

Yes, the boy had an ear infection that week and had slept only in fitful bouts. Yes, he had not really been napping well or even at all.

Yes, she was experiencing intense PMS for the first time in her life, at age thirty-seven.

And it was then, on a regular Friday, in the deepest hours of night, when the boy awoke there in bed, between his mother and father, for he did not—he *would not*—sleep in his own. It was the third or fourth time that night he had stirred. She had lost track.

At first she did nothing, waiting for her husband to wake, which he did not, because that wasn't a thing he ever did. She waited longer than she usually did, waited and waited, the boy wailing while she lay as still as a corpse, patiently waiting for the day when her corpse self would miraculously be reanimated and taken into the Kingdom of the Chosen, where it would create an astonishing art installation composed of many aesthetically interesting beds. The corpse would have unlimited child-care and be able to hang out and go to show openings and drink corpse wine with the other corpses when-ever it wanted, because that was heaven. That was it.

She lay there as long as she could without making a sound, a movement. Her child's screams fanned a flame of rage that flickered in her chest.

That single, white-hot light at the center of the dark-ness of herself—that was the point of origin from which she birthed something new, from which all women do.

You light a fire early in your girlhood. You stoke it and tend it. You protect it at all costs. You don't let it rage into a mountain of light, because that's not becoming of a girl. You keep it secret. You let it burn. You look into the eyes of other girls and see their fires flickering there, offer conspiratorial nods, never speak aloud of a near-unbearable heat, a growing conflagration.

You tend the flame because if you don't you're stuck, in the cold, on your own, doomed to *seasonal layers*, doomed to *practicality*, doomed to *this is just the way things are*, doomed to *settling* and *understanding* and *reasoning* and *agreeing* and *seeing it another way* and *seeing it his way* and *seeing it from all the other ways but your own*.

And upon hearing the boy's scream, the particular pitch and slice, she saw the flame behind her closed eyes. For a moment, it quivered on unseen air, then, at once, lengthened and thinned, paused, and dropped with a *whump* into her chest, then deeper into her belly, setting her aflame.

Goooooo baaaarg EEEEeeeeep, she gargled, sleep-drunk, only half awake. She was trying to say something—*Go back to sleep*, perhaps—but instead the words came out in an undulat-ing sweep of grunts and squeals, sounds she'd only ever heard long before, during her girlhood, from her grandmother's husky as it begged at the door for dinner scraps. She had never liked that dog, first because its eyes were ice blue—the eyes of the undead—and, moreover, because of the way it sounded, almost human. And now those same sounds slipped from her own mouth.

The strangeness of the sound, and then the memory of the husky, woke her more than she would have liked.

Stop! she said sharply to the child, her husband an unmoving mass on the other side of the boy, who rolled and kicked, his cries turning to screams.

Stop. Stop. *Stop!* she barked, rolling over to face the boy.

His fucking binky! she growled meanly to her husband, then turned away from them both and stuck a finger in one ear.

The boy cried and cried, and her husband did nothing and nothing. The fire roared large, larger, blistering hot, until it threatened to consume her entirely, and it was then she rose with a great howl, flung the sheets from her, reached for the bedside light, in her haste knocked the lamp to the floor and heard it shatter, moaned with rage and staggered around the bed, found the other bedside lamp, then turned the switch to find her husband sitting in bed, holding the cowering boy, binky now in mouth.

Her hair was long and unkempt and, suspended within it, small bits of leaves, a dust of cracker or bread, unidentified white fluff. She breathed heavily from her mouth. Smears of blood painted her path around the bed, tiny shards of lamp base now embedded in the tender skin of her feet, though this the mother did not notice, or perhaps she did not care. Her eyes narrowed, and she sniffed the air. She skulked back to her side of the bed, wrapped herself in the blankets and, without helping, without offering a hand, without care, promptly plummeted into a hard and drowning sleep.

In the morning, she stood, disheveled, in the dirty kitchen, drinking coffee, a load of bloodied sheets churning in the washer, her feet washed and bandaged. The boy played with his train set in the living room, cooing and babbling and laughing. Her husband, such a chipper man, buttered a piece of blackened toast.

You were kind of . . . He paused, thinking, then continued: . . . a bitch last night.

He chuckled to show it wasn't meant meanly, just as observation.

Night bitch, she said, without pause. I am Nightbitch.

They both laughed then, because what else were they supposed to do? Her anger, her bitterness, her coldness in that darkest part of the night surprised even her. She wanted to think she had become another person altogether the night before, but she knew the horrible truth, that Nightbitch had always been there, not even that far below the surface.

No one could have predicted such an arrival, for years up until that point she had been the very picture of a mother, self-sacrificing and domestic, un-gripey, un-grumpy, refreshed even after unrefreshing nights of nonsleep, nursing the baby and rocking the baby and shushing the baby while her kind husband snored and slept or, actually, most of the time, was not even there.

He had a job. He made money. He was off on his work trips, *Goodbye!* and *I love you!* and kisses with a brisk wave of the hand and twinkle of the eye. She stood with the babe in arms and watched him back the car from the driveway. Her undergraduate degree was from a prestigious university, better than the one he had attended. She held two master's degrees, whereas he held none. (She also held a baby.) It shouldn't have been a contest, and it wasn't, was it? No, definitely not. She would never think of her husband in such competitive terms, but she did fault herself for choosing such an impractical field as studio art. What a nut she had been, this mother! She was just a lady who liked art, and that was no way to make a career or make money, no matter how much you liked art, no matter how talented you might be at making it.

She pushed to the very back of her mind the fact that she'd had a job, before the baby, to which she'd actively referred as her "dream job," running a community gallery, bringing in artists whose work she felt would expand the collective artistic consciousness of their small Midwestern town, programming art classes, coordinating with schools on student projects, immersing herself in art and the art world and doing something she believed in, and, moreover, actually getting *paid* to do such a job, working in the arts, one of those rare and magical jobs. Of course, the breadth of work required by such a job was not commensurate with the pay, but she had come just to be grateful, you know? Grateful that she even got to work in the art world, despite the amount of work. Her classmates from grad school would kill for such a job, and she did it happily.

But then the baby. She had considered it might present a complication, but not anything she couldn't handle. After all, women didn't have to stop their lives now, in this day and age, for babies. They could work in the office and work at home. They could work and work and work around the clock if they wanted! This was their right. But what she hadn't thought enough about were the show openings in the evenings, and arts classes on the weekends, and early-morning before-school meetings with teachers, and after-work receptions. With a husband out of town and a baby at home, this sort of schedule no longer worked. Who would pick up the baby from day care or put it to bed? She couldn't bring him to a black-tie gala, no matter how progressive the crowd. She could not manage a volunteer docent staff of twenty-five, or lead a strategic planning session with her board of directors while nursing.

She tried. For a time, she did indeed try. After all, she was working her dream job. Her dream job! That's why, despite the baby, the tiny three-month-old baby and the only day care in town with an opening and its nursery lined with cribs and the loud, tired women feeding the babies formula through plastic nipples, she worked. It was a job she had always wanted. She was advancing in her career. She was growing up. She was succeeding. And she had a baby.

And all she could give him was her milk. She could give him two hours after day care, two hours before, countless hours of staring at him as he slept. (She would think: Please don't forget me. Or do forget me if it will make you happier. Or maybe just forget that I left you alone for eight to nine hours a day during your infancy, with women who let you lie on the linoleum floor and cry, cry for hours. He used to cry a *lot*, one of them told her months later, and it was as if, with this offhanded statement of ordinary fact, the day-care worker had sunk a finely sharpened blade into the mother's midsection, violently, for the mother felt severely—mortally, eternally—wounded and, at the same time, murderous: why had the worker not *picked up* her son, most beloved? How had she resisted his cries? To tell the mother casually about her endlessly crying son, alone, on the linoleum floor, was a particular cruelty the mother would dwell on for weeks. After all, wasn't it actually, entirely, *her* fault to begin with that she had to leave her son in such a place? It was. It was.)

And the milk. The milk! The milk was so important! This cannot be stressed enough. It was the most important thing in the entire world of the infant, the books would have all the mothers believe, and this mother believed.

The lactation room might as well have been the smallest, ugliest chapel in the entire institutional building the gallery shared with the university, the holiest little room, with a sink and counter and chair, fluorescent lights, no ventilation.

Where was the mother's hymnal with songs of worship and praise? She wanted to sing about babies and breasts and milk and skin on skin, warm babies that were supple and yeasty like freshly baked loaves of bread, so delicious, smell them. Smell.

Where was her fucking hymnal?

But there was no hymnal, just the pump, a motor, tubing, plastic, static electricity, sweat-dampened clothing, stale air, industrial sanitizer, so much anxiety, and a dream job.

There was no baby.

And the mother wasn't grateful.

She visited the lactation room one, two, three times daily. The tubing and plasticity. The motorized suck. Her shirts with dampened armpits and the static in her hair when she pulled sweaters over her head. The dress with the zipper down the back that was hard to unzip. The slots of time she scheduled on her computer calendar marked PRIVATE. Another angry mother knocking on the door because she was late or early or just wrong. Wrong.

And of course there was the sanitizing, the stiff paper towels, the policy of DO NOT LEAVE BEHIND ANY PARTS TO DRY, PLS RESPECT OTHER USERS, the spray can of industrial sanitizer to clean up the human bodily fluids that might be left behind.

Who ever thought a mother would need to sanitize a counter of the milk meant for her baby? The milk should be sopped up using a ceremonial rag that's then set at the foot of a towering, infinitely beautiful sculpture carved to honor the Eternal Mother, Giver of Life and Maker of All Things. This, or else a small white kitten—preferably the runt of the litter—should be kept in the room, along with a very soft pillow, some good cat food, and cold, fresh water, and this kitten should be offered the wayward drops of milk, the occasional tiny spill.

She left behind a bag of tubing and plasticity one day, because who would steal it? No one stole it, but a part went missing, the part that suctions to the breast. Who would take just that part? Another mother? She might have cried at the loss. She can't remember now. She never left the bag behind again because of this cosmic punishment. That's what she thought it was. That's what it felt like.

(Where does one acquire a new suction thingy? What is it even called, that part of the machinery? She would need to search for it online, commit time to research. She did not have any time for research. She did not have time to procure a name for the thingy, then to procure a new thingy.)

The room was not ventilated, so the door needed to be propped open when not in use, but the triangle stop had been flattened and gnarled. The door was heavy. Who had time to prop? But what of the other mothers? Use the chair instead to prop. Kick the doorstop in harder. Find a way. Consider the other mothers. Be grateful that you have this room. Some working mothers have no such thing. Be grateful.

Always in a hurry. Hurry, breasts. Hurry up and relax, then let the milk come. It's her fault if the milk doesn't come. Too much coffee. Not enough food. You need to figure out a way to minimize stress. Eat an energy bar. Eat these nuts. Eat an entire bar of chocolate while at the same time holding the device against your breasts. Take these special herbal pills. Eat lots of oatmeal. Figure out how to balance it all. Drink an entire liter of water in the hope of let-down. Meditate. Breathe deeply. You have eight more meetings today.

There was never enough milk for the baby. He was getting so big. All he wanted was milk, and there was not enough time or milk or hands. The day care closed at six, so no late meetings, must account for traffic, the walk to the parking garage, weather. Do not forget the milk. DO NOT FORGET THE MILK.

She forgot the milk one evening. She left it on top of the machine where she inserted her parking ticket to pay the toll. Crying, she drove the sleeping baby from day care back to the parking garage, called Security.

Yes, someone turned in your milk, the man said.

She sobbed. And the security guard brought her the lost, and found, milk. He delivered it to her car window, because she could not even get out of the car. There was a baby sleeping in the back. She cried as she drove home.

Imagine this person, finding a small box containing two bottles of still-warm milk, taking that small box back into the small, sad mall attached to the parking garage, wandering to find the security office, saying to the guard, I've found some milk. This must be precious to the owner. I hope it finds its way back to her. And the guard placing the small box in the mini-fridge in his office, shaking his head at the miracle of the find, the kindness of it, or at the mother's loss, or at her lack of care—how could a person be so thoughtless?—or at all of it, all at once.

The mother would like to thank the finder of the milk. She would like to tell the person, You are one of the kindest people I have ever known, even though I never knew you.

As she walked to a lunch meeting—because who needs time to eat when you could also be working?—she began to have suspicions. And later, as she responded to e-mails on her phone with her right hand while pressing both breast pumps to her breasts with her left, the mother's thinking began to coalesce into expansive conspiracy theories, but the kind of conspiracy theories that actually wind up being true.

Her parents would have said she was *touched*, would have called her *touched* and perhaps *cursed* and would have something to add about *the devil,* had they any idea of her thoughts, which they didn't, because they never called and she never called, so they knew nearly nothing about each other these days. The mother was certain they, too, were responsible for the many injustices currently besetting her, as well as her paranoia about turning into a dog, responsible in some foundational way, but couldn't specify exactly how, and, rather, indulged in a general rage directed at the past and to the east, where they lived, hundreds of miles away.

Truly, though, her parents were the least of her worries, since the *whole fucking thing* was a sham, the working and pumping and hurrying and not holding her baby. She inflated with mother-rage and composed elaborate, emotional arguments against the system and capitalism and the patriarchy and then religion and gender roles and biology.

She wanted to share these theories one day at the coffee shop, to which another kind working mother had invited her, a working mother who was also an artist, who had been in the same graduate program, who now taught at the university they had both attended and made art and had seamlessly transitioned into motherhood without so much as a mean-spirited hiccup. The mother had grimly watched at a distance—on social media, where else—as the working mother posted milestones, *First day of day care!* and *Helping Mommy with her installation*, the baby strapped to the working mother's chest as she did something with a pile of chicken wire in a gallery.

Why can't I do that? she always asked herself. How can it be that easy?

So how do you like being a working mother? the other working mother asked, and the mother—the tired, unhappy working mother, working her dream job and not holding her baby—that mother stared stupidly and wanted to present her theories about how this was all a trick, a trick to get them to do everything, a trick they could not escape. Yet her brain no longer worked as it once had. The friendly working mom waited. Was she supposed to say something? What was a "conversation"?

No, the mother finally said. I think *working mother* is perhaps the most nonsensical concept ever concocted. I mean, who isn't a working mother? And then add a paid job to it, so what are you then? A working working mother? Imagine saying working father.

Ha! she spat bitterly, without having even known how bitter she truly was.

The kind working mother nodded with pity on her face. The other mom—the mom who did not sleep and had a baby and worked her dream job, the mom who was perhaps struggling, who needed some support, who was doing her best . . . but yeesh—was not making this look like it should look. Appearances. We can have it all. Why was she so ungrateful?

That night, the mother cried as she held her sleeping baby after work, because she saw him awake for only an hour, maybe two, each day. He refused to nap at day care and came home exhausted, wanting only her milk and to be held and to sleep in his mother's arms. She cried holding him, and then he cried when she put him down. He wanted only to be held, all the time, and really she couldn't blame him, so she strapped him to her chest and e-mailed into the night until she and the baby both fell into bed.

And so, when it had come time to make a baby and then make a decision, it was her husband who made more money and she who made less, which ensured it was she who was made to stay home. It was just that simple.

At the time, when decisions had to be made, she had truly wanted to stay home—she was, in a word, exhausted—though she had never wanted such a thing before. And, honestly, what a privilege. What a treat. She understood that she was just a privileged, overeducated lady in the middle of America living the dream of holding her baby twenty-four hours a day. According to basically everyone's standards, she had nothing to complain about, ever, after that point and possibly even leading up to it. In fact, wasn't it a bit, you know, hoity-toity, a bit oblivious middle-class white lady of her, even to think about complaining? If she read the articles, examined the data, contemplated her lot in life, her place in society, her historical role in the oppression of everyone other than white men, she really had not even a sparse spot of yard on which to stand and emit one single strangled scream.

But, as babies do, hers grew. It widened and lengthened. It grew more charming and less. It walked, but it didn't talk until well after medically-agreed-upon speech milestones had been surpassed, because it had a near-psychic bond with the mother, who could intuit its needs via the position of its eyes or tilt of its hands. In an essential way, at that point in the boy's life, she was the only person in the entire world who could understand him, understand this unspoken language only the two of them shared. He cried when she tried to leave him with a family friend, and then cried when she successfully left him with a babysitter, and then cried even when she left him with her husband because she had to go get groceries and really just wanted to enjoy it, get a coffee and put it in the little holder that attached to the side of the cart, and really examine the produce, you know, look at it and touch it and take her time. She just wanted one shopping trip to herself, and yet they all wound up going together—packing up the diaper bag with snacks and wipes and a bottle of water and a change of clothes and a selection of toys and should we bring a book?—because the boy had been sad to see her go even though his very own father, who was never there, would have finally been there with him, just the two of them, at home, but no, the child would not have it.

Yes, indeed, she was a good mother, one of the very best.

A testament to her goodness: that preternatural ability to wake and wake and wake again, night after night, ever since the day the boy was born. Her husband—bless his heart—had never done well with sleep deprivation, yet she, surprisingly, had taken to it as if she hadn't been a lifelong oversleeper, as if waking at all hours of the night and getting up at 5:30 a.m. was something she was somehow genetically programmed for. While, yes, she had indeed been exhausted by this life, the peculiar thing was that she had not been tired. Overworked, pushed to her limit, bedraggled and bitter and on the verge, indeed, but each morning she rose and stayed upright for the entire day, overcome as she was by a near-miraculous ability to simply *not need sleep* in the way she once had.

I'm not tired! she had said during her darkest days of working, and continued to intone, clear-eyed and astonished after a year at home, mostly by herself, with her young ward.

I'm fine! she declared somewhat hesitantly to no one in particular. And she had been fine. She nursed him and walked through the neighborhood with a cooing bundle strapped to her chest. She rocked him and napped with him and cooked and cleaned. She slept, but mostly she did not sleep, and it was fine, but then the boy turned two, and with that, something in her turned as well.

She didn't want to be Nightbitch, wouldn't have chosen it if she felt she did indeed have such a choice. And her husband: she didn't want always to be angry at him, for she did, she really did, love him. It was just so hard to conjure these days.

Of course, there had been reasons she fell in love with her husband, despite his overly rational tendencies. She was—or at least had been at one point—an artist, and so it seems her husband must have in some way distinguished himself from other engineers, *regular* engineers, and indeed he had. When she first met him, back in grad school, he had been working for a local DNA company and living in a basement apartment with another thin, pale, twenty-something man who rarely talked, preferring the company of his computer to human interaction. The mother had been intrigued by her husband's job—*You make DNA?* she had asked him. *What are you? Some sort of evil wizard?*—and he in turn was delighted by her questions, answering them with a good deal of technical lingo and lab-speak, at which she squinted and nodded, then asked more questions. Yes, he had come to her art shows and had reveled in her work, as much as a DNA technician could revel. And, yes, he had been a good sport. He had enjoyed himself. But what finally made her fall in love with him was a thing he referred to as his Folder.

Would you like to see my Folder? he asked one evening as his roommate silently murdered ninjas on his computer while wearing headphones, because he was, after all, polite. Her future husband's computer was on the opposite side of the living room, and he bade her sit on his lap, and proceeded to open a little yellow folder on his computer that said it contained more than eighty thousand items.

This is where I keep all the good things I find on the Internet, he said, and proceeded to flip through the items, one by one, without explanation. A short clip of a naked woman farting into a heavily iced chocolate cake. A cute white puppy photoshopped with human eyes and teeth. A naked man in a mask peeing on a pile of stuffed animals. A fat cat walking on a treadmill. An old man with a cactus up his butt. A man covered in slices of bread on a beach with a horde of seagulls around him. A sloth sitting at a classroom desk with a notebook opened in front of it. Sex dolls, Furries. Weird little people and weird little situations, inexplicable, funny, perplexing, disturbing. And her favorite: two naked Japanese ladies squatting and peeing on a small octopus, which, understandably, squirmed away from them on the floor.

Wow, she said.

Poor octopus, he said.

Why are they doing that? she asked.

I guess they're into it, he said. I really have no idea.

Although another person might have been offended or alarmed by such an array of the human experience, the mother was not. To the contrary, she absolutely swooned when her husband, then just a strange man she had happened upon and was getting to know, would say stuff like *Just look at these strange humans*—without a hint of judgment or disdain, with nothing but pure fascination, pure wonder. It was this wonder the mother loved then and continued to love passionately: how wonderful to find a person who delighted in all the aberrations and quirks of human behavior. It was, perhaps, the best quality a person could have, she saw in that moment, there on his lap, and she decided she would marry him.

So, yes, he was an engineer, but he also had a Folder, and a collection of messed-up stuffed animals on his dresser (some with their heads on upside down), and a carnivorous frog named Hopkin in an aquarium by his bed. Since she had fallen in love with him, the frog had died and his job had changed, but the Folder abided, though they hadn't looked at it in years now, for she could no longer stomach it, ever since she'd had the baby. Humanity and all it entailed was too much, far too much, given the great new weight of humanity that had entered into their home with the birth of their son.

SHE WAS NO LONGER well rested, well fed, well. She was tired and cranky and worried about her body, whether it was changing and what the changes meant. And she dreaded the nights, those long dark nights, promising herself she would not yell when the boy woke, then yelling, then apologizing, pulling him to her, saying *Shhh* and *I'm sorry* and *It's all right.*

She was so, so tired, was the thing.

You really should stop worrying about your hair growth or whatever and get on top of your week, her husband suggested just before he left again, at the end of the forty-eight-hour stretch of time he had been home that weekend. Structure, you know? Make a plan. Draw up a schedule. Treat it like it's your job. Happiness is a choice, he said.

She wanted to say something, or maybe slap him right across his talking face, but instead she tried to take his suggestion to heart. He only wanted what was best for her. Perhaps he was right.

And so, although it was Monday yet again and, yes, her husband was gone again, she was choosing happiness this week. She was determined to really get ahead of her obsessing, to stop with the negative thoughts, the daydreaming about turning into a dog (even though the coarse patch of hair had lengthened and spread), the worst-case scenarios and hypochondria and Internet searches. She had made a weekly schedule. She had meal-planned.

Since happiness was a choice, today she chose motherhood. Today she chose art. Today she would beautifully merge the two and in doing so find happiness. She loved her positive outlook! She would be present to the child all morning, she wouldn't look at her phone, she would be filled with inspiration by his play, and then, at naptime, she would pull out all her old art stuff and get inspired, start working on something new. That she didn't have a project in mind, that she hadn't been inspired for years, that she feared opening the closet where she had stashed former projects, old supplies—all that was silly. She just needed to have some confidence. Believe in herself. Make the time.

She had once, in grad school, conceptualized an entire outdoor nighttime installation that involved transforming a local playground into a sort of wonderful nightmare, the geodesic climbing dome covered with an enormous many-layered skirt and, atop the dome, her friend dressed as a human-sized white rabbit, wearing the dome skirt. The swings became the flicking furry tails of invisible animals. The metal bars on which they were suspended she covered with iridescent fabrics so as to invoke something reptilian. The main play structure she made into a many-headed and -legged and -armed beast out of whose mouth show goers fanciful enough to take a ride down the slide emerged, coated in glitter and spangles that had been deposited on them as they descended. She got the feeling her professors and classmates did not find this work serious enough, though. She had, after all, included glitter in the final project, and so, when she applied to programs for her graduate art degree, she really laid into her *unique upbringing* in her personal statement, emphasizing her family's *homesteader aesthetic*, the folk traditions with which she was familiar, her desire to *transform and elevate* traditional farm skills and domestic know-how to art. Once admitted, with a scholarship based on her stoic come-to-Jesus Appalachian farm upbringing—which she had actually been running away from since childhood, only to capitalize on it when she decided it would serve her, but whatever—she undertook the collection of the plentiful roadkill found in the area surrounding her Midwestern university.

She took the broken bodies of deer, raccoons, rabbits, coyotes, and stripped the rotting meat from the bones, cleaned and bleached the bones, sanded them and polished them, donning a full-body protective suit and monstrous gas mask to keep the bone dust from her clothes, her lungs. She hollowed the bones with jeweler tools, then plated the insides with gold or silver. When she could afford it, she inlaid gems. She went on to wander through the surrounding forests, identifying cherry and walnut and pine, cutting off branches, and then taking them to be cured. She smoothed and carved the wood, combined it with bones and metals and even some furs, taking these elements and creating the skeletons of new, mythical animals. For this she was praised hugely. The artistry! her professors exclaimed. The skill set required to prepare the bones, refine them, add to them fine metals and gems! She had not only created some truly imaginative and original pieces but also showcased a vast array of sophisticated techniques.

Yet now there was nothing. Not a single creative impulse inside her, no matter how she searched. During her pregnancy, during the sleepless nights in the final trimester, she stared at her phone for hours and became obsessed with what some might call performance artists but what she thought of as people who were *engaged deeply in real-time artistic experimentation*. She read about a married couple who undertook extensive plastic surgery to look like each other, the man getting breast implants, the woman sculpting her nose so as to bring it into closer alignment with her husband's. It was a lifelong project, not quite performance art but something more profound, the line between their lives and their art erased.

The mother became preoccupied with this idea—the idea of no boundaries—and researched more, about the Eastern European showman who had started out early in his career in a traveling circus yet ended up undertaking a series of what he called "performative life experiments": a three-year stint of silence, living naked in a storefront window for a month, and, most famously, inducing amnesia and then working for years to recover the particulars of his former life.

And what about the Frenchwoman who hired private investigators to follow her lovers and then created entire art shows around this? Who put her own psychiatric surveys, given to her by a doctor, on display in exhibitions held at some of the highest-profile museums of Europe?

The mother fantasized about staging the birth of her child as an artistic happening. Could she set up a glass-sided pool in a studio where an audience might watch while she pushed the child from her body during a stoic water birth? Or perhaps she could give birth in a medical theater at the hospital, one of those rooms used for teaching where students sat up above in rows to watch. The performance would be an on-call sort of event, viewable only by those available to come at any time of the night or day.

She felt that such a performance would be better for a second child, when she knew what to expect, and so she tabled the idea, and then the baby came, and then the idea was lost for good.

She looked at her boy on the kitchen floor, playing with a metal steaming device that looked a bit like a spaceship when closed, and a big metal flower when open. He sneezed, then laughed. He was her only project. She had done the ultimate job of creation, and now she had nothing left. To keep him alive—that was the only artistic gesture she could muster.

But today she was determined to go beyond that. Start at the beginning. Back to basics. Whatever.

She masking-taped oversized sheets of paper to the kitchen floor and pulled the finger paints from the cupboard. It was just after breakfast, and the day was bright. The boy seemed tired—putting his cheek on the floor to watch the wheels of the trains turn when he pushed them along their tracks—but they just needed something new, something fun.

She pulled his pajama shirt over his head and yanked off his saggy diaper.

Do you want to paint? she asked, pointing to a plate pooled with every shade of finger paint.

You can put your hand in, your foot, she suggested. He moved his foot toward the plate and looked at her with a question.

Yes! she said, smiling. She put her own hand in to show him, then patted the paper on the floor.

He dipped his toes in, then bent and rubbed his palms in the colors.

Yes! she encouraged him.

His face lit with delight as he patted his hands on the paper and then put his whole foot on the plate, stepped backward, slipped, fell, and caught himself, but not without getting paint on his cheeks. He laughed, and she did, too. She helped him up and showed him the handprints she'd left on his belly, and he took both hands and put them in her hair.

Okay, she said, pulling them out. Okay.

The boy stood, then screamed with excitement and ran around in a circle, shaking his hands and spraying droplets of paint on the chairs, the curtains, the stove.

On the paper, honey, she said. Isn't this so fun? Yes. On the paper, though.

He jumped on the plate, then jumped on the paper, then hopped like a bunny across the wood floor, grabbed a towel, and threw it up as high as he could.

On the paper! On the paper! she said, as she tried to grab him, then slipped herself, catching the open cabinet door on the way down, which she pulled cleanly off its hinges and finally held, detached, in her hands.

The boy was now rolling on the paper, in the paint, cackling. She examined the door, the hinges, and as she did the boy took off, into the living room.

No! she yelled, nicely.

He laughed, delighted with such a game, and she said, with a very, very serious face meant to communicate just how very, very serious the situation was: I mean it. This is not a game.

This game? he asked, naked, smeared with paint.

Noooo, she warned as she edged toward him, eyebrows raised and mouth set in a stern mom-line. Not a game. You're messy! Let's stay in the kitchen.

She lunged to grab his arm, and he screamed and catapulted onto the couch, up onto the big cushions, burrowed down behind one the way he liked, to hide.

After she'd given the boy a bath, she spent the rest of the morning washing the paint from the floor, the chairs, the stove, the cabinets, the rug, the couch, as he watched cartoons. Naptime, she told herself as she cleaned. Naptime.

She put the boy down for a nap in her bed after lunch, read him books and snuggled him and sang him songs until he lay still on his back in a tangle of sheets, rosebud lips open ever so little, his long dark lashes twitching with dreams.

Really, it was her fault he needed her to be there as he fell asleep, her fault he was still sleeping in bed with her to begin with. When he was an infant, she had nursed him in the night whenever he cried. It was so easy. They lay on their sides, facing each other in the dark warmth, the baby latched to her nipple, his small, soft hands touching her chest. She fell asleep as he nursed, and he fell asleep as he nursed, rolling onto his back, a drip of milk trickling from his open mouth. The night fell quiet and thick, and they slept and slept until he woke again. So easy. So nice.

But *easy* and *nice* is how bad habits form, after all. She should have *sleep-trained* the boy, should have forced him into his own crib, his own room. She should have let him *cry it out.* She should have nursed him when he woke instead of before he slept. She never should have cuddled him to get him to bed. All the books said so. She had done it all wrong. Really, she had only herself to blame.

She had been in bed with him for an hour when she fell asleep, too. She awoke groggy in a panic, heavy with the weight of her ambition, with her failure, so heavy she could barely pull herself from bed. It was four o'clock, and the day was lost. She groaned and told herself she'd try again tomorrow, which made her feel worse instead of better.

For dinner, she made the meal she had planned—turkey loaf full of grated veggies, and roasted potatoes, and a green salad—and even though the week before the boy had liked all of these things, he refused to eat them that night, screaming, *Macaroni, macaroni!,* until she relented and made him macaroni and cheese and peas. He ate two bites of each, then dumped the rest on the floor.

The magic-hour light cast everything in melancholic tones—the gelatinous bits of noodles left on the boy's plastic plate, the vagrant peas beneath his high chair, the clutter of wayward puppets and matchbox cars strewn across counters and beside the cat-food dish. In such moments, she could almost touch her loneliness, as if it were her second child.

How could she possibly get through two, three more hours? How could she possibly read five books, make up a bedtime story, lie in bed for an hour, two, waiting for him to fall asleep? She was very tired, despite her nap. Feelings were just unreal things that moved through a person, right? That's what her husband said. You could choose to attend to them or not. She told herself to be a detached observer of her emotional landscape. In her mind, she repeated the phrase *emotional landscape* and then saw it there, a gray silhouette against a gray sky. She drew the bath. She read the books. She told the stories. She lay in the darkness, waiting, waiting.

That night, as she waited in bed beside the boy, her husband lounged in a hotel room somewhere, reading a book or watching TV or playing video games, eating from a room-service tray laid out on the bed. Even if he was working on spreadsheets or filling out service reports on his laptop, the image of him there, by himself, in a quiet space, seemed luxurious and exotic. In her darkest moments, she imagined that her husband craved this time away from them, a wave of relief washing over him each Monday as he pulled out of the drive. Four whole uninterrupted nights of sleep! Blackout curtains!

A discrete, achievable task to accomplish that day! A paycheck to expect at the end of the week!

Did he ever stay away a day longer than needed? Delay his departure from St. Louis or Indianapolis with one more cup of coffee? Anger ballooned inside her as she imagined him dallying on the Internet in a café. He should leave the moment he was finished. He should get up early—as early as she did—and get his work done quickly so that he could rush home. That's what she would do if she were away.

Her problem was that she thought too much—"toxic thinking" and so forth—so she tried to stop, but a physical sensation of exertion remained.

Was it her fault that her husband made more money? That it made more sense for her to quit her job than for him to quit his?

Was it her fault that he was always gone, rendering her a de facto single mom for the majority of the week?

Was it her fault that she found playing trains really, really boring? That she longed for even the smallest bit of mental stimulation, for a return to her piles of books, to her long-abandoned closet of half-formed projects, to one entire afternoon of solitude and silence?

Was it her fault that, though she longed for mental stimulation, she still found herself unable to concoct a single original thought or opinion? She did not actually care about anything anymore. Politics, art, philosophy, film: all boring. She craved gossip and reality TV.

Was it her fault that she hated herself for her preference for reality TV?

Was it her fault that she had bought into the popular societal myth that if a young woman merely secured a top-notch education she could then free herself from the historical constraints of motherhood, that if she simply *had a career* she could easily *return to work* after having a baby and sidestep the drudgery of previous generations, even though *having a baby* did not, in any way, represent a *departure from work* to which a woman might, theoretically, one day *return*. It actually, instead, marked an *immersion in work*, an *unimaginable weight of work*, a *multiplication of work* exponential in its scope, staggering, so staggering, both physically and psychically (especially psychically), that even the most mentally well person might be brought to her knees beneath such a load, a load that pitted ambition against biology, careerism against instinct, that bade the modern mother be less of an animal in order to be happy, because—come on, now—we're evolved and civilized, and, really, what is your problem? Pull it together. This is embarrassing.

Actually, if you thought about it, it really wasn't fair to call her a night *bitch*. Such a gendered slur didn't account for the fact she had made a boy with her own body, nurtured his multiplying cells for months and months to her own detriment, to her own fatness, to the decline of her youthful sex appeal, which wasn't supposed to matter. A real feminist wouldn't care about such things as *the shape of one's body* or *being thin* or *appealing to heteronormative cis men*, and actually she did not care about this, but she did care about being hot in her own eyes. It's just that a person has ideas about herself, has a vision for herself, and her vision for herself had not been of a mother, but now that she was one, she felt strongly that she needed to be a hot one.

But there wasn't really a commensurate word to degrade men, was there?

If she was Night*bitch*, was the boy, then, a *rotten little cock* when he looked her in the eye and then proceeded to dump an entire bin of freshly collected toys on the floor, his only explanation afterward that of *macaroni*? No.

And was her husband, in turn, a *computer nutsack* when he was *leveling up his Pit Lord* for long hours into the night, thus effectively curtailing the potential for a satisfying sex life, thanks to his absence in bed and also to the fact that he was playing video games? *Was he a nutsack?* Maybe.

Bitch just had a ring to it, that condemning, inescapable ring, a ring that *fucker* or *asshole* could never fully conjure for a man. Bitch was flat and sharp and final. She thought of a bored, small-town bureaucrat in a shabby little office with orange carpet and flickering fluorescent bulbs stamping official yet pointless documents with clicking, metal thuds. *Bitch. Bitch. Bitch.* Thank you. Have a nice day.

The house waited silent and clean, the paint smudges of that day a distant memory. The boy, beside her in bed—bathed not once but twice, for he needed a midday bath and then a night-night bath, to calm him, to try to soothe him into sleep any way she could—was also finally, gloriously asleep. She inched from bed, down the stairs, into the bathroom. She had bruised her tailbone in the fall earlier, or else the tag in her pants had been irritating her back. In indistinct yet nagging discomfort, she reached toward the base of her spine. Her finger found a swollen lump, and when she checked it in the mirror, she saw a raised mound, hot to the touch.

She pressed the spot at the base of her spine with two fingers and flinched at the pain, then twisted around again to examine it in the mirror and, when she couldn't get a close enough look at it, retrieved a hand mirror, which provided little enlightenment as to the nature of the bump, then opted to take a picture of it with her phone, only to find a blurry red mass on the screen after repeated tries. She thought she felt a hair protruding from the bump and decided tweezing it would relieve her discomfort, and so picked at it blindly for a time, only exacerbating the pain and causing the thing to begin to seep.

Fuck it, she said to no one, and stomped to the closet in the guest room to retrieve a box of her old art tools. As she opened the lid, the pungent smell of the paints and putties and the noxious tang of old glues calmed her and immediately transported her to those long hours alone, fingers dirty and sore, every manner of clay and paint and glue splatter on her clothes. She inhaled deeply, intoxicated, before steeling herself against the tears she felt welling from a place of profound and desperate longing to return to her projects—any project—and the complete inability to do such a thing. She quickly sorted through a shallow tray to find a sharp X-Acto knife—what she had been looking for all along—then washed it at the kitchen sink and held it above a flame on the stove. In the bathroom, she traced the tip of it down the red lump and felt instant relief as it oozed open. She held a hot washcloth to the lump, pushing to drain the fluid, then dabbed it with a hand towel. When she looked again, it had deflated. A flurry of hair poked from the incision she had made. The only word she could think to describe it was *tail*.

YOU NEED TO CONSULT with a medical professional, her husband said kindly. I can't believe you cut into the cyst. It's unsafe.

Okay, but can you please address the fact that I have a tail?

He laughed. He was always laughing at things she said.

I'd hardly call it a tail. Cysts in that region are known for their hair.

She knew all about such cysts. When located at the top of the tailbone, they were called pilonidal cysts, and they were most common in young men and often contained hair and skin debris. She had, of course, searched the Internet for such cysts, looked at pictures, watched videos of them being drained and extracted, and none of them looked like what hers looked like, a plug of dark hair that resisted plucking and that she could almost imagine wagging when she was happy, though whenever this feeling overtook her she quickly quashed it, because it was too strange to imagine such a thing: *wagging*.

Actually, honestly, she allowed herself only one good wag a day. Other than that, it was off limits. Who knew what else would develop if she gave in to these urges? Who knew what would transpire if she fully embraced her desires to wag, to lovingly lick the fine hairs of her son's head, to trample down a nice flat area in the bedsheets before herself curling there— chin resting on her forearms—and falling asleep?

She wasn't turning into a dog. She did not have a tail. Her teeth had not sharpened. And the hair that now covered the entire back of her neck was not fur. Her husband was right, and she truly needed to hold fast to reason in times like these. Oh, she simply could not let herself imagine such fanciful things, and didn't, except at night, once the boy was asleep, when she sat, panting, at the window, staring into the open, dark night.

THE NEXT MORNING, SHE did what any reasonable person would do and went to the library. Never mind that she had not showered since the weekend, and it was now midweek, her hair an inexplicable blend of oily roots too thick even to run her fingers through and ragged, wavy ends curled like dry grass and rustling about her face in a frizz of autumnal foliage. Add to that the dark circles beneath her eyes, which resisted every form of concealer, and which she now explained as genetic, though neither her father nor her mother had this same feature; it had the unfortunate effect of making the mother look as though she had been punched hard in both eyes, or else had leukemia.

She had (unsurprisingly) not slept well the night before,

kept awake by her worry—A *tail*!? Really???—and so simply had to go to the library and get some books to quell her incessant theorizing and diagnoses. The Internet was truly a horrid place, wasn't it, what with its endless information, infinite search terms, images and videos and articles, databases, discussion boards, quizzes to see whether or not you did in fact have leukemia. The mother had not known prior to the night before that the search phrase *looks like I was punched hard in both eyes* would produce not only a list of seven common eye injuries but also endless scholarship on traumatic brain injury, concussions, and chronic headaches. Deeper still into the search, she scrolled through allergies, to pollen and food, to solvents, to everyday air pollution, sensitivities and inflammations, and then there she was, at autoimmune diseases, sick women with no discernible diagnosis, pains and bruises and aches and anxieties without cause, women who hurt in any number of ways, who were consumed by their bodies and, at a loss for someone to turn to, turned to each other, each one staring into her own white square of light.

Oh god, the mother thought, in bed. Oh, dear god, she did not want to be one of the sick, scared mothers on the Internet in the middle of the night, discussing the hairs springing from their cysts, threads unspooling from their pores, microplastics uncurling from a pimple, *photographic evidence!*, and so forth. She did not want to be one of the women with an indefinable *something*, a woman at whom sidelong glances and dubious stares were directed. How much easier it would be to have two black eyes, or an easily defined disease, a wound, a broken bone, anything that could be seen and understood, an explanation inscribed in her flesh that could be shown to any person who might inquire, *What's wrong?* Anything to point to and say, *Aha! This must be the cause of everything!*

And so, in light of her completely reasonable and non-emergency condition, it seemed the right thing to do to calm herself at the library, such an unfraught nexus of all things researched and thought through, of stuff that had been written and rewritten, fact-checked, considered by any number of smart and unsmart folks before an investment had been put into such thoughts and words, into spreading them out into the populace. The library was a balm. She could almost feel her heart slowing as she and the boy neared it. She breathed deeply of the completely unscented air once they were inside.

At the library, she retrieved one medical text about cysts, in particular those called dermoid cysts, which contained within them on rare occasions hair, teeth, eyes. She wanted to see every abhorrent thing a body could grow, and imagined teeth popping from the cyst on her back as if produced by assembly line, one by one in steady succession. The other book was one she had found in the library database and then searched for in the stacks in haste, for the boy was, as they say, *melting down,* there on the second floor of the library, right at the place in the Dewey decimal system where one finds Folklore and such, in the 350-to-412 aisle. The boy lay on the floor and stomped his feet, for he was bored and irritable in the nonfiction stacks.

GoooooooooOOOO! the boy wailed as she searched for it, for 398.3 WHI, then grabbed the tattered spine from the row. Her back ached as she peeled the boy off the floor and toted him down the stairs to the toy trains in one corner of the children's room. From her seat, as her son tooted and chugged, now happy, she saw the dreaded Book Babies happening in the little activity room.

The problem was, she did not enjoy the company of moms. Certainly, if she happened to meet an interesting, hilarious, beautiful, sharp woman with whom she hit it off and then discovered this woman was a mother, that was fine—more than fine, even. It was wonderful. A wonderful woman she could bitch with about kids. A woman who didn't mind getting a little tipsy on rosé on a Tuesday afternoon. While she would not actively avoid a friendship with a woman because she, too, was a mother, she felt that to begin one merely because of this shared motherhood was repugnant. She found being in a room full of mothers and their wards most dispiriting, each woman clutching her crumpled plastic baggies of snacks, on the way to sniff a diaper to check if the child needed a change, or wielding a tissue like a weapon as she stalked a child to wipe its nose. Those mothers, taking turns staring blankly into the middle distance as their children ran and screamed, peed their pants, knocked into each other, screamed more, cried and laughed and ran . . . You could always tell a mother by that look, she had come to find, one that encompassed not only exhaustion and boredom, but something more. It was as though the mothers were staring toward something they had lost, something they couldn't even remember. What was it . . . ?

She knew the look so well because she was the very mother staring absently so often. She caught herself doing it at story time, at playtime, during trains, during cartoons. A blankness overtook her, and she realized it only once she came to, there beside her son, as he honked like a dump truck.

So she actively resisted making friends in a mom context and objected to the sort of clapping and cooing that went on in the library room, the floor play that would be mandatory, the group peekaboos and collective itsy-bitsy-spidering, the happiness and positivity that would also be mandatory. It was a veritable embrace of All Things Mommy, and the mother certainly did not want to embrace anything of the sort: she was indeed a mother, but she wasn't *that kind* of mother, the sort that built her entire life and being around her child, who filled her days with baby groups and baby activities and fully submerged herself in the mommy current, moving through her days and weeks according to library schedules and civic events, texting about splash pads and jungle gyms, sharing warnings about ticks, about pesticides on fruits and vegetables. But there they were. She saw them through the windows framing the door. Those mommies. Those happy mommies.

Chief among them was the blonde mommy—the *Big Blonde*, she always thought to herself whenever she saw her at the library or glimpsed her at the edge of a playground or texting furiously in the play space at the mall—with her blonde, blabbering twins in coordinated jumpers embroidered adorably with deer and owls set against the enchanting woodland scene printed on each skirt, their silky tresses collected in pigtails tied with pink velvet bows. As they crawled around, one might glance at their yellow ruffled diaper covers peeking from beneath each skirt, the name of each child embroidered on the butt, *Celeste* and *Aubergine*. She was the Ur-mommy, perfected and monumental, despite the fact she had named one of her children *eggplant*, but French. She didn't even care! Not even a moment of shame for the embarrassingly vegetal name as she smiled and laughed and chatted and exchanged and hugged and fed and generally joined in wherever joining in was possible. Now, as the mother watched from a safe distance, one of the Big Blonde's girls baby-sign-languaged at the Big Blonde, who, in turn, signed to her other daughter, who then responded in kind, after which the Big Blonde collected them both in a big squeeze as they all succumbed to a fit of giggles, after which she pulled from her diaper bag two red apples, which she handed to the little girls, who looked on in absolute wonder and gummed the succulent fruits.

It was then that the Big Blonde looked up and caught in her line of sight the bedraggled mother—that tired-looking mother over by the trains in the rumpled shirt, poor thing, always alone with her son (what a *doll*), and an odd look in her eyes, why doesn't she just come join the group?—then offered a tiny wave and, with a quick and cheerful word to the mother beside her, dug something from the depths of her diaper bag and rose to walk with intention toward the mother, who pasted on her face the best approximation she could of a friendly little smile while, on the inside, chanting, *Fuck fuck fuck fuck fuck.*

Oh, hiiiiii! the Big Blonde crooned as she approached. The mother thought for a moment this might be a true apparition, for the Big Blonde was so perfect, her lines so cleanly drawn. She brought with her, as some women are magically able to, a symphonic olfactory experience, even while still half a room away, which delighted the mother so intensely she felt a slight stirring at the base of her back—A *wag*!? she wondered in horror—and, meanwhile, forgot momentarily how much she deplored this woman, this Big Blonde, now a mobile sniff party: a touch of dryer-sheet freshessence from her no doubt newly laundered white shorts and cashmere-soft tank, something earthy yet also extraordinarily refined, as though patchouli had been manufactured in a French parfumerie and then dabbed lightly on the Big Blonde's wrists and behind the ears, and then, beneath each smell, a sweet pink candy scent of strawberry, like a memory from the mother's own childhood, a big chunk of bubble gum too big for her mouth, the syrup dripping down her chin. A charm bracelet on the Big Blonde's wrist jingled, and then the mother was back from her sensorial reverie, there at the train table, to offer an inadvertent grimace and her own tiny little wave.

The boy who had been so diligent with his trains looked up to offer his own wave with a dirty, dirty hand, and it was then the mother apprehended the profound filth of her child, his hair unbrushed and shirt stained with juice from breakfast, pants stretched and saggy at the butt from days of repeated wear, diaper as saggy and wet as a mop head. And what of her own appearance, which she considered with a silent and consuming terror. Had she put on undereye concealer? Deodorant? *When was the last time she had washed her face?*

Hey! the Big Blonde offered with an air of ease and familiarity the mother secretly wished for herself. How's it going? We've seen each other around, right!? she asked as she pointed one finger at herself and one at the mother, and then toggled them back and forth amiably.

You guys should come over to Book Babies, she added.

Oh, he's obsessed with trains though, the mother said, gesturing at the boy, who was already back at it, honking loudly.

Sure, sure. Well, next time you're around . . . Here she paused for dramatic effect, and then offered conspiratorially: Me and the girls are starting a new business. We're selling herbs! It's really exciting. And, I mean, you look like the sort of woman who would really be into herbs, right? Like, all-natural and stuff.

Ummmm, maybe! the mother offered as brightly as was humanly possible, as though selling herbs were the most ordinary thing ever, as though she knew exactly what this mother was talking about, as though she, too, were excited at the prospect. She was just about to inquire further, because it would be polite and normal to do such a thing, and she was very much trying to be both these things, when the caterwauling of the Big Blonde's twins wafted to the train table. At the sound, the Big Blonde backed away from the mother, rolled her eyes in a gesture of *Kids, amirite?* and said, I gotta go, but I'll see you around, yeah?

Okay! the mother said, with gusto that she hoped communicated a believable enthusiasm and good-sported-ness.

The Big Blonde laughed and waved before jogging back into Book Babies and collecting her sobbing wards in her arms to boop their snotty noses with delight.

Hooooooooooonk! the boy yelled. Hoooooonk!

Honey, she said to her dirty little son, suddenly tired, so tired, so very, very wanting just to get back into bed. Honey, let's go.

THAT NIGHT, AFTER THE boy had fought his way into sleep for more than an hour, the mother flung herself on the couch, rubbed her eyes, then dug through the tote bag of books she'd collected from the library.

A stack for the boy, fire trucks and buses and front loaders galore, but then two for her, a pair of books she hoped in some way might shed light on her current condition, though she greatly doubted they could. At least, perhaps, something to take her mind off her constant worries—off her teeth, which might or might not be sharpening, a tail that might or might not now be in a constant state of near-sprout, the carpet of fur creeping, creeping down her neck.

The medical text was too cerebral, too long, too-small font, so she opted instead for the second one, *A Field Guide to Magical Women* (publication date 1978), which featured on its cover all sorts of fantastical creatures done in a style she associated with the 1970s and Nancy Drew and B-movies, lots of shadows and inky renderings, the edges of everything a bit blurred. She looked at the spine to confirm that it was, yes, *nonfiction*, which seemed curious, then opened to the first pages.

Though the mother had assumed *A Field Guide to Magical Women* to be a compendium of cheesy middle-grade stories about feminine monsters of yore, once she began to peruse the book she saw it was, yes, more a field guide than anything. As the author, Wanda White, wrote, "I went in search of mythical women, a research expedition that took me to all seven continents and spanned my entire professional career. This book is the culmination of that work. While colleagues have claimed that the field within which I'm working—namely, mythical ethnography—isn't a viable field of study, I present in these pages irrevocable data that counter their claims."

"By understanding these creatures' habits, diets, and patterns," she continued a bit later in the text, "you too will be able to encounter them in the wild and experience their magic firsthand."

In the foreword, Wanda White explained she was "interested in the ways in which womanhood manifests on a mythical level" and was particularly drawn to "the experience of motherhood and how this complicates, deepens, or denies womanhood," then went on to ask:

> To what identities do women turn when those available to them fail? How do women expand their identities to encompass all parts of their beings? How might women turn to the natural world to express their deepest longings and most primal fantasies?

There was no author photo of White, just a short biography at the back of the book, which read: "Wanda White holds a Ph.D. in biology and teaches at the University of Sacramento. She has worked her whole life in the field of mythical ethnography."

The mother considered all this with the demeanor of one observing a faith healing or a time-share sales presentation— that is, with mild, bemused interest and good-natured skepticism. Yet, still, she kept reading.

In the first chapter, White explained that the Bird Women of Peru lived in the tall, leafy boughs of the rain forest, where they constructed intricate and artful nests from sticks and reeds. The pages showed a number of habitats, one of them a round orb with a small hole in the side perched nearly seventy feet up, another an artful multilayered structure on par with the work of Andy Goldsworthy. The Bird Women fed on fruits and insects and regularly ate communally, sharing their food and squawking back and forth for hours. The Bird Women were not born as such but, rather, sprouted feathers and beaks in their sixties, but only if they had never married or had children. It was unclear what precipitated such a transformation; people in small Peruvian villages often explained the disappearances of older single women by saying they gave in to "the calling of the birds." The villagers would gesture toward the forest and point at the sky, flapping their arms as they tried to explain. The Bird Women spent the latter parts of their lives flitting from tree to tree, producing the loveliest calls, and learning how to fly. White claimed to have once witnessed a Bird Woman take what White referred to as the "twilight flight," both the first and last flight a Bird Woman would take, for once she learned to fly, her maiden trip into the sky would lead her away from the nest she had constructed and toward the horizon, to an unknown destination. All White knew was that Bird Women who learned to fly, once they departed, never returned, and the other Bird Women would sing for days after with a sound that she described as "mellifluous, virtuosic weeping on par with the likes of Beethoven or Mozart, had they been birds."

This was as far as the mother could read before she fell into sleep, there on the couch, to dream of a tree that surged with leaves and birdsong, a pyrotechnic sunset, and then, an inhale. A plunge. No weight, no body, just movement and sky. An endless fall.

ON THURSDAY, SHE WOKE with dirty hair, in the same sports bra she had been wearing for far too long (through night and day and night and day), at the same moment the small body in bed beside her woke, whatever the hour, and there was no doing otherwise. Had he already woken her in the night? Twice? Even thrice? Had there been a bad dream? A need for 3:00 a.m. water? A lost binky? Never mind, the child rose with the sun, and she lay in bed with her eyes closed. Maybe if I don't move, he won't notice me. That was always the hope that ran through her head, but he climbed on her chest, put his face in hers.

Mama, he said. Up. Up up up up up.

Okay, she said, not moving.

Mama up, he repeated. Play trains.

She put on the crumpled pants from the floor, the only slightly worn top from a drawer, still in a state of half-sleep. The boy was already downstairs in his saggy nighttime diaper, at the train tracks covering the living-room floor. He laid his soft little cheek on the cool wood planks to watch the wheels of the trains move.

Uhhhhh uhhhhhhh, he honked. Uhhhhhhhhhhhhh.

Every morning, it was the same: six o'clock, the train tracks on the living-room floor, a heavy skillet on the kitchen stove, a pat of butter, frozen hash browns retrieved from a wrinkled bag in the freezer, a dusting of salt, a carton of yogurt in the fridge, wash his plastic bowl left in the sink from the night before, wash his tractor plate because it was the only plate on which the little prince accepted his food, flip the hash browns, fill the bowl, wash his fork and spoon, hashies on the plate, plate on the little plastic table in the corner of the kitchen. Milkie or juice, honey? Milkie or juice?

She ate a banana, which he wanted, too—not his own, but *hers*, the rest of it—because, yes, he was still hungry. He wanted to push the button on the blender when she made her smoothie, but he was afraid of the noise of the machine, so he threw himself on the floor in a frustrated rage, because he didn't want it to be loud when he pushed the button, and he must push the button.

Honey, she said, you know it's loud. Every morning, it's loud.

No, Mama. NOOOOOOOOOOOOO, he screamed.

Every morning, the same. Every day, the same. After breakfast, play with trains, read a book about trains, read the same book again, again, this is the last time, and one more time, okay, just one more, then walk down the block and cross the busy street and run across the church parking lot to the train tracks up on a little hill. Examine the train tracks. Sift through the rocks. Don't throw the rocks, honey. We don't throw them. Balance on the train tracks. Grow frustrated. Scream and kick rocks. Calm down and discuss different train cars. Would a train be coming soon? She didn't know. They would just have to wait and be patient.

Was this boring? Yes, she knew it was, and she wanted someone, anyone, to understand the monotony, the mind-numbing routine, the way in which her mental activity began to slow the moment she woke each morning, beginning with high hopes, thoughts of art projects and energy, a sunny day and happy boy and goals fulfilled, and the slow yet steady grinding down of hopes to rote considerations of *what to eat* and *what to clean*, the slow agony of The Schedule—time for breakfast and time for a walk and time for lunch and time for nap and time for snack, time for pooping, time for dinner—this and then that and then this again, until every single thought had been emptied from her head and left in its place only the physical sensations of exhaustion, a pain in her lower back, greasy hair, a bloated feeling from eating too many fish-shaped, sodium-laden crackers. She spoke in toddler talk and was constantly asking different questions about poop.

Poop in the potty, she suggested when the boy's tummy hurt. He was now well beyond his second birthday and should be pooping in the potty. He willingly sat on the potty, and she read him a book called *Potty*, about pooping in the potty, and then, when he finally had to poop, he demanded, Poop in a diaper.

But, honey, try the potty.

No! he said, standing up. Poop in a diaper!

She sighed.

Sure, she said. Okay.

She put a diaper on him, and the boy went behind the overstuffed chair and stuck his head around the corner.

Go poop, he said. He grunted and pushed, making eye contact with her as he shat, the way he liked. When he emerged, the diaper bulged with his work.

Wipe my butt, he said to her.

And later that night, the boy would not go to sleep. For hours and hours and hours, they lay side by side, dueling. She did not allow herself to growl, to bark ferociously, to show her teeth, to narrow her eyes and pull her ears back closer to her skull, though she would have liked to do all these things.

Their house was a mid-century bungalow with odd angles, built by a builder who didn't know how to build. She had thought the house the height of charm when they moved in—had in fact convinced her husband that this was exactly where they needed to live, despite the questionable wiring and single bathroom—but now she was angered by the doors, all too narrow or too short. None of the corners were right angles. And no matter how much she cleaned, the place never felt clean. This house, she thought, growing angry, angrier. This fucking house.

And instead of counting sheep, there in bed, as she waited for the boy to go to sleep—as he rolled and tangled, then untangled his legs in the sheets, as he asked for water, for food, complained, tried to play with her, pouted when she shushed him and said, Go night-night, it's time to let your body rest—as he resisted and tossed and she lay still and quiet beside, she imagined punching holes in the plaster walls.

How satisfying to summon the strength of her body, to feel her bones jar as her fist contacted the hard wall. Her hand would bloody. Her knuckles would probably break. But the give of the wall, the crumble, the damage. There was a relief that could come with violence, she now saw.

Punch, punch, punch. An hour there, beside the boy. Punch. Two hours. Still awake. On another night, she would have cried. On another night, she would have gotten out of bed and gone downstairs and ignored him as he snuck from the bedroom and edged down the steps, would have read on the couch and not acknowledged him as he cuddled in the crook of her arm, would have done whatever she pleased and let him fall asleep whenever he wanted, wherever, because she couldn't. She simply could not lie in that bed with him for one more godforsaken moment.

She should distract herself. Read something. Anything to get her mind off of the disappointment and despair welling inside her. And there it was, on her nightstand, the *Field Guide*. Of course.

She was not reading her *Field Guide* straight through, but instead felt called to allow the tome to spill open where it might and take up with whatever she found there. For it did feel as though the book was not a stagnant thing that existed but, rather, an entity unto itself that actually had things to say, and spoke, to her specifically.

What do you want to talk about now? she'd think as she pulled the book from her bag at the park, and, as if in response, the book would blow open to "An Excursion in Antarctica" or "Some Thoughts on Transformation."

On this night, as she waited for her husband finally, blessedly, to arrive home the next day, she lay in the stuffy heat of the bedroom, her son now snoring beside her (it had taken only between two and three hours!), and flipped the book open to the section entitled "Domestic Varietals."

Per White: "While my research abroad has certainly been some of the most engrossing and fascinating of my career, the domestic breeds of magical women cannot be overlooked and, in fact, absolutely merit their own frank and serious consideration."

Well, then, the mother thought. Here we go.

On these pages, she found the Slaythe,

. . . a type of modern creature drawn to and focused on all things related to her career, success, financial earning, and power. This creature is not specific to any particular field, but you can find her in the highest echelons of her chosen area of expertise.

She will dress as she sees fit, in any sort of style, but should you be unlucky enough to engage with her in antagonistic business negotiations, be on the lookout: a slicing look can leave you incapacitated for days. A sharp word is able to inspire a profound and crushing doubt of all life decisions. Sometimes—though this is as yet an unconfirmed theory of mine, albeit based on years of observation—the Slaythe may ever so slightly edge into sharpness, with her actual corporeal body taking on a new pointedness, her face narrowing outward to a point as her forehead and nose and chin shift into a sort of precipitous range. Perhaps this is magic, or perhaps this is aging. (With the right funding, I would gladly design a proper study.)

The failed Slaythe is a sorry creature indeed, though no less caustic. Outside the realm of business, you will find her within an immaculate home, her children obedient, her mate equally docile, the household observing a strict schedule. Nothing less than perfection will be accepted by this breed of Slaythe, whose dreams, now diverted, express themselves even more viciously. I wish her family well.

Slaythe prefer ambiguous domestic partnerships with other

women. Whether sexual or not, you will most likely never be
able to discern.

One might imagine other women would hold the Slaythe
in contempt of the cooperative and selfless spirit that often
animates female social circles, but I've found that, more than
not, the opposite is true instead: beta females in proximity
to the Slaythe will hold her in high regard and feed from her
power, growing into their own animations, over months or
years, of their own Slaythe selves.

The mother closed her eyes. What must it be like to sit
among women with the same animating vitality? To build
vast empires and heretofore undreamt worlds? To control the
exchange of ideas, the evolution of a society? She had never
really been all that interested in traditional success or power,
but for a moment she saw the appeal of it, of an empire ruled
only by women, and then the appeal of wielding might that
could bring it all down, on a whim. An entire ruined kingdom as manifestation of one woman's rage. A crushed and
crumbling room. Anything to put what she felt outside her
own body, for she had borne it long enough and did not want
it anymore.

IN ADDITION TO THE hair spreading on her neck and
now shoulders, her pointy teeth, her tail, the next morning
her breasts were swollen and tender, and her lower back was
cramped. A thick, heavy headache thudded beneath everything she did. This she knew. This was normal, or at least
normal ever since her period had come back a year after the
baby, a bright deluge or a muddy trickle, a week of flooding or
a couple days of next to nothing. She could depend on nothing reproductive now, other than the suffering.

Never had she felt this sort of agony before her periods,

a state so acute that she now understood those women who had murdered their husbands, then claimed PMS as a defense. Her only instincts during this time were toward violence.

Adding to her premenstrual agony, the fat black cat with its unkempt fur sticking out at odd angles, big green eyes devoid of intelligence, rawled and rawled at the exact frequency that inspired homicidal rage.

Did she perhaps kick the cat a little—mostly by accident, since the thing was always there at her feet, asking for more food, but also the smallest bit on purpose, just enough to loft a fount of gleeful murder-joy inside her chest? Yes.

Out out out out outoutoutout, she grunted, thundering around the kitchen to try to catch the animal, who skittered between the chair legs, then under the kitchen table.

The mother stomped to scare it out, then grabbed its oddly rotund midsection. The cat deflated ever so little and squeaked like a toy. Its tiny legs wiggled as she carried it to the door and propelled it onto the porch.

She used to love the cat, back before she had her son. It was a beautiful creature, pure black and fluffed extravagantly, with big green owl-eyes and a tiny, high-pitched princess meow that sounded like a bell. She was astoundingly beautiful and, to the same degree, astoundingly idiotic. She meowed frantically until someone walked over to the bowl and pointed at her food and shook it around a bit, at which point she began to eat as if starved. She always darted in the same direction the mother was walking, and then got stepped on, then made a horrible noise and rocketed off to the basement. She ate too much and had become overweight and could no longer properly clean herself, so the mother had to, weekly, wash matted poop from her butt hair, and did so with great disdain. Such a cleaning was necessary since the cat was prone to urinary-tract infections due to what the veterinarian had called an "anomalous vulva."

But we made it here together! her husband would say warmly whenever she complained about the cat. He cradled the stupid thing in his arms and argued: just think, we and this cat all evolved from a single-celled organism and made it to this moment in history, together. We did it!

The mother would let out a bark of laughter, for of course she had never thought of it in such terms before, and it did at least for a time make the cat more a triumphant comrade than a worthless pest, but that camaraderie soon faded.

Oh sure, yes, they had all made it. But, honestly, this cat never would have made it without human intervention. Her breed would have been a palace cat, the cat of the queen, a cat who sat on a silken cushion all day and was fed minced meat that a ruddy cook had prepared. The cat did, then, in a way, deserve to die, if you were playing by evolutionary rules.

Now the mother did not want another thing needing her, needing to be cuddled, fed, washed, cooed at, and doted over. Now she wanted only silence and not to be touched.

Her sense that society, adulthood, marriage, motherhood, all these things, were somehow masterfully designed to put a woman in her place and keep her there—this idea had begun to weigh on her. Of course, it had crossed her mind before, but after her son arrived it took on a new shape, an unwieldy heft, and then even more after she quit her job, as her body struggled to regain its equilibrium. And once she was stripped of all she had been, of her career, her comely figure, her ambition, her familiar hormones, an anti-feminist conspiracy seemed not only plausible but nearly inevitable.

She needed to get cat food and other groceries that day, and she did not want to get cat food and other groceries, but she went to get them anyway.

At the grocery store, she could not get out from inside this thinking, that she was trapped, that it was all a plot, and she spiraled into an even worse mood, despite her efforts toward positive thought and the choice of happiness.

She wondered whether she was being hysterical as she wheeled the cart through the produce and past the deli. That was the last thing she wanted to be. She had always prided herself on not being a hysterical woman but, rather, a smart woman with good points who sometimes got a little upset but was mostly cool to hang out with.

Of course, she knew that the concept of "the hysterical woman" was itself a sexist creation, and she rejected the label altogether, but she also made sure no one would ever associate her with such a label to begin with.

The boy babbled, Cookie, cookie, cookie, from his seat in the cart, then did his sign for *please*, rubbing both his palms up and down on his chest and looking at her with big eyes.

She smiled and touched his nose and meandered distractedly toward the bakery department.

It wasn't hysteria if the claim one was hysterical about was true, if the systems of which one was a part were set up from the start to put women at a disadvantage. In fact, even though a loose historical definition of hysteria would indict the uterus and out-of-control female hormones, it was *these very things* that did not handicap women but elevated them, sharpening their minds, availing to them the realities of gender politics and honing critical thinking skills until razor-sharp.

Yes, certainly, her emerging rage was in part a by-product of physiological processes, but how could you *not* be pissed after having a baby? she wondered as she picked up a wedge of cheese and sniffed it, registering a depth of smell hitherto unknown to her—hay, smoke, honey, a fungal musk, a sweet-rotten tang. Amazing, she thought as she set it back down. A premenstrual sensitivity, she told herself, even though what she feared—with a sharp realization—was that this was yet another canine development, this heightened sense, which only grew stronger and stronger as she moved through the store: the ripe yeasts of the bakery, the baking soda and bitter cocoa of the boy's chocolate-chip cookie, the milks in all the states of freshness and souring, vinegar from the olive bar, the deadened fields of grass in the bagged-bread aisle, high sharp notes of fresh coffee grounds.

She was alive in a new way as she walked about the store, the boy's happy face covered in chocolate. She smelled the dark tea and damp dirt of the aged urine in his diaper, then the salt and green of the seafood section. The boy liked to look at the lobsters in the tank, claws banded, wallowing in a pile in the murky water. They stopped to watch the animals tumbling over each other and knocking against the glass.

The grocery store is a locus of oppression, she thought as she wheeled onward, past an old lady who worked at the store and cooked fish-fillet samples in an electric skillet at a small lectern.

Bite? the mother asked the boy, pointing to the cookie. Share?

He held the cookie out to her, and she nibbled on the edge. *Thank you*, she signed, and he clapped his dirty hands. She wished she had an entire cookie, a dozen cookies. She was suddenly ravenous, but, no, that wasn't right. She didn't want cookies. She went to the meat counter and bought three thick rib-eye steaks, the smell of pennies and blood and death spinning her into a depthless hunger. They were so beautiful! How had she never before noticed their beauty, the deep red of the meat set starkly against the white swirls of fat. Each a tiny masterpiece, she thought, licking her lips. She asked for more: two pounds of ground chuck. On second thought, make it three. A half-dozen bratwursts. What about that stew meat? It looked delicious. How about a pound of that? And look at that top-round roast. That one that's the size of a possum, she said, pointing, to the butcher, who chuckled as he retrieved it from the case. And some premade kabobs for good measure, for vegetables, because that was healthy, she said, getting hold of herself.

Yes, vegetables were very civilized. Dogs wouldn't buy vegetables.

Listen to what you're saying, she said to herself.

Stop it, another self said. Stop talking to yourself.

Shit, she thought.

It was a Friday, and her husband would be home from work later that day. She had upward of ten pounds of red meat in her cart. They still needed juice, wipes, yogurt, bananas, crunchy snacks, and a bag of utterly civilized carrots.

Imagine trying to shop for crunchy snacks with a toddler and heightened near-animal sense of smell while the enormity of patriarchal society loomed behind every box of farm-themed crackers, in the crackle of every pretzel bag you picked up.

As she walked through the automatic sliding doors of the grocery store to the parking lot, someone behind her said her name, and she turned.

Sally—single, cute, young, happy, blonde Sal—waved and nearly skipped toward her with glee.

Hey, how's it going!? she asked, hugging the mother and ruffling the boy's hair. I haven't seen you in *forever*. Do you love being home with this guy? I bet it's so fun.

Sal worked at the community gallery where she had been director before she stepped down. It had been the right choice. It had. Being at work while her infant lolled on the day care's linoleum floor had been agony, but being at home was also agony, just of a different sort.

She wanted to tell the girl: It's complicated. I am now a

person I never imagined I would be, and I don't know how to square that. I would like to be content, but instead I am stuck inside a prison of my own creation, where I torment myself endlessly, until I am left binge-eating Fig Newtons at midnight to keep from crying. I feel as though societal norms, gendered expectations, and the infuriating bluntness of biology have forced me to become this person even though I'm having a hard time parsing how, precisely, I arrived at this place. I am angry all the time. I would one day like to direct my own artwork toward a critique of these modern-day systems that articulates all this, but my brain no longer functions as it did before the baby, and I am really dumb now. I am afraid I will never be smart or happy or thin again. I am afraid I might be turning into a dog.

Instead, she said, smiling, I love it. I love being a mom.

I'VE BEEN TRYING TO come up with a new project, she said, standing in the bathroom doorway that evening—Friday!—as her husband dumped warm water over the boy's head. Something that has to do with smashing things, maybe? I'd love to use a bat. Or an ax.

Ooh, what about painting with a mace? her husband said.

Yeah . . . , she said, unconvinced.

He laughed and sudsed the boy's hair.

Something about moms and rage and smashing stuff, the mother continued. But, you know, artful.

Moms, he repeated.

They're angry, she said.

Angry? he said.

Never mind.

If I had to guess what your next project was, he said, I would say you're training to be a butcher, because we have a fridge full of meat.

Not full of, she said. There are other things.

Do you still think you're turning into a dog? he asked, eyebrows drawn up in that way he had that communicated, *I am totally joking but also think you are sort of a dumbass.*

Shut up, she said. I'm fine. We even went to Book Babies this week. Well, we *saw* Book Babies when we were at the library.

How was it?

Unbearable, she said, and they both laughed.

She was grateful he was bathing the boy, though during said bath he had asked that she put the boy's towel in the dryer to warm it, that she bring in a piece of toast for the boy to eat, that she fetch the boy's pajamas from his room, all as the man sat on the closed lid of the toilet, next to the tub, reading something on his phone. Sure, she would do these things, even though all week she had done them herself, without even the option of help, and wouldn't it seem petty to point this out? She really just wanted to sit on the couch and stare blankly out the window for a time—even for just ten minutes—but her husband liked it when she was upbeat and talkative upon his return. He had, after all, just been in the car for hours, all the way from Minneapolis or Chicago—and he, *too,* was exhausted, for he had stayed up late that week at the hotel, reading or looking at the Internet, or he had simply *not been able to sleep* for any number of reasons—the room was *too quiet,* or he had *ordered room service too late,* which caused indigestion. Really, it was a challenge to be in a hotel all the time, he reported.

If, when he arrived home, he was greeted with the mother's complaints or the boy's perturbed demeanor or a house that was a mess, it *stressed him out,* and couldn't he just have a calm re-entry, some time to decompress from driving, an hour or so on his computer. The mother had been indulging him for years now, and she reminded herself—again and again and again, she simply must remember—he was not a bad man.

She did night-nights after the bath, for the husband needed to *wrap up some work e-mails,* even though he had had the entire week to do so. Really, she would have liked to leave the house altogether and go to the coffee shop for the entire evening the moment her husband got home, either that or shut herself in the guest room and simply imagine—art projects or outfits, a future vacation. She wanted to exit, but it would really be inconvenient for her husband, *for the entire family*, as he put it, so she stayed.

Maybe she actually was in a good mood, even though she thought she was pretending? Maybe it was actually fun to stay and be together as a family as soon as her husband arrived home? Each week, she considered these potentialities, trying to convince herself.

After she coaxed the boy to sleep, her husband said how happy he was to see her happy, how much he just wanted her to, you know, find her groove. They sat on the grungy old couch as the television murmured a foreign movie that her husband had selected. He stroked the soft hair on her forearms, then reached beneath her pajama pants to feel the hairs on her shin, running his fingers up to her thigh—not prickly, as they usually were, but lush with regrowth, for even though she had shaved her legs at some point that week, the hair was already back in full force and then some.

Mmmm, he said, burying his head in her neck and taking the back of it in his hand, a fistful of hair in his hand.

Oh, he murmured as he kissed her, surprised.

Just . . . , she said, moving his hand to her waist and offering only tight-lipped kisses, for fear of slicing him with her canine teeth. He moved his hand to the small of her back, and she squinched her face and pushed him away.

The cyst, she said, scooching away from him to the other end of the couch. I just feel out of sorts. I'm getting my period.

Well, how about . . . , he said, pulling at her waistband and bowing his head with that sly smile on his face, but the mother said *no* and smiled and kissed him and turned to the TV, and that was that. How could she show him the four new spots on her torso, raised and pink? Surely he would just say they were moles, but she knew better.

Nipples. They could only be nipples. Six now in total, including the ones on her breasts.

SATURDAY MORNING, AND THE mother jumped in the shower, for how long had it now been since she bathed? Three days? A week? Before she could even glob a pile of shampoo in her hand, her husband was in the bathroom, saying they were out of milk, and then the boy was crying and pulling at the shower curtain before he picked him up and whisked him away. She could hear her husband in the kitchen, telling the boy to calm down, while the boy screamed MAMA! in response.

One minute! she sang, scrubbing furiously at her scalp. Take care of your child, she wanted to scream. Just take care of it! What was so hard about it? Give him something, anything. Make a silly face. Put on a goddamn cartoon.

She could not comprehend her husband's great expertise with complex machinery yet complete inability to trouble-shoot their child. She hopped from the shower before she'd properly washed her face.

We're out of milk, her husband said again.

I know, she said, taking the crying boy from him and kissing him on the cheek.

Why are we out of milk? he asked.

Because he drank it, she said, gesturing at their son.

Milkie, the boy said.

Well, obviously, he said, an annoyed edge in his voice, as if she were wasting his time instead of the other way around. But did you know?

I knew we were running low, she said. She focused to keep her voice even and calm. It was on my list. But somehow I overlooked it. He sighed and went back to his laptop, open on the kitchen table.

Wrapped in a towel, hair dripping, she held the boy, who was reaching for his father.

Dada, the boy said.

Why don't you just leave? she thought. Go away. In some ways, it was easier with him gone. She could take care of the child without a constant stream of commentary, questions inspired by thinly veiled judgment, condescending soliloquies on how her husband would do whatever it was she needed to do if it were his job, how he really had it all figured out, how it was simple, just a matter of some perfectly reasonable X, Y, or Z.

Sure, yes, in retrospect, it wasn't *that* big of a deal for him to ask her about the milk, to need her help with the child since he had not developed her same skills in all his time away, but couldn't he see how she struggled? Was he capable of acknowledging all she did? He made it seem as though she were on an extended holiday. If he could not offer his actual hands-on help, at the very least he could offer his gratitude with a shower of thank-yous every waking moment he was home. Instead, when she tried to bring up the division of labor, the invisible labor of her life, the psychic load, he would offer something like *I suppose the money I make means nothing*, and of course that wasn't what she was saying, not at all.

She carried the whimpering boy upstairs with her and positioned him at his train table in his bedroom, then found a sports bra, comfy pants, a tank top. This was what she wore every day.

On Monday, after that weekend spent abiding her husband, for that's truly how it felt, she hugged him unenthusiastically and directed a psychic *fuck you* as he pulled from the driveway. She collapsed into a chair at the kitchen table with her lukewarm coffee to collect herself and watched the boy as he methodically pulled a baking sheet, a muffin tin, a skillet, the grater, from the cabinet next to the oven. Though she did not want to and would never admit that her husband's advice regarding happiness and schedules could perhaps be of the *good idea* sort, she did not want to begin her week and then continue forward in her current state, in this sour anger, so mad she found herself on the verge of tears. Not productive. No good for anyone, really, most of all herself.

Okay. So maybe there was absolutely nothing wrong other than she had too much time on her hands. That was the problem. Not that she had time to actually do things she enjoyed, like make art or read or exercise in a meaningful way. Rather, she had time—*so much time!*—to take the boy to the play area at the mall and take him to the play area adjacent to the pool and take him to the Tot Lot at the community gym and take him to a morning or afternoon story time—*Why not both?*—at the public library.

I'd be ecstatic if this is what I got to do all day, her husband always said whenever she complained, which she didn't even really *do* anymore, because she was trying to embrace his perspective and truly be ecstatic for her stay-at-home lifestyle filled with a toddler and lots of time and kid-related activities.

This week, she would try even harder to *get out of the house* and *connect with others*. She would *remain positive*. She packed the diaper bag and hummed to herself as she dressed the boy and tapped his nose to make him laugh and then brushed her hair.

She was doing *This old man, he played one* with the boy as she exited the house, bag on shoulder, boy in arms, and then stopped short and gaped at what she saw on the lawn.

Dog, the boy said, pointing.

Yes, three dogs in fact, in the shade of the silver maple: a golden retriever, a collie, and a basset hound. She had always thought of these breeds as dogs that girls in the 1980s loved. She had, in fact, in the 1980s, loved such dogs and, as a child, fantasized about brushing their hair with a pink hairbrush and decorating the dogs with lavender bows and naming them Lisa or Gem or Mr. Belvedere. Also, the dogs would save her if she ever accidentally tripped into the street in front of an oncoming car or fell into a very deep hole.

But now they were there, on the lawn, and all turned, panting, to look at the mother and her child.

Oh, come on, she said aloud.

Yes, it was a ridiculous sort of situation, but, truly, her heart thudded with a horrible terror, a horrible delight. Was she, in fact, going insane? Did domesticated dogs roam in packs? And why were they on *her* lawn, as if they were convening some sort of society and wanted to initiate her into its ranks? The boy wiggled against her hold, she let him down, and he bounded into the yard and right up to the dogs, who wagged their tails wildly. They pushed their wet noses toward his face, and he squealed and turned and ran back to his mother, who waited for him, speechless, on the porch.

Hey, dogs, hi, she said, as she approached them, then knelt and held out her hand. The hound was first to trot over, with the collie and retriever shortly after. The hound plopped in the grass between her feet while the others jumped to put their paws on her stomach and shoulders, lick her face, sniff all her parts that needed sniffing. Normally, she would have recoiled at such a show of unrestrained, obsequious affection. Dogs. So easy, so loving. She had grown to have a very certain disdain for dogs and their willing, uncritical love. They should demand more, be moodier, have more conditions. But, no, it was always happiness, an open mouth and a wagging tongue, a light in the eyes that begged to be loved in return.

Something had shifted, however, and these dogs—these 80s dogs—and their wet tongues and needy paws and warm, thudding bodies were so lovely. She opened her arms and drew them in to her. They knocked her on her back, and she lay there laughing, with the dogs walking all over her and wagging and licking and, finally, lying on her. The boy screamed with joy and piled onto her as well.

She would be covered in hair and dog musk and slobber and grass clippings and dirt, but it was okay. She loved these dogs and, my god, what was happening?

She and the boy spent the morning on the front lawn, petting the dogs and asking them questions and telling them they were good. The mother retrieved an assemblage of balls from beneath the couch and in random corners of the garage, and the boy threw them one by one, screaming with delight.

The retriever outplayed the others, a beautiful sight to behold as she leapt in the air, ears alert and eyes bright, to snag a ball midair with her teeth. She landed solidly on the ground and then turned swiftly, sprinted to the boy, dropped the ball at his feet.

After the boy had tired of fetch, the retriever came to where the mother sat on the porch steps and placed her head gently on the mother's leg. The mother stroked the animal as she watched her son trundle after the collie and the hound, arms outstretched, squealing and cackling. She stroked the retriever's long silky blond hair, softer than any she'd ever felt, as if it had been shampooed and conditioned, then blow-dried and brushed lovingly.

Did you just get your hair done? she asked the dog, and it nuzzled at her neck, then licked the palm of her hand.

She pulled the body of the dog to her and hugged, burying her face in its fur, which smelled of strawberries and soap.

Strawberries! she said, holding the dog's face and looking into its soft eyes. What a good, pretty, perfect dog. The retriever smiled, and she could almost see something familiar in her eyes. She squinted, tilted her head, then murmured to the dog, Oh my god, do I know you?

The dog gently fit its mouth around the mother's hand, then tugged her up from the porch, into the lawn, toward the sidewalk.

Come, it said. The dog's teeth dug into her skin and she vaguely wondered if it would bite her.

But where would I go? she thought absently. Where would a dog even want to take me? To her home? To a wide-open field full of supple green grass through which we could run and run and run, feeling the full power of our bodies, the blood careening through our muscles and fasciae, a place where our lungs would open and we could take into us the entirety of the sky, a place where there were no humans but just the throb and thrust of life, life, life?

She let herself be led, and shuffled through the lawn, the day now slowed and sparkling with the air of a waking dream.

In the long green grass of the front yard, the boy lay on his back in a patch of shade, collie and hound on either side of him. The collie knelt beside him and placed one paw on the boy's chest in the same manner as the mother laid her palm there just before he fell asleep. The hound's long ear swayed as the animal whispered something in the boy's ear. A story, perhaps. A lullaby.

Why, they're putting him down for a nap, she thought. How lovely.

As she passed, the collie and hound both looked her in the eye and nodded.

It will all be okay, they said to her. Go on. And the retriever again tugged on her hand, leading her away from her home and the boy and the life she both wanted and didn't.

A bird called, high and shrill, and the mother started. She looked down at the retriever, then over at her son, those other dogs. She pulled her hand from the dog's mouth, horrified, then darted toward her son and yelled at them all as she grabbed the bewitched boy from the ground.

Shoo! she shouted with a flip of her wrists. Go home! she insisted, and they moved toward the street, casting their big sad eyes back to her on the porch. You evil beasts, she scolded, go. And then, without thought, she tilted her head back and howled from the cavern in her chest where everything was, the crushing anger and joy of that morning, the wealth of golden sunlight, how she hadn't slept a whole night in two-plus years, her loneliness, her ugly desires, how silky her son's blond curls were—all of that came out of her in one giant sound. The dogs froze in the middle of the street to listen, and then, when she was done, sprinted back from wherever it was they had come.

A PACK OF DOGS? her husband said over the phone. It was late Monday night, and the boy was in bed, and she was scared and crying.

I'm covered in fur and I have a tail, and then these dogs, she said and gasped. I don't even like dogs, and now I want one.

Honey, he said evenly. She could hear cable news playing in the background. I'm sure this is all just a hormonal imbalance. Have you made an appointment yet with the doctor?

No, she said, blowing her nose. She didn't want to go to the doctor, have him tell her that everything was fine, that this was all in her head. Everything wasn't fine. This is what she had been trying to get across ever since that first night, when she had awoken angry and then stayed angry. Nothing was fine, despite how other people reasoned away her worries and anger, said that this was just how things were, that things would get better, that she really needed to calm down and not be so angry, that she really should be grateful and happy, that happiness was a choice, that she was privileged and bratty and wanted too much all at once.

Add to this her anxiety over a quietly forming theory that she violently pushed from her mind each time it managed to whisper itself inside her: that the golden retriever and Big Blonde—both immaculately groomed, both exhibiting the same vitality and excitement for life, both inexplicably smelling of strawberries—were one and the same.

Look, call Animal Control if they come back, her husband said, his mouth full of something—a late-night room-service order, perhaps. She saw a warm brownie topped with a perfect scoop of vanilla ice cream and cascading hot fudge.

Are you eating? she asked.

Don't play with them, he said. For god's sake, don't encourage them.

Fine, she said, and then didn't say anything else for a while.

Are you mad now? he asked.

I just need to go to bed, she said, and hung up a bit too quickly, but not so quickly that she didn't retain plausible deniability that it was accidental.

She brushed her teeth and washed her face, willing herself to stop crying, to pull herself together. You are an adult, she told herself as she flossed, the most adult thing she could think to do to reinforce said adultness. This is life. Deal with it. But she could not push from her mind the simple questions that plagued her: Why couldn't her husband say something kind or comforting, *I'm so sorry* or *Thank you for all you do*? Why did he not grasp the transactional emotional norms of customary human interaction? Was he able to empathize, or was he actually, as they sometimes joked, a sociopath who had had a very stable and loving upbringing and thus did not kill people but, rather, couldn't recognize emotions and hurt her feelings some/all of the time?

She lay in bed beside the boy and stared at the indistinct shapes of darkness, the softly pixelated ceiling, the charcoal maw of her closet. She wished she hadn't cried on the phone. Perhaps her husband would have taken her more seriously. To be understood by him, she needed a different approach, but she hadn't been able to maintain her composure at such a late hour, after such a peculiar day that occurred amid a run of peculiar days.

He didn't understand anything, not her sadness or her anger, not why the dogs had been so oddly disturbing. And she hadn't even begun to try to explain how she had felt called by the retriever, how it had somehow spoken to her, how it had been so alluring, so comforting, as if it understood all her woes, all her innermost urges and struggles. No, she would never try to explain such a thing to her husband. It would ruin whatever small bit of credibility she had left. Her intuition, her feelings didn't matter to him—they were *unbelievable*, in fact. That was the precise word—*unbelievable*—in the manner of tall tales, urban legends, folk remedies, aliens, mythical creatures rumored to roam the woods, and so her feelings were immediately discounted, even though she knew them to be the truest things in her human experience, a light to show the way.

She dug through the pile of storybooks beside the bed until she uncovered, by the faint glow of the nightlight, her *Field Guide,* which she flipped open despite her exhaustion, for Wanda White always seemed to have the precise passage to soothe the mother's soul.

Wanda. Wanda. How she yearned to meet Wanda, to weep

into her powdery-smelling chest and have this older woman stroke her hair as her own mother never had. To be babied inside the softness and warmth of a cardiganed embrace. A morsel of tenderness . . . Oh, dear Wanda.

"After all," the mother read, her night vision honed more now than ever, "what is more unbelievable than pushing a small human from a small hole between your legs, or having a masked, robed stranger slice open your belly and pull from it a mewling, bloodied babe? Both are absolutely preposterous propositions, not able to be believed and yet undeniable in the presence of the child, a factual reality."

She paused, tears in her eyes, which she harshly rubbed away.

As if the book itself was her most cherished friend. As if its pages knew her heart. She kept reading.

> . . . the unbelievable is not only credible but essential, and has a very real place in the world. I will go so far as to attest that the unbelievable is another way of knowing, an organizing principle that does not run in contradiction to but, rather, in communion with the organizing paradigms of science. The unbelievable, while perhaps not communicating straightforward truths, can communicate deeper truths if a person is willing to be patient, to listen, to contemplate.

THE NEXT MORNING, SHE woke with *the unbelievable* still alive inside her, under what felt like a spell. She rose to make the boy breakfast, and as her son attempted to eat a bowl of yogurt—spreading most of it across his face and pulling it through his hair—the mother absently washed dishes. *Who is Wanda White?* she obsessed. She imagined Wanda White's office on a sun-dappled campus, the many tweed jackets and skirts hung in an uncluttered line in her closet.

She picked at a spot of hardened egg yolk on a plate and positively knew that Wanda White wasn't married and was in very good health. She always wore sunscreen and liked to eat vegetables. She was happy and fulfilled, traveling the world to study creatures in which no one else believed, then coming back to campus to spend long quiet hours in her office poring over her notes and turning them into something smart and useful. Perhaps she was the campus kook, her scholarship considered unserious and hoaxlike by others in the department. Well, then, why had they hired her? Her work was more interesting than the rest of the university's combined, more groundbreaking. Then why have I never heard of her? the mother wondered as the boy screamed and clapped, flinging yogurt droplets that landed on the already dirty kitchen floor. Why has she never been on a morning show? On NPR? In the newsfeed on the mother's phone?

Perhaps she was just a charlatan, but if so, why was she employed by the university? Obviously, her work *was* dubious. Bird Women of Peru, though they sounded lovely, did not sound altogether factual.

Wanda White was housed within the Philosophy Department, which did indeed seem the wrong place. Shouldn't she be in some science department? Anthropology, perhaps? That her discipline fell under the umbrella of philosophy made the mother wonder if her book and scholarship might pointedly have been crafted so as to make a reader consider whether it could be true.

After breakfast, she sat on the living-room floor with the boy, rolling a cement truck back and forth to him as he cackled with delight. On her phone, she scrolled through the University of Sacramento website to find Wanda White's faculty page. No picture. Only the scantest of information. An e-mail address, though, which she pasted into a new e-mail and then closed, still blank, saved to a draft. She would collect all her questions and thoughts, all her many ideas about White, and write them down tonight, after the boy was asleep. She watched him as he now put marble after marble into the plastic tubes he had fit together there in the living room, awestruck and delighted as they slid from top to bottom, spinning whirligigs and dropping through chutes with a satisfying, crisp *plink*. He squealed with delight, clapping his hands or placing them on the floor and jumping into an astoundingly vertical donkey kick. This boy. Her boy.

She took him to the park a few blocks from their house, because the day was gorgeous and the park near. Really, they should be going there more frequently, probably every day. It was the perfect sort of afternoon in the warm summer shade, the boy climbing and squealing and putting wood chips in his mouth and then taking them out, and the mother alone with her thoughts about White and magic and women and whatnot, until she heard what sounded to be a pack of jackals, and turned her head, and there they were. She recognized them from her infrequent trips to Book Babies. They were the mommies. The Book Mommies. A nausea overtook her, though she could not have specified exactly why. What even were the chances, the Big Blonde in the lead with an all-terrain side-by-side stroller that the mother knew for a fact cost well over a thousand dollars, and her sidekicks in tow, the mommy with the mopey little boy whose nose was always running, and the mommy with a hyperactive three-year old prone to throwing pebbles. The mother collected her son as quickly as she could, for she did not want to make small talk, did not actually have any interest in selling herbs, did not want to be polite about the weather or naps or potty training, for she didn't care and did not want her communion with White, with the day, and with this lovely afternoon, to be broken by these women and their children and their wretched contentment.

Oh, hiiii! the Big Blonde said and waved, and the mother said, Hi! We were just leaving!

Even in her haste to collect the diaper bag and sundry toys strewn about in the grass, to retrieve the blue sippy cup and wayward bag of dry cereal, she couldn't help but notice the women accompanying the Big Blonde, the same two always at her side during any activity. The mother of the mopey boy was short, with stubby legs and arms, ponderous eyes framed by extravagantly lush lashes, and straight hair that hung in hanks just to her shoulders. The other woman was all athleticism and yoga pants, her dark eyes exuding an alert intelligence echoed by the pert, sharp features of her poreless face. She twitched her head to and fro to track her ward's erratic movements, and in the process emphasized the volume of her thick, flat-ironed hair.

The mother could not avoid passing in close proximity to this little group, for the park was fenced and the mommies surrounded the only exit.

Hi! the mother said as she neared the group, but what she really hoped to communicate was *Bye! We have such a full day! Really need to get to it! Not a moment to be wasted!*

I don't think I ever properly introduced myself, the Big Blonde said as she positioned herself in front of the park gate—*purposefully blocking it,* one might even say—and shook her head in feigned exasperation at herself.

What a silly! she squeaked to her twins in their stroller, as mothers sometimes do, having entire conversations with their children which actually are directed at other sentient adults nearby.

Oh, that's fine, the mother said, looking to the gate in a silent and what she felt was very polite request to pass.

I'm Jen, the Big Blonde said, and this is Babs and Poppy. Here she gestured in the direction of the short woman, who tipped her head to one side and offered a sad little smile, and the athletic mom, who nodded and displayed her recently whitened teeth.

So nice to meet you! the mother offered hurriedly as she eased between the strollers and, for perhaps the first and last time ever, softened with relief upon hearing her son's wail of pain, for she had accidentally knocked his little shins up against another stroller in her haste and, as such, simply *had to* attend to him and *get him home to lunch quickly*, for certainly he was *famished*, and now it was an *emergency*, a *meltdown*, and she must reasonably exit this situation immediately, which she did.

Okay, sorry, the mother said. Oh my god, so nice to meet you, but I just have to . . . She gestured to the weeping boy, then glanced at the three women, who were considering her, not meanly exactly, but skeptically, no longer warm, as they had been moments ago, but hands on hips and eyes just narrowing, as if to ask, *What is your problem?*, which was a very fair question indeed.

She had been a bit rude, she decided later, when she thought about it. She must be more polite the next time. She could have at least introduced herself. Asked about herbs. What *was* her problem? That evening, as she began a letter to Wanda White, she believed earnestly that White was her only hope, though of precisely what, she did not know. She had convinced herself, at least a bit, that the *Field Guide* had magical properties, that it was in conversation with her thoughts, that she had a psychic bond with White. She realized there was no rhyme or reason to these conclusions. But still.

WW—

I've recently come across your book *A Field Guide to Magical Women* and the research you've done around the world. I have so many questions, but I'd like to begin by asking—if I may humbly take up just a few minutes of your time—whether your research is, well, "true" in a scientific and rational sense, or whether you're instead *performing* scholarship so as to make larger points about, say, the limits of knowing and the failure of science to fully describe the world?

I realize this is a somewhat philosophical question, but I also saw on the University of Sacramento's website that you are part of the Philosophy Department and thought that such questions might not be outside your purview and even welcome.

On a personal note, I've recently embarked on a peculiar and unexpectedly fraught era of my life—motherhood, to say it as plainly and simply as I can, though certainly motherhood is in no way plain or simple—and find myself coming up against questions that seem to intersect both philosophically and experientially with your work. All this is to say I look forward very much to hearing from you and thank you for any time you're able to offer to my queries.

Yours,
MM

The mother read and then reread and then read again her very first note to Wanda White, at the glowing window of her laptop, at the dark kitchen table. She did not want to come on too strong, did not want to sound entirely irrational by bring-ing up her transformation right off the bat, wanted instead to present herself as a thoughtful and engaged reader interested in the same questions and pursuits. The cursor blinked in the darkness of the kitchen, for it was now late—early morning, really—and her son had been asleep for hours. She would be a wreck in the morning, but she didn't care. Her thoughts had stretched toward Wanda White all day, and she simply had to remove them from her brain and send them off to the shadowy academic in order to unburden herself.

As soon as she hit SEND, her entire body went limp, so limp she found it hard even to get herself up the stairs to the bedroom to tip into bed beside the boy. So relieved was the mother that she was very nearly asleep before she reached the bed, now in a state of sublime relaxation, the likes of which she hadn't experienced in years.

Imagine, then, what force of nature or god or magic it must have taken to exhume her from the delicious depths of sleep to which she had descended. Imagine the power it must have required to pull a mother from her first restful night in years—entire body slack and dead, breathing slowed to nearly not even there, her dreams as real as life itself. She moaned as she was achingly pulled from the molasses of sleep to the *clickety-clack* of her blood and a stomach sick with adrenaline.

Outside her bedroom window, things scratched and snarled, huffed through wet snouts, gurgled and tongued. She sensed bodies moving in a frenzy, among and over one another, impatient, anxious, on edge, and waiting.

Jesus, she thought hazily. What in the fuck. What in the fucking fuck.

She touched the boy's chest as he snored softly beside her, then rose and threw on sweats. In the kitchen, she grabbed a butcher knife, then thought better of it and instead went to the hall closet and found the baseball bat. She was tired and enraged and would beat to death anything she found out there. She would kill it with her own hands.

She peered out the high window and in the light of the full moon saw them.

Dogs. So many dogs. Fifteen? Twenty? She scratched the coarse hair that now covered the back of her neck and her shoulders, then bared her teeth. She could hear every sound, smell every smell. She slowly opened the side door and stood behind the screen, looking out into the night. The mother smelled her before she saw her, the strawberries and soap of the retriever, and there, at the top of the steps, she sat. Beside her, the pudgy basset hound, with her pretty eyelashes, and the collie, her body tensed with energy even in the middle of the night.

Behind them, scores of other dogs—more even than twenty, she now saw.

I know you, she growled at the canine trio, not altogether meanly but more like *I'll be damned, waking me up in the middle of the night, I really should have been more polite to you today.*

They had come for her, as she had both feared and hoped they would. They wanted her to join them, to take her, but she wouldn't go, she would not. Something inside her quickened despite her resistance, an elation at the thought of joining them, yet not nearly as articulated as that. More a sense that her body might leap forward and tumble down the steps and out into the night without first consulting her. That she would succumb to the delicious buzz of the late-summer cicadas and dewy weight of the pollen-heavy air and be seduced by it, pulled into its warm embrace, were she not careful. Besides, what she was seeing simply could not be real, had to be a waking dream, some sort of hypnopompic hallucination brought on by stress and exhaustion. She shook her head back and forth violently and then shimmied all the way down to her tail, as if she'd just emerged from a pool and was throwing off droplets of water.

Beneath her sweatpants, her tail twitched instinctively. She suddenly had independent control of each of her ears, which she moved back and forth to listen to each and every breath and whine and gulp of the dogs.

This is not real, she thought as she ventured out onto the porch, then down the steps, propelled by a guttural longing, the polyphony of night-noise, so many luxuriant smells.

What's to lose? It's just make-believe—a thing she often told her son—just a game.

She had left the bat by the door and, once in the driveway, saw that the dogs filled the pavement and spilled out into the street, then back into the pools of shadow darkening her neighbors' lawns.

The retriever took her hand as she had yesterday, and led her through the sea of animals, each one of them as alert and still as the night around them.

In the middle of the driveway, in the middle of the dogs, she was not afraid. She waited. They waited. Then, from somewhere on the outskirts of the fray, a dog let loose with a high and plaintive bray—the first note of a hymn, the mother thought, a call to worship.

With the note, the retriever took the cuff of the mother's sweatpants in her mouth and began to pull down on the material.

Hey, stop, she said, laughing at first and then stopping, because the retriever did not let go, would not let go, and the collie started in on the other leg, pulling at the fabric, so the mother had to hold tight to the waistband to keep her pants up.

Stop, she insisted, now more firmly, kicking first at the retriever and then at the collie. They did not let go, merely held tighter as she pulled against them.

Oh Jesus, she said.

The collie grabbed higher up on one leg, and then a bushy shepherd with different-colored eyes started on the other. A muscular black Lab hopped up on its back legs and nipped at the hem of her T-shirt, its teeth ripping holes as the Lab came back down to the ground, mouth still closed hard on the fabric.

The mother flailed, panicked. She kicked at the dogs and knocked at them with her hands, but more and more teemed toward her. She was jarred to one side, then the other, then forward onto her hands and knees, and there was no stopping them at that point. She covered her head with her hands, and they ripped at her clothing, pulling apart the back of her T-shirt, easily rending the thin fabric of her underwear.

It was over as abruptly as it had started, not a paw on her. She panted on the ground in the fetal position, naked. Her ears twitched, and she could hear only the gentle breath of dogs all around and smell their exertion.

She raised her head. The dogs paced about her, whined and pawed the ground, side-eyed her, stopped and stared, fur raised along their spine ridges. She curled her fingers against the pavement of the driveway, showed her teeth. Her eyes lit with fire, and she could feel the hair on her head growing, her mane expanding into a monstrous spectacle. The muscles in her haunches rolled. One thought came and then left as quickly: *you are an animal.*

She didn't want to think, only to act. Only to survive. She snarled, then lunged blindly into the throng of bodies surrounding her, teeth searching for flesh. She was hair and blood and bone. She was instinct and anger. She knew nothing but the weight of her body and the pull of the earth against it, the particular wetness of the night air, the bats that flew through her periphery, every movement of the paws and legs and heads around her. She searched the night with her mouth, wanting to sink her teeth into anything. She closed her eyes and became pure movement, pure darkness, a twitch and surge, the animal's first dream.

SHE AWOKE THE NEXT morning in bed, T-shirt and underwear on, sweats in a pile on the floor beside the bed. She grimaced and stared at the sweats for a while, tugged at the neck of her T-shirt.

Though she knew she should be worried, should wonder whether she was losing her mind given the state of her fully intact clothes—knew she should call the doctor immediately and make an appointment, should probably be evaluated by a psychiatrist, should probably be placed on an assortment of drugs, should confide in her husband as soon as he returned home and relate to him this break in reality she had experienced, the coming of the dogs, the rending of her garments, and then, there, in the morning light, her clothes whole and untouched—even though she knew all this, as she lay there in bed, the boy crawling over her, she could not help but bubble with a near-religious ecstasy, something bright and pure. It welled from her core.

She grabbed the boy and threw him into the air again and again, until he was breathless with laughter. She buried her wet nose into his neck, nuzzling him, and he screamed with delight and tugged on her ears, freshly fuzzed. She took his arm gently between her teeth and he screamed again and ran from the room. She pounced from the bed and followed him, on all fours, to his bedroom. Her hair was long, longer than it had ever been, and streamed down her back, over her haunches, the ends tickling the backs of her legs. They played until they both couldn't play anymore, and the room was ravaged, train tracks scattered, stacks of books now toppled, the bedsheets in a pile on the floor.

Downstairs, she whistled as she made the boy's breakfast. What had happened last night? She understood she should be scared, but she simply wasn't. A fresh power animated her body, and she loved her body, loved being a body, and loved the boy, another body she had made.

Maybe this was what happened to all moms and no one had told her, just like how she hadn't known her feet would widen and extend after her son's birth and her hair would come out by the handful in the shower. Maybe this was one of *those* secrets of motherhood. The boy ate his hash browns, and she sat in the tiny plastic chair next to him at his tiny table, looking out the window absently, stroking the hair on the back of her neck. She rose and took a steak from the fridge. She cut off two very tiny pieces from the slab of meat, then threw the rest in the skillet.

Shall we try this? she asked the boy, taking him the bits of raw meat. Should we be doggies? she asked. He nodded and smiled, his mouth full of food. They each took one of the small red pellets of meat and put them in their mouths, chewed. She growled and tickled him, and he laughed.

We're wild animals! she said, and the boy said, Go outside!, and she agreed.

The boy ran to the door while she finished cooking the steak and then put it on a plate. As she turned from the counter, plate in hand, the boy bounded back into the kitchen and shouted, Look!

He held up a dead mouse, and she screamed and then laughed.

Where did you find that? she asked. Yucky!

No yucky, he said. Come, Mama.

She followed him, and he stuck out his fat little finger, eyes wide, and watched her to see how she would react to the pile—a literal pile—of mice and squirrels and rabbits and even one flaccid raccoon which had been left just outside the door, on the porch.

She gasped.

An offering. A sign. A welcome.

VORACIOUS WITH DEATH, SHE and the boy descended midday on their favorite lunch place downtown, just across from the library. One of those boutique grocery-and-deli places, with aisles of upscale cookies and crackers, imported jellies. Hot and cold buffets for the college kids, but also a favorite of the mommy set. A person could select just a pile of mac and cheese and three fingers of chicken if she wanted. She could purchase an entire plate of grapes. She could, if need be, arrange on a plate two cheese cubes as eyes and a kiwi slice as a nose with a splat of strawberry yogurt below for a mouth. And there was also wine by the glass.

The boy loved going there and instructing his mother exactly what to put on his plate. He pointed like a little general, grunted commands, clapped and sulked and bullied his way into precisely what he desired. The mother piled meat-loaf slathered with ketchup, crumbly pieces of pot roast, more chicken fingers, a mountainous pile of a lovely baked corn concoction the immensity of which made her son clap with joy, for he, too, loved the baked corn. In a separate small bowl, she dolloped mac and cheese.

At the cash register, the store girl weighed her pound-age of meats and allowed herself a momentary glance at the mother, for which she had been waiting. The mother smiled and the boy laughed, and she said, Totally PMS-ing, and the girl laughed uneasily and pressed buttons on the register.

Totally, the store girl said.

It cost upward of thirty dollars for their food, so large was the mother's hunger and, in turn, her lunch.

She and the boy sat at one of the outdoor tables where other mothers tended to their children, insisting they eat a green bean or offering yogurt, wiping schmutz from chins and cleaning up spills.

The mother and her boy sat side by side. She set the bowl of macaroni before him and cut a chicken finger into small bites, which she arranged on a napkin. She was unusually silent as she did this, distracted by her hunger and the smell of the meat. The mother may have been in some sort of ani-mal trance—cutting the chicken finger, yes, but doing it without knowing what she was doing. She could focus only on her hunger, a hunger that filled up every space inside her until she was nearly crazed. She turned to her plate.

Oh! The glory of the meatloaf! The suppleness of the muscle fibers as the pot roast fell apart! She used a fork and then she used her hands and then she simply allowed her face to fall upon the pile, and you could suppose this was some sort of worship, the mother with head bowed, taking the foodstuffs directly into her body. There was a purity to such an act.

The boy watched with wide eyes for but a moment and then screamed with glee and did the same, plunging his face into the mac and cheese and then sitting up with a noodle stuck to one cheek, cheese on his eyelids. He clapped.

The mother continued in her fugue, the feel of the meat in her throat filling her. The boy reached over to take a bite of the corn and she growled low and quiet and he retreated, to pick up the chicken tender in his mouth and shake it side to side.

She gulped the meat down and moaned with the taste of it, snuffled and chomped, and then nudged the pile of corn with her nose toward her son. He picked it up with one pudgy hand, slammed it into his mouth, and closed his eyes as he chewed.

She ate and ate and ate; with a singular animal focus she ate. She licked the plate clean, and when she arose, she saw that all the mothers around her had quieted. Even the businessmen were off their phones, watching.

She picked up her napkin and calmly wiped her face. She took a very deep breath. She would act natural, play it cool. She would not cry. She would not cry!

Horrifically, she met eyes with a man at the next table over, a guy with a smart haircut and an open-collared button-down, his briefcase beside him on a chair.

Hungry, he said, not a question but more a verbal fist-bump, a somewhat awed acknowledgment of what had just transpired.

Oh, she said, as her face flushed red. She turned away quickly and tried to laugh.

Ruff! she said playfully to her son, unable to muster a lighthearted chuckle. They were just playing! It was doggy games! She was a good mother, and this was just a game, she said to herself, to anyone who might have asked.

Ruff, ruff! the boy barked back, his face alight with joy and slathered with cheese. She patted his head and wiped his face, and he dived back into his food and the mother had a very dignified sip of water.

It seemed that folks had gone back to their lunches, but she did not altogether look, because it was too horrifying, this loss of self-consciousness she had experienced, the overwhelming hunger that took her and drove her into some other state, in which only smell and taste and hunger mattered.

Okay, she said quietly to herself, taking deep breaths. Okay.

Mama! the boy screeched. He loved her, every way she was.

Be doggy, he said, and she smiled and signed *All done* as she said it, flipping her palms toward him. All done, honey. More doggy later. He barked and went back to his food, content for now.

The mother felt a hand on her shoulder and turned to find an older woman there. She smelled of sweet powders, and her short gray hair was styled elegantly. Everything about her was pleasant: her soft makeup and clean glasses, the wrinkles around her smiling eyes, the fuzz of her cardigan on a summer day.

What fun it is to have a boy! she said.

The mother laughed.

Ah yes, she said. So fun.

And what a mother you are, she added. What a wonderful mother! To have such fun with your child. I remember the days.

Oh, thank you, the mother said bashfully, somewhat amazed—this woman who was not chiding her but instead reveling and remembering.

We used to play doggies, too! she said, now talking to the boy. My son and I! It was so fun, and he just loved it. Errrrr, she said, showing her teeth to the boy and waggling her head back and forth, then chuckling as she patted the mother's shoulder again and walked away.

The mother watched the older woman and wished she would stay, sit down and chat, tell her about her life. You used to play . . . *dogs*? Really? Did people think you were strange? How old is your son now? How is your relationship with him? Did you work when he was young? What were your passions? Did you make the right choices? What would you have done differently, looking back now? Can you please tell me what to do, how to be happy and fulfilled? Can you please tell me the secrets? Because I know there are secrets, and I would like to know all of them.

She nearly wept with longing, to sit down across from the woman, take her old, soft, highly lotioned hands in hers, and ask her questions, so many, many questions. Her own mother, who was far away, rarely called, and when she did spoke only of the garden and the weather, the shortening days, how they were in dire need of rain. She had once, while pregnant, attempted to talk to her about childbirth, what to expect, how she was scared of the pain, and how had her mother managed, to which her mother had only the offer of *It's called labor because it's hard work*—which she understood as a consolation. Sure, her mother was saying, it's bad, but since you are a woman, this is your lot in life, your work, to do what's hard, what's unspeakably painful, and then to keep this covenant of silence.

The mother packed up her things, wiped down her son, delivered the dirty plates to the bus tub as quickly as she could, then ran out the doors, following her son, to the playground. She scanned the playground and storefronts for the woman but couldn't see her anywhere.

Her son barked somewhere on the playground, bidding her to play hide-and-seek. The mother turned her face to the sun and howled, then sprinted toward him, to play.

YOU'LL NEVER BELIEVE IT, she said to her husband on the phone that night.

Mmm, he said, distracted.

This morning, on the porch, there was a pile of dead animals.

Excuse me? he said.

Rabbits and squirrels and maybe some mice. A raccoon on top. She let out an elated whoop of a laugh.

That's strange, her husband said, and she said, Well, I guess it is, but it's also sort of fun.

Are you okay? he asked.

I feel wonderful, she said. Better than I have in months!

Well, that's good news, he said.

Is it? she asked, laughing. I mean, is it good news for *you*?

What's that supposed to mean? he asked.

She laughed and laughed and laughed.

WW—

I have been considering what really matters in life. I realize this isn't an original question, but still wanted to present my ideas to you, in case you had been thinking along similar lines.

Before my child, I had never longed for a family, or even to be married. Instead, I fantasized about the echoing rooms of a museum, the expanse of dustless floors and white walls, the certain sacred hush that comes with such spaces, and then my work there, in that space. This was the first fantasy, when I was a child, the most generic of fantasies, but over the years, it inflated and morphed. I thought only toward expensive haircuts with very little bangs and trendy eyeglasses, a sun-washed studio in which many interesting projects were under way. Friends with lots of opinions and good taste, trips to Europe, summers at residencies, and on and on. I won't bore you. What I'm saying is that I had imagined this entire life. I had dreamt it.

But then my body. Then a child. And, yes, he has brought me great joy—being a mother, despite my loudest protestations, has been pure and sweet and true—but there is not room for the child within the sun-washed studio. Or, rather, there is not room for art within my house with my child. It is as if all my dreams have been reset. The walls are blank, and with them I am blank, too.

All this is to say, what should a woman fight for? Given her limited resources, limited time and energy and inspiration, what is worth fighting for? Is it art? In the grand scheme of things, it sometimes seems so pointless, even selfish. To force one's point of view on the world—who really needs it, especially when a child needs a mother so immediately?

I don't have any answers other than that art seems essential, as essential as mothering. In order to be a self, it is essential. I should perhaps cease being a person without it.

Is that enough of a reason, that it matters to me?

MM

THERE ARE SCRATCHES ON the door, inside and out. The edges of the books are chewed. One of the pillows is ripped and ruined. She will not leave the house and go into town; she does not want to. She and the boy play with Play-Doh and bake a pie and dance to songs in the living room. Her entire body is covered in hair. The cat—its fluffy tail, its supple belly—is irresistible. She loves to run and run and run outside on the lawn with the boy. They play catch. They play fetch.

Should we get a dog? she asks the boy, and he says Yes.

Maybe we'll ask Daddy, she says, and then she says, Or maybe we won't.

They walk to the neighborhood hardware store and get dog treats and a shiny stainless-steel bowl for water that she likes very much. She tries out the bowl once they get home, and the boy laughs, then he tries it, too. He wants to drink all his drinks from then on from the dog bowl, like a dog, and she does also, so they do. They share with the cat, because they're good dogs.

She is becoming a better mother because she is becoming a better dog! Dogs don't need to *work*. Dogs don't care about *art*. Why had this never occurred to her before?

She *likes* the idea of being a dog, because she can bark and snarl and not have to justify it. She can run free if she wants. She can be a body and instinct and urge. She can be hunger and rage, thirst and fear, nothing more. She can revert to a pure, throbbing state. She had that freedom when she gave birth, had screamed and shat and sworn and would have killed had she needed to. Her husband nearly passed out from the noises coming from her mouth. That's what he called them: *noises*. For a time, she lay with one leg in the air, and her doula told her this was the position she would have put her in had she not done it herself, to help the baby turn, but the mother had known instinctively. She had followed her body. What else was there to follow? If she could not be part of the world of ambition and money and careers, she wanted to leave it behind entirely and recede into the wildness of her deepest dreams, of her corporeal yearning. No more reading about who was in what juried show. No more berating herself for not trying, each day planning to get back to her work and every day failing. She would simply give in to what she felt she was being called to be: an animal taking care of its young with no wishes or cares beyond that. Fine, then. She could almost feel the hairs sprouting from each and every pore on her body.

She barked from sheer happiness and the boy barked, too, then scratched her on the head.

"... **FOR WHO IS TO** say what wonders and mysteries women grow within themselves?" the passage read, in the dim lamplight, before she drifted away on the couch in that late afternoon, after their daylong canine reverie, the boy snoozing on the living-room floor in just his diaper.

Who is to say what feats and follies, what absolutely notable-even-to-be-imagined modes of existence women have accessed since the dawn of human history? A woman, when pushed to her limit, will call on all her faculties, all her skills, all the biological tools and tricks at her disposal, not only to survive but, moreover—for those who have reproduced—to care for her young. As such, the mother's powers supersede

*that of the un-childed woman, for the mother—especially
the mother of infants and very small children—occupies
that peculiar space of in between—not fully human or fully
animal—and it is in this liminal otherworld where we find
many of the most compelling magical women. In this space
her powers are at their most formidable and her constitution
at its most volatile, creating a nexus of unmatched capacity.*

She sank deeper into the sofa and blinked to stay awake, for
the writing seemed to emerge from somewhere deep inside
her, even though it was right there, on the page. . . .

*Perhaps most peculiar: most magical women are not aware
of their powers and proceed into the realm of the magical
without so much as a parting glance. To them, this journey
is as natural as breath, as falling into sleep. To pass from the
world of the known to that of the unknown often happens
unconsciously, but whether conscious or not, it marks the
beginning of what the Kwolo call her aga, or second life.*

HER HUSBAND RETURNED HOME Friday evening. It
was late in the summer, so late that if you squinted you could
begin to see the leaves of the trees turning. It had been a beautiful day and, even after a five-hour drive, he was in a great
mood, because why wouldn't he be?

The side screen door was unlocked, and the heavy winter door behind it ajar, as they often left it in the summer. A
breeze pushed in through open windows, and music played
softly from the living room.

Hello, he said, kicking off his shoes and leaving his suitcase by the washer.

The kitchen was orderly and clean, the bathroom shady
and smelling of bleach. The beds were made and the carpets

vacuumed. Beside their bed sat a new kennel, bedded down with a soft throw blanket, a down pillow from the bed. No dirty clothes on the floor, as there usually were. No wayward toys strewn hither and yon, as there usually were. Twilight breathed in and out of the open windows, moving the gauzy curtains.

He walked through the house and called for his wife.

Honey, he said, where are you?

In the living room, he found the boy—happy and clean, in only a diaper—sitting beside a dog who was stretched out on the clean rug. The dog was enormous and reminded the husband of a wolf, with a thick coat of silver-and-black fur. It opened one eye to watch the husband.

Baby, where's Mama? he asked. The boy clapped and laughed.

Dog! he said joyfully, then wrapped his doughy arms around the neck of the animal and laid his tiny head on her chest.

The animal rose as the husband approached it, hands in the air as if he were being robbed.

Good dog, he said. Good.

The animal pulled back its lips to show its teeth, then snarled, quietly, from deep in its chest. In one sharp move-ment, the dog rose and sprinted to the back of the house, to the French doors, which had been left open, and out onto the lawn, where the long day was darkening. The child screamed with glee, and the husband chased after the dog, out the same open doors. His wife, he thought, moving toward the coming night. She must be out there.

two

In the distance, she heard her husband in the backyard call for her, but she was not that woman anymore, that mother and wife. She was Nightbitch, and she was fucking amazing. It seemed she had been waiting for this for a very, very long time.

She charted her path by keeping to the shadows. She trampled the carefully planted petunias along the house where her across-the-street neighbor lived, a man named Stanley who voted Republican and would never loan out a tool from his sizable collection, would barely say hello when she passed, would not abide for even a moment her son walking on his grass, which the old man tended with the care of a doting nursemaid, would in fact glare at the small child and cross his arms as the mother chastised the boy and bade him come to her, would not even smile when she apologized and tried to make a joke of it.

His fucking grass, she thought as she crouched by the side of his house and took a monstrous shit. She clawed at the grass beside the pile and ripped up clods of turf, then went to the edge of the green expanse where Stanley had thrown fresh grass seed on the patchy dirt and kicked it onto the sidewalk.

She made her way through back lawns and along fence lines, avoiding the pools of light cast by streetlamps, to the tunnel that passed beneath the train tracks, and then the small park that ran along a small stream. She knew that homeless men slept on the benches there, and once, while riding her bike, had happened upon a group of young men passing around a pipe. She usually tried to avoid the park, because she was afraid of what might happen to her there, but tonight it was the only place she wanted to be. Her heart thudded as she smelled all the animals, smelled the pungent men asleep on the benches.

I could rip out their throats while they sleep! she thought, as a giddy power surged through her. She was overwhelmed by her strength. She was awash in her own violence. She wanted to howl, but instead crept down the path that cut through the woods, stepping gingerly so as not to make a sound. The cold woodland creek moved in the periphery of her consciousness, and she thought toward its midnight chill and furtive, relentless flow. In these ways, it was her kin.

Within the moonlight, she could see the life of the night not normally available to her senses. Bugs crawled on leaves, and a bird startled high up in a tree. Beneath the grasses and old leaves, a snake pushed its way toward a mouse, moving the air around it ever so slightly. The whole of the night clicked and purred about her. The moonlight itself seemed to vibrate and bring to life each and every thing.

She froze beyond stillness when she glimpsed the rabbit by a cottonwood tree. The hair on the back of her neck rose, and she bared her teeth. She lifted one arm and set it down, then raised the other. Her movements became almost mechanical, slow and measured. She meant to be a shadow that folded and fluttered through tricks of light.

The rabbit twitched its nose, an ear, then sprang toward the darkness. Each muscle in her body tightened and then exploded with movement. She surged after the animal, crashed into the bushes and ripped through weeds, to trap its hind leg before it could disappear into a copse of briars.

She clamped her teeth around its neck, and the small animal breathed inside her mouth. She slung it violently back and forth. Her eyes blazed, and she threw it to the ground to see if it would move, then picked it back up and shook it again.

The musk of its fear!

The warmth of its blood!

The give of its skull as she crushed it between her teeth!

She carried the dead animal in her mouth back through the night, the neighborhood, until she was behind her house, in the farthest corner of the lawn, digging a shallow hole in which to bury the creature, her treasure, her prize.

Afterward, she paced the lawn. She smelled the spot where her son had lain in the grass earlier that day, and the path he'd walked from door to lawn, the places where his hands had touched the blue ball still at the side of the driveway. She smelled the dirt and she smelled the car tires. She smelled the back steps, where the cat liked to sit in the sun, and then she smelled the path the cat took to the patio and through the lawn, followed the smell to her spot beneath the crab-apple tree. Beneath the tree she smelled the crab apples and all the phantom scents of chipmunks and squirrels and birds. She lay down and rolled in the grass to collect the smells in her fur and moaned with the joy of it, then proceeded to the compost bin, and the little rock garden where she liked to plant spring flowers, and there was her smell, her human smell—she knew it immediately.

She couldn't have known that what she had needed all along—more than medical attention or psychotherapy, more than choosing happiness or adjusting her attitude—was to sink her sharp teeth into something living and bloody and feel its essence drain away until it was simply a rotting and unmoving thing.

Not iron deficiency or episode. Nothing "wrong" with her. Just one night. One night of violence was what she needed. One night to not care what anyone thought, to shit where she pleased, to not be needed by any living thing, and to be only a body in motion in the dark, a shadow, a ghost of herself, who listened only to the mandates of her body.

Exhausted, she curled in the grass to sleep.

NAKED AND DAMP WITH dew, curled into herself, she awoke the morning after her midnight escapade with an overwhelming sense of well-being heretofore unknown to the mother—or, should we say, to Nightbitch. The sun crested the far edge of town and bathed the backyard in a clean and even light. Every blade of grass glistened. Every bird sang.

She was well rested despite her few hours of sleep beneath the crab-apple tree. Her body felt strong and alive, and she was not chilled even though she was naked. She was awake in a way she had not been since her child was born, maybe even before, not groggy, not grumpy, but enthusiastic and, she imagined, completely capable of going on an early-morning jog, though she had never done this in her life. Her sinuses were clear and her eyes bright. Her hair felt clean to the touch, and she imagined her skin dewy and unmarked by the years of not enough sleep and not enough water and not enough sunscreen and not enough salad.

She unfurled her limbs, spooled out each arm to feel the pull of skin against bone, unfolded her legs slowly, and then wiggled her toes until they snapped. She stood, and her spine popped from bottom to top, then stretched her arms to the sky and yawned wonderfully, as she'd only seen actors do in movies.

She gazed over the backyard, the bees and bugs coming to life, the soft morning sunlight peeking between branches, the big shiny leaves of the hostas. She didn't know she could feel this good, this happy, this awake and sated.

She crept to the garage and typed the code to open the door, stayed bent and low as the door rose with a too-loud mechanical grind, then retrieved the extra key from inside. She scuttled to the side door, covering herself, and let herself in, feeling as Eve must have that first morning out of the garden, but, honestly, what a relief. To understand yourself anew. No longer to linger in the *what ifs*. To now know the truth.

The bathroom mirror revealed to her a being hitherto unmet, hair matted and mud-clotted, face smeared with blood and dirt, nostrils caked with a tarlike soot. Her hands looked as though she'd been gardening for weeks. Red scratches crisscrossed her legs. She pulled a thorn from the bottom of her foot, then stepped into the shower.

She warmed her skin beneath the hot water and watched as coarse hair and fur rinsed down the drain. Mud from her hands and feet. Bits of leaves and sticks from her hair. Even what she assumed were the points on her canine teeth chipped off, and she spat them into the murky water.

An overwhelming sense of rightness, of *I told you so*, of profound sanity gripped her as she dried herself, slipped on a cool, clean shirt, and then slipped herself into bed between her dreaming husband and dreaming son.

THE FACT OF THE matter was that she had not been wrong about anything. She had not been wrong about the creeping hair on her body or the sharpening teeth. She had not been wrong about the tail or the pack of dogs that arrived inexplicably on her front yard. Her feelings, in fact, about every single thing had been reasonable and precisely on point, not only about the dog stuff but even before, how she was so angry and tired, how she didn't feel it right that she was now at home, out of the workforce, career on hold, art on hold, life on hold indefinitely, while her husband fulfilled himself. Not right that her work raising the child was devalued, women's work, housework, that once she became a housewife she began, ever so slowly, to disappear, until she only fully existed in the presence of her ward. When she considered how she spent each day, it was fair to wonder: without him, did she even exist at all?

Yes, it could be concluded that she was indeed the winner, though of which argument in particular might be more difficult to pin down. She felt she could safely assume she was the winner of *all* arguments, at least recent ones. She felt she could safely trust her instincts and judgment from here on out, even if at first such instincts seemed insane. She could and should feel vindicated, could revel in her rightness, yet how truly infuriating that she could reveal none of her rightness to her husband, now sleeping beside her in bed.

No, certainly, she could in no way, not ever, reveal her transformation to the good man. Though he was a kind man, a reasonable man, she could not be sure of what he might say, what he might do, were she to show him the truest part of her true self. Would he force her to see a doctor or, worse, a psychiatrist? Would there be many orange bottles of prescription pills to dull her transformative jubilee or, worse, halt it altogether? Might he institutionalize her? Separate her from her child? Would she waste away in a bright white room, arms and legs tied to a chair, wearing a soft and downy robe, her eyes blankly staring out the window? Surely he would in no way be able to see how natural her transformation was, how healthy and restorative. Certainly he would not be able to see that their child was well cared for despite her canine propensities, despite their doggy games.

YOU SIMPLY CAN'T DO that, her husband said in the kitchen the morning after her transformation, a look of concern on his face. I get home and you're not here? The boy's alone? And that dog?

Nightbitch stared flatly. She crossed her arms, then uncrossed them in a small gesture of magnanimity. She told herself to try to remain friendly during this conversation, not to snarl, not to show her teeth, not to participate in any aggressive displays, because, truly, she did want to work this out with the smallest of fusses, mostly because she did not want to reveal to her husband what she had done last night, or why she'd had to leave early. She wanted her secrets to remain secrets. Her secrets were the only things these days that were purely hers, things apart from *mother* and *wife* and *middle-aged woman*. Now her secrets were nearly as precious to her as her art had once been, and, as she thought about it, there was something that had been secret about her art, too. The dreaming of ideas, the excitement she held silently inside as she began to work, the heights to which she fantasized a project might grow, the hours of work alone, the thinking and imagining, the conversations with herself. There was something beautifully, deliciously secret and intimate and intoxicating about that life, the art she had made.

To talk about a project too soon would ruin it. And to talk about it too much after it was done would also turn it into something common.

The best way was to make something, silently, secretly, and then have it appear in the world in all of its magnificent and surprising glory. Like birth, she thought. To push a thing from the most private part of yourself. To have it scream upon its arrival. To have it be perfect and glorious, to not have to say a word about it, to simply hold it in your arms, to extend it to the world with just one word of imploration: look.

Yes. Her art. Her secrets. She must keep them as her own, whatever small bits of them were left.

Her husband still waited for an answer, some sort of response.

I left you a note, she said, refusing to apologize, refusing to concede. It wasn't as if she had disappeared inexplicably and completely. The note she had been smart enough to leave behind on the kitchen counter plainly said that she had gone for a long walk and wouldn't be back that night, that she just needed some space, that it was no big deal and not to worry, that she was sorry she'd left the boy by himself but she could tell from the map on her phone that her husband was close by in the car—blocks away, really—and nothing would be hurt by leaving a few minutes early, the house was driving her bonkers and she just needed to get out, she loved him and she loved the boy and she would see them in the morning.

After all, her husband never conceded. He never apologized. He simply argued his way out of everything, or tried to. He simply stood his ground and explained himself evenly and didn't ever undermine his own self-interest. And now this is what she would do as well.

Had he apologized when he knocked over her peanut plant, which she'd been tending for a year, coaxing it bigger and bigger—why was it growing so slowly?—moving it from window to window based on the season, feeding it blue water fertilized with blue powder? Annoyed one Saturday morning when she had dared sleep in, in the middle of making the boy breakfast and reading the boy a book and trying to dress the boy, he had gone to throw a banana peel in the trash and had somehow, in his flummoxed clumsiness, knocked the peanut plant from the windowsill, hastily brushed the dirt back into the pot, and only superficially pushed the plant back into the dirt. He had done all this and not mentioned it, and when the mother saw the mess, the dirt that had not been cleaned from the floor or the windowsill, the already wilted plant— when she had found this and confronted her husband about it, he said with annoyance that the plant had been perched precariously and really, truly, it was bound to fall, suggesting he had merely fulfilled its destiny rather than made any mistake himself.

It had been folly to try to grow a peanut plant. Who grew a peanut plant? And would one even flourish at such a northern latitude? How long did it take them to mature? And how did a person even go about roasting a peanut? Of course, all these and more questions had occurred to her, but still she persevered, because it was *fun,* because it was a project that was just hers, because it was a mother's artistic gesture in the face of obliterating domesticity.

It shouldn't be *dying,* he'd said, annoyed. There's no reason for it to die. Just put it back in the dirt. Water it.

I did, she'd said.

Well, it doesn't make sense that knocking it over would have killed it, he continued matter-of-factly, as if his rationale would bring it back to life.

All you have to say is you're sorry, she said. That will make it all better.

But I want to fix it, he said. *That* will make it better for me.

Just say you're sorry, she said, and instead he went to the plant and fiddled with the dirt, held the plant up, and then watched it fall back down when he let go.

Finally, after all that, he had walked by her, on the way to the living room, and mumbled, Sorry.

She had wanted to bite him by the throat or pummel him with a baseball bat or scream at the top of her lungs, but instead she'd started washing the dishes he had dirtied from breakfast.

And so she emphasized her points, emphasized that she had left a note, did not apologize, said this had been what she needed, and had anything been hurt? No. No! The husband listened, objected, listened more, finally calmed. She made coffee, and they both stood in silence, drinking it. Their son babbled in the living room, playing with—what else?—his trains.

I was afraid for a second *you* were that dog, the husband said sheepishly.

Oh sure, she said. I turned into a dog. Do you hear what you're saying?

Well, you've been saying . . . , he began, then trailed off, unsure of himself and this irrational territory into which he had wandered.

You aren't seriously going to . . . , she added.

They paused, then doubled over with laughter. He grabbed her around the waist, and she jumped in to him, and they tumbled together onto the floor, and then the boy came and tumbled onto them, too.

There was a wonderful emptiness to the house that Saturday morning as the family wrestled on the floor and laughed, touched each other's clothes and stroked the soft skin of arms and legs. They sat on the floor, telling stories and jokes, playing hand games and tickles. The boy brushed his mother's hair, and Nightbitch brushed her husband's hair, and then they read books for hours.

The cat meandered through the living room, meowing horribly, and the husband got up to trundle after her, hands outstretched, a game he played only when in the best of moods.

Kitty! her husband said, stalking the animal as she waddled away from him, wide-eyed with panic. I'm going to throw you on the roof and let you starve to death up there, he said, grabbing her on either side of her convex belly and making her deflate, then squeak, like a rubber chew toy.

Maybe a chicken hawk will swoop down and grab her with its talons while she's up there, Nightbitch suggested, picking a dust bunny from the cat's flailing paw and laughing at her terror. Then take her up into the sky and drop her from a great height into a deep quarry, where heavy mining equipment with caterpillar treads will repeatedly run over her broken corpse.

Wow, the husband said, impressed. Very specific.

Thanks, she said.

Nightbitch and her husband made love that afternoon as their son napped in his shady room in the cool breezes of the ceiling fan. In their own shady room, they united as they never had. Her husband, the engineer, put in a particularly sensual performance, which she knew was a stretch for a man of his disposition. But this once, it seemed he let himself go, biting her shoulders and licking her neck, kissing her deeply and hungrily until they were both, finally, free of the weight of their human minds, their mortgage and bills, the dirt on the floors and ants in the cupboard—all of it gone and only them there, together, animals alive in a house.

Fling wide the doors. Open every window. Welcome bugs and dirt. Welcome allergens. The family moved freely between worlds for a time, in and out, as the wind did.

Yet wasn't it peculiar—indeed, perhaps even more peculiar than the mother's transformation itself—that the husband did not, in a real and searching way, attempt to get to the bottom of the presence of the dog he had seen that evening he arrived home to an almost empty house? Wasn't it indeed perplexing that this detail remained largely uninterrogated, given that he was a man of science and reasonable explanations? And odd, too, that the mother had felt no real need to account for the dog at all?

Perhaps we can assume that even the husband—the good, stable, reliable husband with his engineer's reasonableness, his common sense, his strong hold on reality—had also, in some small or large way, been bewitched?

—

ON MONDAY MORNING, SHE did what any totally and completely normal person would do who had recently transformed into a dog and sat on the toilet with the lid down, searching the Internet as she listened to her husband and son move about the house. She started with *werewolf facts* and *real monsters*, then moved on to *shapeshifting* and *shapeshifting Native American*, then *skinwalkers* and *Navajo witches*. She read and read, but what she wanted to find was a mother who turned into a dog—a regular domesticated dog capable of being a pet, even—and so she kept on, with *mother myth* and *madre perro* (thinking somehow the Spanish would produce more desired results), *hormonal extremes hair* and *postnatal hair abundance*, *humans killing animals with their mouths*, and then, because it occurred to her, *cannibals* and *headhunters*, and it was at this point she knew she had wandered too far astray and stopped altogether.

Despite her cleaning that week, the bathroom remained a mess, mildew crawling between the shower tiles, hairs mingling in every corner of the room, a lone Q-tip beside the trash can. The towels hung haphazardly, and she whisked a hand over them in a halfhearted attempt at tidying.

She would not properly clean it. She wouldn't. In fact, it simply *could not be* cleaned, no matter how hard she tried! And now she was done trying. She would let it grow dirtier and dirtier until, one weekend, her husband would finally notice and do something about it. What if I just didn't do a thing? she wondered. What if I just stopped? Would he notice? Would he do anything? So far, her findings were *no* and *no*.

Though their weekend lovemaking session had indeed been restorative for their marriage and for Nightbitch's attitude toward her husband, that enchanted honeymoon of sorts had lasted but a day. Sunday morning, she rushed from bed to the bathroom, for she felt the impending blood-fall waiting inside her, a deluge that gushed into the toilet when she sat down and provided her great relief while, at the same time, inspiring a wave of ultimate exhaustion, an unwieldy project she must now attend for the next week. With the blood also came all the old resentments. The bathroom was, yes, dirty. Her husband was, yes, leaving *again*. And whether or not she would *be happy* and *succeed as a mother and person* this week were again pending and open questions, hanging there, taunting her.

She rose from the toilet and stretched. She looked herself in the mirror, considered the dark bags beneath her eyes, then pulled her top lip back to check her teeth for signs of canine activity, of which she found none. She was determined, yet again, to get out of the house. They would go to the library, to Book Babies, so she could prove to herself that she was in no way *going crazy* or *on the brink of something insane*. Even more, she would get another good look at—good sniff of—Jen and her sidekicks, just to assure herself that they were, you know, mommies. Women. *Homo sapiens* who desired to sell herbs and nothing more.

Yes, she was on the reasonable path, she told herself as she packed her bag with toys and diapers and wipes and snacks and water and a change of clothes for the boy just in case. She felt oddly cheered as she kissed her husband goodbye and was out of the house even before he was, watching him wave from the stoop as she departed—the man looking a bit deflated, to be honest.

Okay, *byeeeee*, he hollered as he waved.

She wanted to know how a person—after spending the night romping through the neighborhood, shitting and killing and howling—how that same person might rise just days after to take her child to something as quotidian as story time at the public library.

How am I doing this? she asked herself, examining her hands on the steering wheel. The only physical remnant of her transformation was a dark swath of skin on her forearm, a birthmark of sorts. She had an urge to lick the spot but resisted.

Though much of her fur was now gone, the tail lying somewhere in the underbrush, her claws receded back into her fingers, she still felt very much the pulse and pant of the animal she had become. Her sense of smell had distracted her that morning, causing her to clean more and more obscure corners of the kitchen in an effort to get rid of every last trace of mold and onion and meat. She longed to tend to her son the way she felt she should, licking him and biting at his feet lovingly, yowling as they played, and feeding him raw meat. And though the animalness of her being remained, she was also inside her full human-mother being, back to the usual worries and insecurities, the thoughts of career success, the burden of failure, the marital resentments, feminist rage, and so on and so forth. All of this was back, yet somehow transformed. She felt she could abide it as long as she still had Nightbitch. As long as she had that.

Nightbitch felt she was owed her secrets, but this did not preclude feelings of profound guilt inspired by said secret-keeping. Not to tell her husband of her transformation, to keep it as a silent and seductive memory inside her, to pretend that something extraordinary and life-changing had not occurred, that life just moved on as normal, the boy in the living room playing with his many-wheeled toys, the husband off on another trip, and the mother who remained, unchanged, simply undertaking her domestic duties, her simple life—to carry on as if all of this were true did indeed evince in the deepest parts of Nightbitch a swirl of dread. She did not usually lie to her husband, and certainly not about events as monumental as this, but it felt very important to keep this her own.

At Book Babies, mothers and children crowded into the library's back room, where a chirpy librarian showed them books and puppets and sang songs, after which toddlers crawled and walked and teemed over one another, a squirming mass of fists and baggy diapers and too-big heads. Sure enough, there were Jen and Babs and Poppy, engaged in their usual happy, animated conversation. Nightbitch sat in the only open space still available on the floor, closer to Jen than she would have liked, for she wasn't sure what to say or how to be. Nightbitch nodded formally, awkwardly, when she caught Jen's eye, then flushed red.

Were they!? Weren't they!? How preposterous even to entertain that these women had visited her house, ripped her clothes from her body, then left behind a pile of dead vermin for her enjoyment.

She was just going to sit there and participate and be a normal mom! That was it!

She listened as the other mothers, the contented mothers, talked about their best recipes that the kids would eat. They all seemed to be friends. She didn't make eye contact, instead looked at her phone and felt slightly superior for not caring about leggings and essential oils. She felt educated. She felt interesting and independent and did not want to be like the happy mothers. Was it that she didn't want to be happy? That wasn't it. It was that she wanted another option.

All the while, she shot surreptitious glances at the hard-core Book Mommies—those mommies who were *really* into being mommies and selling herbs and enriching their children all the time—chief among them, of course, Jen, her curled eyelashes and penciled brows, concealer that must have been painstakingly applied so as to cover every blemish, the smallest imperfections. Her fingernails were manicured, as were her toenails. Her legs were shaved. She smiled and chatted easily about herbs, how she *loo-ved* Mombie (whatever that was) on those days when she woke up with the grumpies, as if this mother, this *Jen*, even had a true, working understanding of the grumpies.

Nightbitch wanted to say, You don't even *know* what the grumpies are! Have you ever yelled at your twins, in full voice, in the middle of the night? Yelled at them to go back to sleep, pumping your diaphragm with rage and sound? Have you sobbed beside them when they asked for another glass of water, another snack, at ten at night, just really let go and had a full-on snot fest in front of your children, so they were the ones comforting you? Have you ever locked yourself in the bathroom for twenty whole minutes to peruse your phone while your child bangs on the door and yells MAMA as loud as he can, until he is sobbing and, probably, permanently traumatized?

Sometimes—Nightbitch longed to say, stunning all of them into a sweet-smelling silence—I fantasize about getting in my car and driving through night and day, as far south as I can go, until I get to a dirty beach and check in at a cut-rate motel where I'll drink horrible piña coladas all day in a faded beach chair.

Sometimes—Nightbitch imagined uttering plainly to their beautiful, happy faces—I imagine abandoning my family, abandoning this entire life.

So don't invoke the grumpies unless you've really got them, she wanted to scream. Just don't.

As the librarian read about a sad giant who just needed a hug, Nightbitch studied Jen down to the tiny wrinkles by her eyes and the white tracks of foundation collecting in the folds. Had this other woman, this perfect mother, turned into a dog recently? Had she gallivanted about town? How was a person to tell which mothers changed and which didn't? Surely she couldn't be the only one? A horrible loneliness bloomed in her chest when she imagined herself the only mother in the room, in the entire world, to roam the silent lamplit streets, part woman, part animal.

Nightbitch ballooned with anxiety. She must make a friend of one of these mothers! She must open her mouth and say something! She must at the very least try: a small smile, a single word. She must, must, must forge a real human bond, or she might actually go insane, if she hadn't done so already.

All she had to do was say, brightly, *Your son's so cute,* or, understandingly, *We love pretzels, too,* or, with a roll of the eyes and a gesture in her son's direction, *He's obsessed with wheels.* She could very simply just ask, *So what is it about these herbs?* Just a little throwaway, anything, something to open the door to extended mindless conversation. Why was it so difficult?

She looked at the mom on her left, ready to smile, but the woman was busy digging through her diaper bag as a small girl screamed, snot-faced, at her side. To her right, Jen had her eyes closed and was humming as she rocked one of her smiling twins back and forth in her arms.

The librarian read the last page of her book, and Nightbitch brushed her son's unruly hair with her fingers, then absently, instinctually, bowed her head and licked the cowlick swirled at the center of his scalp.

Mid-lick—really, even before she could get in a full and proper lick at all—Nightbitch jolted upright, as if shocked with electricity. Her entire body flushed with heat and then cold and then heat again, and blood flooded her ears, turning them red. She stared straight ahead and closed her eyes, took a deep breath.

No one saw, she told herself. Everyone was busy getting

ready to go. It was just a small lick—a touch of the tongue, really, not even a complete full-tongued lick. It was fine. Not even that weird.

She calmed herself by repeating things she knew were not true over and over again.

Eventually, she forced herself to open her eyes and glance around with the coolest of nonchalance, the most even and unperturbed look on her face. Nothing was wrong. She had done nothing weird. And so what if she had licked his head? Maybe she was just eccentric? It was only a singular, weird thing she had done, not evidence of her canine escapades. No one would have seen that and thought to themselves, Oh, that mother must turn into a dog sometimes.

She was fine.

The mother of the snot-faced girl was now cleaning her face with a wet wipe. The child was no longer crying and was eating Cheerios from a purple container. On her other side, Jen chatted with other Book Mommies. The children were all now playing with toys the librarian had brought out from the closet: plastic car ramps and plush colorful balls, animal finger puppets and germ-infested LEGO.

Yes, everyone was chatting mildly, and no one had seen. Nightbitch let out a long stream of air and watched as her son pulled back a toy car, let it go, watched it speed and crash into the wall, laughed.

Jen went on about herbs, and then Babs started talking about leggings, and Poppy picked up with essential oils. They complained about their husbands, how the men wanted to know what they were doing with these herbs and such, the amounts of money being spent on such things.

I mean, basically, at this point, if he doesn't agree with me, I just bite his leg and stay like that until he sees it my way, Jen said, then tilted her head back and laughed big and loud.

You just need to train them, Poppy agreed.

Jen looked directly at Nightbitch, who had been eavesdropping on the conversation.

You know what I mean? Am I right? she asked Nightbitch, who startled and smiled bashfully, smiling and saying, What? Oh . . . what? Ha-ha. Sure. Yes.

I mean, you just *errrrrr*. . . . Jen growled, showing her teeth and shaking her head side to side, eyes wide. The Book Mommies chuckled, and Nightbitch only opened her eyes wider, a faint, unsure smile turning her lips.

Ha ha, Nightbitch said. Yeah? Okay.

Look, Jen said, I have *got* to tell you about these herbs.

I don't really *need* herbs, Nightbitch said, packing her bag, stuffing it with a water bottle and a squeezie packet, a wayward truck, for she didn't know what else to do.

Hey, here's my card, Jen said, digging through her purse, then leaning close to hand over a crumpled rectangle. I meant to give it to you the other day. And I don't give it to just anyone, only people who I really think will excel. I mean, you'll make so much money. It's a great opportunity. She paused and made meaningful eye contact with Nightbitch, eye contact that felt scripted, as if she had practiced this very move in a circle of chairs beneath the fluorescent lights of a hotel conference room.

Nightbitch did not know how to move her face, what show of emotion to arrange there. Not only was she stunned because of Jen's show of animalistic behavior—teeth baring and head shaking, particularly weird because it seemed so out of character for a normie blonde Midwestern mom—but, even more, because of the distinct and unmistakable smell *yet again* of Jen's hair as she bent close to hand over her card. Strawberry, strawberry, strawberry shampoo.

Nightbitch told herself that, of course, this was all in

her head. I mean, strawberry shampoo certainly isn't all that uncommon? And perhaps she hadn't even smelled strawberry exactly. Was she sure? Could it have been raspberry? Mango?

So what if this perfectly nice mother with lavishly styled blond hair had the specific aroma of a mysterious dog who'd shown up on her lawn and tried to lead her away from home while two other dogs put her son down for a nap? She eyed Babs and Poppy, who flanked Jen. Poppy with her long, bushy, ombré hair, and quick, athletic build. Babs, yes, a bit jowly, a bit of what one might call a "hangdog" face. Nightbitch would have laughed were she not so stunned. It was all too preposterous to entertain even for a moment, these completely normal mothers leading double lives as dogs. Yes, she had longed to find other mothers like her, but now that this desire hinted at becoming a reality, Nightbitch began to sweat and grow dizzy from the eye contact, from the whiff of strawberry, which had already abated, from the strangeness of all of it, what had happened that weekend and what had happened there in Book Babies, and god knows what else might happen in the future.

Oh my god, you're flushed, Jen said, her face contorted with concern. Nothing a little Balance won't fix, she added, and again began to dig in her oversized bag.

Oh, no thanks, Nightbitch said, looking at Jen's card, which proclaimed her an "Herbal Ambassador" with the tagline *Live the Life You Deserve.*

Thanks, Nightbitch repeated, but I don't need anything. Then she lay flat on the floor and gulped deep breaths and told herself this was all in her head.

Jen's face filled Nightbitch's line of vision, and she dangled a little packet of Balance in front of her. Take these, she said, and you'll feel fine. I'll find you online!

She dropped the packet on Nightbitch's chest, and with that, Jen was gone, and Nightbitch was left on the dirty industrial carpet with her son crawling over her and over her again, then sticking his hand in her mouth and saying *Mama*.

Nightbitch had held it together exceptionally well up until that point. She had continued on with her life despite extremely perplexing and magical events. And so, given Jen, her snarling and show of teeth, her scent of strawberry—given Babs and Poppy and their maybe canine features if you looked at them in the right way—Nightbitch would persevere.

She wanted to call after Jen, *Wait!* and *Please come back! I have so many questions for you!* But how could she possibly ask her, Well, hi, I know we don't know each other, but do you, well—ha ha, isn't this so funny?—do you happen to change into a golden retriever sometimes? I was just wondering, because it seems like you use strawberry-scented shampoo. . . .

But the moment had passed.

THE NEXT MORNING, HER son pulled her from her sleep by jumping on her tummy from the top of the couch, where she had fallen asleep reading from, once again, the "Domestic Varietals" portion of the *Field Guide*. It had become her favorite section these days, for she found in its pages women she used to know or could imagine one day befriending. The night before, Nightbitch had read about the Blues, such a lovely varietal, which reminded her of a friend who had moved away long ago and whom she now, inspired by the passage, missed immensely.

"Born close to water," White wrote, "be it on a coast or the shores of an inland sea, the Blues are known for striking and vivid eye color ranging from silvering indigo to a deep and meditative navy.

Prone to song, they are apt to take up the mandolin or ukulele—really, any small, whimsical stringed instrument will do. The Blue, without exception, will be deeply spiritual (see: Rituals [Solstice], Herbology, Volunteerism) though not eager to join standard organized religion, and will draw to herself an eclectic and accomplished circle of artists, musicians, recovering addicts, fallen capitalists, the elderly, the poor, the romantics, seekers of all sorts. This endearing breed is most easily identified by her ability to sync all other women around her to her own monthly cycle, since her fecundity is among the strongest on the planet (though you will almost never find her the wife of any man). Her houseplants are among the healthiest you will find in a home. Catch her feeding them with the water used to rinse clean her cloth menstrual pads, and you are certain to have found a true Blue. Count yourself very lucky indeed.

She fell asleep reading and then dreamt of cauldrons full of sweet-smelling brews, blood-red rain, footprints of soot leading down a sun-dappled wooded path, the sound of female voices singing an old song somewhere far ahead.

So, when the boy woke her from this dream by jumping on her in a way that made it feel as though he had actually and completely flattened her liver, she howled, and as she did so longed for a Blue to appear in her living room to do something motherly and witchy, burn some weeds and sing a song, whatever, to make it all right.

Arooooooooooooo! she moaned, so long and loud that the boy began to cry.

Oh, I'm sorry, honey, she finally said, clutching her side. I'm sorry. I'm not mad, she said, stroking his head and pressing her tender stomach with the tips of her fingers.

As the boy ate his breakfast of dry cereal and sliced bananas, she checked her phone. A call for submissions to a juried art show. Delete. A newsletter from a gallery where she had long ago had a small show. Delete. And then a friend request and message notification, JEN!!!!!, writ beside the smiling profile pic of, well, Jen.

She accepted the friend request and scanned an accompanying in-app message as the boy began to cackle, throwing his cereal to the floor. Jen opened with *So great! to see you! yesterday at Book Babies!!!!!*—which Nightbitch actually admired for its mid-sentence exclamation audacity. The exclamation points gave way to ALL CAPS in subsequent sentences, which reiterated that she should definitely come to the *UPCOMING PARTY* that would feature the *TEN-DAY EXPERIENCE PACK* as well as *WINE* and *lots of other moms/representatives who will share experiences of SUCCESS and FULFILLMENT with the brand.* It ended with promises of a *KID-FRIENDLY* environment, should she need to bring along her little one, thus creating a *totally barrier-free community of motivated and ambitious work-at-home moms.*

An invitation followed, and Nightbitch clicked *Maybe,* because Jen had said WINE, which she felt was the most persuasive part.

Jen's entrepreneurial positivity-speak, her liberal use of exclamation points, her promises of fulfillment and work-at-home success filled Nightbitch with an unrelenting darkness, as if the sunny shell of her message contained within it a meanly pulsing vein that insisted on something sinister and toxic. Or maybe Nightbitch was just projecting.

Either way, she didn't want to get sucked into some herbal-remedy hustle, yet the prospect of camaraderie, she had to admit, was the smallest bit enticing, despite her former disavowal of mom friends. There must certainly be at least one mom cynical enough to sip wine with her in a corner and crack dark jokes about killing cats and shitting on lawns. Just one. That's all she needed, all she could hope for.

She'd think about it. She'd wait and see and think about it and try to have a more positive outlook and an open mind about people who were different from her, even if they were into herbal remedies. I mean, maybe she could be into such a thing ironically?

In Wanda White's book, she had read about a kind of mother who appeared and disappeared at will. Some were said to fade in and out, always there in the right light, at the right angle, but often translucent, whereas others took on more of a coyote quality, showing up unexpectedly in the corner of a room, or disappearing at the precise moment they were needed. These mothers, to whom White referred as the Flickering, were thought to be nearly extinct, yet there were still random reports of them around the world. A mother in Buffalo had been reported to fade away just after bedtime. Her children claimed they could find her nowhere when they rose from bed for a glass of water, or else could see only her shadow as it moved always one room ahead of them, flitting from wall to wall, eternally elusive. Their mother reported she did feel not "altogether there" in the evenings, after long days spent with her four children, cooking and cleaning and ironing and bathing and singing and dancing and hiking and romping. "Might the mind-body connection be so strong that these women are in fact able to disintegrate their physical selves via intense maternal ennui?" White pondered. "I, for one, think not, for the motivating maternal impulse is toward creation rather than destruction, and so I challenge both the reader and myself to consider the Flickering within a transformational framework. In this way, we are better able to undertake the profound philosophical work needed to understand such a creature."

But on this day, Nightbitch was thinking of another Flickering, a mother in Barisal, Bangladesh, who was reported to appear sometimes as a playful mongoose and other times as a mother. Nightbitch had been pondering this particular magical woman, for, though the woman had rodent-like tendencies rather than mongrel, the ways in which she appeared and left, and her relationship to her children, Nightbitch found quite interesting indeed. In particular, she noted how this creature was said to show up just as her children began a game outside, a beautiful mongoose with silky, gold-flecked fur who stole their balls and ruined their games and made them laugh. The children claimed it was their mother, because the mongoose answered to *Ma* (pronounced May) or *Chokkabanijjo*, their mother's given name. And more: the fur, they said, felt just like their very own mother's hair, exactly the same color, and smelled just like her, with notes of sage and soap. Their mother, in mother form, had the same teeth as the mongoose, unnaturally sharp and biting. And never did the children ever see Ma the mongoose and Ma the mother in the same place at the same time.

The mother never disabused her children of this notion, and did not disabuse Wanda White of it, either, instead eluding the question, mischief a-sparkle in her eyes. She told White that Ma watched over her children when they played in the streets, that she had trained the animal to do this, that the mongoose had in fact been hers as a child. And when pressed about the age of the mongoose, how it could possibly have survived long enough to watch both mother and then her children, Ma simply shrugged and tilted her head. She initially claimed that it was descended from the whistling Indian mongoose, then that it had first appeared in her family after they read a fable in which a mongoose saved an infant from a tiger, and, finally, that her great-grandmother had purchased it at an open-air market nearly one hundred years ago. "In the end, she advised that knowing was not necessary, only experiencing," White wrote, "and suggested I stop asking so many questions."

And, in fact, this is what Nightbitch had remembered most clearly, this directive to enjoy oneself within the mystery. So much effort and worry put in to understanding and explaining and thinking and thinking and thinking. At least for an afternoon, couldn't she just *be*? They were downtown, after all, on a beautiful midweek summer day. She had even pedaled the boy down on her bike, pulling a blue bike trailer behind, just as she had imagined she would back before she had the child, in her most idealized fantasies of motherhood.

She found this line of thinking to be incredibly reasonable, incredibly levelheaded and healthy, the sort of thinking her husband would no doubt support unilaterally, and in this moment of full-armed embrace of the unknown, she found herself inspired to play—to real, fullhearted play—with her son, on the playground next to the library, on a late and sunny summer afternoon. Certainly she had played with him before, but all too often her efforts were uninspired and weary, unable as she was to shirk the burdens of adulthood and reality. On this afternoon, however, they slid from her as easily as a silk robe, and there she was, resplendent in the afternoon light, hair unspooling behind her as she dashed toward the small boy, who screamed with delight.

The boy cackled at her on the little metal bridge, his face squeezed between two of the uprights, and she lunged at him and barked brightly. He turned and ran. A dirty girl in a tutu giggled on the steps leading up to the structure. Another little boy stared in openmouthed puzzlement.

Yip! Yip! She yipped at each of them—causing the girl to scream and the boy, no more than eighteen months old, to begin to sob gently—and then took off after her boy, up the steps and up, up, up, to the little turret from which a curvy red slide descended precipitously to the ground.

Get me! her son yelled, and she fell to all fours and growled, stalking him now, her movements measured and precise.

Mama, he uttered, part question, part delight, and she

let out a slew of murderous barks and growls that sent him screaming down the slide, after which she followed, panting.

It went on like this, her romp over and across the play structure, her son's delight, other children joining in or running away in terror, depending. Soon, she had a whole herd of children who bade her, chase *me!*, and she did as they instructed, chasing and barking and panting, and the children, in turn, offered their own joyful yips, until the entire playground sounded like a kennel, the growling and barking tremendous. The smaller children sorted themselves out along the edges, on parents' laps or tucked into strollers sucking on their thumbs, for what they were seeing did not make sense to their small minds and instead challenged their sense of all that was stable and ordered in the world.

It was quite a scene, this vigorous mother and her barking, the children erupting in glee. The tutu girl brought her puzzled father a stick in her mouth. A redheaded boy put his muddy hands on his mother's clean white shirt and barked in her face, to her great dismay.

As the sun set, the crew there worked themselves into a frenzy of which the awaiting parents who surrounded the playground had never quite seen the like: a pack of children, feral and barking, sniffing, chewing, chasing, and a mother orchestrating it all, with her long unkempt hair and puzzling face, which seemed to grow more and more canine in the lengthening shadows.

Soon the other parents grew uneasy with the play, or else their children tired as bedtime approached or, you know, it was time for dinner. One way or another, the crowd thinned, then scattered, until it was just Nightbitch and her tired boy, curled together in the little playhouse nestled beneath one of the structure's platforms. She licked his head a bit, and he licked her arm and nuzzled her face. She was hot and dirty and sweaty as the boy closed his eyes.

She would tuck him, half asleep, into his bike trailer, swathed in blankets, buckled tight, and use the might of her legs to propel them both home. But before that, under cover of the child's playhouse, she spied in her peripheral vision a little bird hopping close, closer, too close, until, with a flick of her wrist, she reached out and grabbed it in one deft movement, so smooth and liquid her son did not even stir as she brought the small, beating body to her chest and twisted its head with a near-silent *snap*.

THEY WERE REALLY ON it now, on the mommy schedule, the mommy fast-track if you will, Book Babies and the playground and today—how could it already be Friday!? such a beautiful day!—Tyke Hyke. Next week, it would be Play Space at the mall and Gymnastic Jam. Nightbitch had already scheduled it! Really, the sky was the limit—literally. Balloon Babies was all the rage now, a hot-air balloon experience that encouraged overcoming phobias / a love of heights.

She surged with mommy adrenaline, the knowledge she was doing what was best for her child and focusing on his needs. *How can I be a more perfect mother?* she wanted to know. She was nearly foaming at the mouth with the question, with projecting the most mommyishness she could. Of course, there would be some dog in there, too, but she could just tuck that in behind everything, behind her most excellent motherhood.

The boy had a runny nose and a horrible little cough, and during the entire drive to Tyke Hyke the sweet little prince had been kicking the back of her seat, despite her calm implorations that he *please stop* and that it *wasn't nice or funny* and that she would *take away cartoons,* a threat she seldom carried out, because she, too, wanted the boy to watch cartoons.

She wanted it so badly, so that she could stand at the kitchen counter and eat coins of dry salami on buttery crackers and think about nothing. So that she could clean her pores in her magnified mirror for a full episode of his favorite doggy cartoon, or lie in the middle of the living-room floor and close her eyes without the threat that any small person, in that particular cartooned moment, might pounce directly on the fleshy middle of her and bruise a vital organ, or kick her head, then trip and fall again onto her fleshy core, or spit in her general direction, because how remarkable that a body could produce its very own liquid! Just like that! Look, Mama! Look!

And so the boy kicked her seat, and she seethed, and very soon they arrived at the trailhead for Tyke Hyke. She told herself to calm down, not to get angry, no yelling and absolutely no barking, and then she told him there were no doggy games on the hike, and he instantly began to weep because, you see, the boy had been anticipating his doggy games in the great outdoors, in the woods! where there were so many smells! and sticks! and bugs! a doggy would like.

It really was her own fault. She had allowed the child to wear his brand-new blue collar with a shiny silver tag that flashed in the sunlight and made a satisfying *tink* when it tapped against the other metal parts of the collar. She had allowed him to wear this around his neck in the car, just for fun, and had not properly warned him that it would need to come off upon arrival at Tyke Hyke.

Moreover, she had also agreed that he could hold his brand-new retractable leash and play with the quick-release button while they drove and, again, had not warned that this was simply—at least for today—a car toy that must be abandoned once they came into contact with other, normal-seeming humans.

But we're people, she said to the screaming boy as she

stroked his head. He was still strapped in his car seat, and she bent over from the now open door, to talk to him, trying to muffle his shrieks with her body.

Honey, you don't need your collar to run and play with the other kids, she reasoned. You can be a doggy in your heart and a boy on the outside.

Noooooooooo! he shouted, completely unreasonable. Doooooooooooogggyyyyyyy!

The other mothers—the on-time mothers with their obedient, uncollared children—who had collected at the trailhead turned, and Nightbitch gave a little wave.

Honey, she whispered to her son, *please*. She unstrapped him from the car seat. He would not get out of his own volition, so she hauled his solid little heft out the low-profile back door, banging both his head and her own. He was deadfishing it and, once out of the car, slid through her hands and into a sobby little puddle on the asphalt.

Honey, she said.

No walk! he yelled.

We're walking, she said firmly, and he howled like a sad puppy, so that all the waiting mothers turned again, and one even took a few steps toward Nightbitch.

No, no, we're fine. Just a minute and we'll be there, she said brightly, waving them off.

Okay, she whispered again to the boy, you may wear the collar, but we don't need the leash. Doesn't doggy want to run free?

Play leash, he said, then rubbed his palms on his chest in his amended sign for *please*. Peas, Mama. he begged. Peas.

He stopped with the screams and sobs to look at her, rubbing his eyes with two little fists and then taking the back of his hand and smearing snot from cheek to cheek. He was sick and tired and just wanted to play, and why was she denying him that?

So what if the other moms thought it was weird?

It was creative and sweet and fuck them.

Though she wanted to efficiently lick his face, she knew they were all watching, and instead took a used tissue from her pocket and wiped the boogers from his rosy cheeks.

Okay, honey. Fine. You can be a doggy. But the other kids might think it's weird.

The boy glowed and *arf*ed and panted with his little pink tongue. He was horrible, and she loved him. She gave him a kiss right on his wet nose.

Nightbitch smiled tightly as the boy led her on his leash across the small parking lot and right up to Jen from Book Babies. The boy *arf*ed at Jen, who laughed, then sat beside her and arfed again, waiting.

He wants you to pet him, I think, Nightbitch said, playing along as if she just did not have a *clue* what had gotten into this boy, and wasn't he *so* funny??? I mean, surely it was *just a phase,* and tomorrow he'd be back to trains or monster trucks, you know how it goes. She communicated all this with a raise of the eyebrows, a tired smile, the faintest eye roll and shake of the head. It was the universal mom sign for *Look at this psycho he is breaking my spirit in some small way, every day, yet still I adore him and will go to the ends of the earth for him and also allow him to pretend to be a dog and wear a collar and I will walk him—I WILL WALK HIM—because I am a wonderful mother.*

Well, look at you, Jen said to the boy, patting his head. The other mothers, among them more than a few Book Mommies she recognized from the library, smiled dubiously or offered polite chuckles.

He wanted to be a dog, Nightbitch said. I mean . . .

Sure, sure, Jen said. They're always being something.

As the hike commenced in the shadowed cool beneath the tittering canopy, the mothers grouped in twos or threes and took up exclusive conversations difficult to insinuate oneself into. The children rolled like a single organism ahead of them, moving like a flock of birds from one side of the path to the other, but her boy held back, walking politely at the end of his leash, and pulling out more leash only to chase a butterfly or to smell a flower.

Dead snake! Dead snake! a big boy yelled up ahead, pointing next to a fallen log.

Her son pulled on the leash and turned back to his mother. Go! Go! he said, pointing, and she unhooked him, and he took off toward the other children, a boy again, or perhaps still a dog of a sort, but one that wanted to see the dead snake, prod it with a stick and, if he was brave, touch its skin.

The Book Mommies hung back, in a clump now, in watchful silence, until Jen turned to their new recruit.

Hey, she said.

Oh, hi, Nightbitch offered nervously. I'm so sorry I haven't replied definitively to your invite yet. I'm just not sure.

Oh, whatever, Jen said. We're all busy. But you should come. The herbs are amazing.

Without waiting for a reply, she continued: One to make you big and one to make you small. One to make you happy and another to make you fall asleep.

I love the Mombie blend! one woman with an infant strapped to her chest added or, rather, yelled. It is full of energy! she said loudly, her bugged eyes gleaming with a youthful mania.

We know you're into that Mombie! Good for you, Jen said to the mommy, then turned back to Nightbitch. We all sell them. But mostly we just get together and drink wine, she whispered conspiratorially yet loud enough for all to hear. A way to pass the time, she said. Maybe you make a little money or maybe you don't, but either way you can always say, once the hubby gets home, that you need to go and work on your business and can buy a few hours to yourself. But, really, it's a way to feel as though you have something that's just yours, you know?

Oh, Nightbitch said, smiling. She wanted to say, But I'm an artist, I don't have time for that, and then remembered that she wasn't an artist anymore and did, in fact, have time for herbs, but still.

She wanted to say, But isn't turning into a golden retriever the *thing that's just yours*? Be honest!

Instead, trying to be polite, she said: I don't think that's really for me.

Don't make a decision so fast, silly! Jen said, slapping Nightbitch's arm. You have to come to a party at least! I'll give you free samples. Jen shook her head at her, as if to say, You don't even know what's good for you. Just come, you stupid.

I mean, I'm not really into beauty or leggings or whatever, Nightbitch tried again. I didn't even brush my hair today, she added, though the truth was, she had not brushed her hair all week.

Well, this is sacred healing medicine! You'll feel so great that you'll want to put on that makeup and wear something cute! Jen said.

I'm sorry, but what exactly are these herbs? Nightbitch asked. The packet of Balance that Jen had tossed to her as she lay on the floor earlier in the week, at Book Babies, was still at the bottom of her bag and had somehow ripped open a bit, to coat the entire bottom in a fine dust of sweet-smelling leaves and twigs.

Oh my god, it's Chinese. It's Thai. It's Japanese. Jen circled her hands in the air and widened her eyes. Her voice rose in excitement. It's all the ancient wisdom of the great healers in a bottle. She dropped her arms and linked one in Nightbitch's, as if they'd been friends forever. But let's not get into facts and figures now. You'll just have to come over. Oh! And make sure you have access to a little extra dinero. Six hundred or so? she whispered. You'll thank me.

That afternoon, another message appeared from Jen as Nightbitch put her son down for a nap. She tucked him in with a fuzzy yellow duck that squeaked when he bit it, and a little quilt she had made for him covered in bones and puppies, and a fabric that featured photo-realistic meat. She sat on the bed to read the note.

Most notable, on first read, were all the lines—in fact, just about the entire message—that seemed to have been lifted from some sort of recruitment template located in a glossy pamphlet encouraging women to *reach out* and really live up to their *full potential.*

I am looking for motivated and driven people to partner with me, Jen began without so much as a transitional greeting or other sign that she was a sentient being rather than some sort of modern automaton programmed only to recruit and sell. *You have such a vast network already,* she continued, and *This model appeals to busy moms.* Next, claims of unidentified *doctors* and their dubious *credibility* to deliver a *number-one-selling product on a global scale.* Anecdotal tales of *high-school friends* who had had *successful careers as lawyers and teachers and dermatologists* before having children, at which point they *made a commitment* to become *work-at-home moms* who fit their sales into the *nooks and crannies* of their lives, in between naps and meals, e-mailing on their phones at the park or library. *It is truly a company that is too good to be true . . . yet still is!* she wrote, before ending with talk of how she really thought Nightbitch would be *wildly successful* with tons of *referrals* and that she really should not pass up this opportunity for *significant residual income for years to come.*

She lay in bed while her son clapped and giggled beside her and stared at the fan lazily spinning the softly pixelating late-summer afternoon. Jen's strawberry-scented hair, her perfected mommyhood, her herbs, her unrelenting recruitment. A lawyer mom who now stayed at home with her kids and sold herbs was the most depressing story Nightbitch had ever heard, possibly even more depressing than her own life. There was no way that mom had a rich and weird internal life that colored her otherwise monochromatic days in magical shades of dog. She was a lawyer who was doing the reasonable thing, feeding her kids applesauce and picking up a side gig to contribute just that little extra to the family finances and really solidify herself as a loving mom and contributing earner.

Was that mom happy? Was she fulfilled from downing handfuls of unidentified herbs with her Venti coffee while incessantly texting other mommies similarly stoned on herbs and frantically pushing toddlers on kiddie swings? Maybe she didn't need to be fulfilled in the way Nightbitch herself needed it? Maybe her kids were enough? Nightbitch desperately yearned for such a thing, for her son's delirious cackling and pudgy little wrists and garbled, lispy words of love to obliterate every last smidge of ambition. Why couldn't mothering and cooking and grocery shopping and cleaning and laundry and Book Babies really fill her with glee and well-being and a sense of a life well lived? Perhaps she needed to take the herbs and go to the parties and be a joiner for once in her life, and she, too, would be satisfied?

WE HAD A WONDERFUL time this week! Nightbitch reported to her husband when he arrived home later that day. He was still in the car, window rolled down, idling in the driveway. She held the wet cat, wrapped in an old beach towel, in her arms in the front yard as the boy ripped at grass and then played doggy and then sniffed some flowers. Her whole aura had changed, her husband said. She glowed. She was barefoot, and her face was freckled, her cheeks sun-kissed red.

We went to Book Babies, she said, cradling the cat like a baby, as her husband exited the car. She had just washed the cat's butt, again. Nightbitch's eyes glowed as if lit with a fire burning inside her head, and her hair wisped about her face in the breeze. We played on the playground, didn't we, honey? she asked the boy, to which he brightly replied *Arf!* as he dug in her flower bed with his two little paws.

Well, the husband said, unloading his suitcase and slamming the car door, at which the cat started but did not escape from Nightbitch's grasp.

Oh. One thing, she said. The cat destroyed my headphones.

Again? he asked, scratching the animal's head. She's horrible.

I would love to punt her like a football, she added as she cradled the jittery animal.

Imagine her little paws, the husband said.

I really hate her so much, Nightbitch added.

Yeah, her husband said. I'm going to murder you, he told the cat, playfully.

Nightbitch looked into the cat's big green empty eyes. The cat's black nose twitched in a way that was very adorable but not adorable enough; then it flattened its ears against its head and hissed.

I think this cat gave me toxoplasmosis, she said.

Oh? he asked.

I read an article, and it says there's a relationship between explosive rage and toxoplasmosis. I mean, they don't know if there's a cause-and-effect thing going on, or what the cause is and what the effect is, but there's definitely a link.

Her husband said nothing.

Do you think I'm mad because I have a brain parasite? she demanded.

I mean maybe, he said, but you'd probably be mad either way.

I fucking hate this cat, she said, at which the cat hissed again, and this time wriggled free to skitter across the front lawn and under the porch.

IT WAS THAT SUNDAY morning when the boy crawled into the living room on all fours. A raw steak, beautifully marbled with fat, dangled from his mouth. He dropped the slab of meat at his father's feet.

Ruff! he barked, then panted, his little tongue jutting from his open mouth.

Dude, the husband said, what are you doing?

Doggy, the boy said, then licked the husband's leg. He looked up again, a grimace on his face as he worked his tongue inside his mouth.

Hair, he said, grabbing at his tongue with his fingers. Hair! he screamed.

Here, the husband said, show me. He examined the boy's tongue, picked the hair off. All better, he said. But, sweetie . . . , he continued. We don't put raw meat on the floor. Or in our mouths, for that matter. Yucky, he said, making a face.

The boy shook his head.

Mama, he said. Yes, Mama. Meat. Yes!

Honey! the husband yelled toward the bedroom.

Nightbitch heard all this from the bedroom, where she was, per usual, putting away clean clothes while her husband scrolled infinitely on his phone. Though she had warned the boy that their doggy games were strictly Mommy-son enter-tainment, and tried to impart to him that Daddy wasn't interested and that the boy should never ask him to, say, drink water from a dog bowl or fetch a stick in his mouth, she had been dreading the day when he would inevitably introduce the husband to the games they played while he was gone.

Shit, she said under her breath. Fuck. Shit. Fuck.

In the kitchen, the husband picked debris from the meat at the sink, and the boy whined at his feet.

Bite! he cried. One bite!

Yucky, the husband said again. I have to cook it first, sweetie.

No, he cried, then, seeing his mother, Mama, bite.

She patted the boy on the head and said as nonchalantly as possible to her husband, He likes raw meat. What can you do?

Excuse me? her husband said, looking at her with annoyance, disbelief, that *I-knew-it-ness* he was so good at telegraphing with just a wrinkle of his brow, as if she were destined to fuck things up.

The kid has a refined palette, she continued. Beef tartare. There's nothing wrong with it.

When did our son start eating raw meat? the husband wondered. I mean, how did he figure that out?

Hmmm, Nightbitch said, smiling at the boy and then reaching out to tickle him and send him into a squirming fit of giggles on the floor.

I guess I was cooking dinner and he must have stolen a little piece of raw meat, she offered as she retrieved a glass from the cupboard.

No, the boy said from the floor. Mama give meat. Yummy. Doggy.

Honey, she said to the boy kindly, then, to her husband, He's so silly, isn't he?

My little doggy, she said to the boy, stroking the silky hair on his head. The boy closed his eyes, relishing her touch.

Have you been feeding him raw meat? her husband asked.

A little, she said defensively. It's fine.

What about parasites? He could be infested, the husband said.

I hardly think so, she said, pointing to the boy, who was, yes, the picture of health: shiny blond curls and rosy cheeks, a big belly left over from his baby days that she hoped he would never lose. The boy smiled at his parents, each now paying attention to him, and tipped his head back to let out a bright, clear *Arf arf.*

Sure, he *seems* happy, the husband whispered later that night, in bed, over the boy, who slept between them. He wouldn't let the issue go, as was his custom.

He *is* happy, Nightbitch whispered back.

I just think the dog stuff needs to stop, the husband countered.

But he loves dogs, she insisted. There's no harm.

The meat, her husband said. And there's a dog kennel just to . . . play in? In the living room! It's not natural. It's too much, he concluded, as if this were the final word on it, as if he'd drawn a conclusion that they all must now accept.

She rolled her eyes in the dark.

It's not like he even eats that much, she said. And it's great to pretend. It's all fine.

If he gets sick, it's on you, the husband whispered sharply. If other kids think he's weird, that's you.

Of course it is, Nightbitch said. It's *all* on me. Every part of it.

They lay there in silence. They'd had this fight a million times. She waited for him to say more, but there was only the sound of her son's even breathing. She fell asleep imagining the taste of fresh blood.

———

ALL NIGHTBITCH WANTED WAS never to do night-nights again for the rest of her life. It was Monday, her husband had left that morning, and she and the boy had baked muffins and played with trains, played with Play-Doh, gone for a walk to the train track, taken out the hose and attached the sprinkler and had a go of that, played chase, played ball, played fetch inside and out. Their feet were dirty and their noses were dirty, and they ate peanut-butter-and-jelly sandwiches on the porch steps as the sun eased toward night. Their muscles were hot and tired and happy, and the boy stared with vacant exhaustion, mouth slathered with jelly.

Oh yes, Nightbitch had with great folly believed that night-nights would be easy on this night, a breeze! Just a smooch and snuggle, and then the boy would be gone. In fact, such a night-night had never once occurred in the boy's entire life, though Nightbitch refused to acknowledge this and instead embraced that positive attitude and productive thinking.

Yes, it would be a wonderful Monday night-night, she told herself as she washed the boy and slipped on his little pajamas and then slipped the whole boy bundle between the cool blue sheets of her bed.

Yet, as soon as she lay beside him, she was horrified to see the folly of her hopeful thinking as the boy began to thrash under the sheet, ask for fresh cold water, ask for a cool washcloth, ask for a carrot, an apple, animal crackers.

No, she said, and then no again. It's time to go to sleep, not time to eat. It's time to let our bodies rest. Time to be a good doggy and keep your body still.

When attempts to engage his mother proved fruitless, the boy sat up in bed and attempted to play patty-cake with himself, clapping and slapping and then laughing hysterically, delirious with his weariness. She was so very, very tired, so incredibly exhausted, and wished she could sink down

into the memory-foam bed or else have a night off from the
tedium of bedtime, reading the same books over and over,
telling a story, another one, then playing a song on the phone,
lying there, waiting for the boy to go to sleep.

It was true that she had been responsible for putting
the boy to bed nearly every night since he was born. Certainly
she had been the only one able to get the boy to sleep when he
was an infant and all he wanted was to nurse until he slipped
into dreams of big fleshy pillows and oceans of warm, warm
milk. So wasn't she, in a sense, owed an innumerable amount
of night-nights by her husband? Shouldn't he, whenever he
had the chance, undertake night-nights happily, gratefully, in
honor of the many nights—the years—when she had been in
charge of the task?

Yes, this would be the fair way, but, of course, it wasn't
how things went in their household. Even after her husband
returned from his week of work, she performed night-nights
on Friday, because he was tired—he was, indeed, always tired,
and sometimes his tummy did not feel so well, because he
had been chugging coffee and eating corn nuts on the way
home, perplexed by the ensuing nausea . . . and he really just
wanted to get back to his computer, his video games and
browsing and folders, relax a little, you know, and Nightbitch
did not want to throw a fit or cause a scene or really engage
with any confrontation whatsoever, because she had nothing left. The lack of fairness surrounding night-nights was
yet another source of rage for Nightbitch, lying there in bed
as the fireflies blinked outside and the boy tossed beside her.

One hour, two, of the boy talking, laughing, clapping,
tossing, crying, asking for big cuddles, rejecting big cuddles
because they were too hot, asking for fresh cold water again,
crying because she wouldn't bring it to him, then tossing
some more. All this was enough to make Nightbitch desperately want to die.

I am spending my life lying in a dark room, she thought to herself. I am spending my most productive years in unproductive, supine waiting.

Please go to sleep, she pleaded, and then cried quietly in bed because she was so tired, wanted just an hour without the child at her side, an hour of television, an hour of sitting on the couch and staring at the wall, just an hour. Anything. Instead, she lay there and lay there and lay there, and then it was ten o'clock.

She had been putting off weaning the boy from the binky, for why would she want to make bedtime even more difficult, her life even more tedious. The binky was, in fact, a constant source of battles these days and, once carelessly dropped on the ground, inspired a fount of screaming from the boy when he saw the bits of dirt and pine needles and bark adhered to the plastic nipple and could not immediately put it back in his mouth.

And, of course, there was the matter of waking in the night, the constant and endless waking when the binky fell from the boy's mouth, the searching in the darkness, the panic, then the consolation. If she could just get one entire night of sleep . . . She fantasized about this, about how her body might feel that next morning, of the dreams she might have. Who would she be with a full night of sleep? Someone else entirely.

Plus, the boy was too big for the binky. Other kids at the library his age didn't have a binky. She pointed this out when they were there. See? Only babies. But the boy shook his head and held tight to the binky, sucking stubbornly.

I baby, he would insist. I baby.

So this Monday night, when she was doing night-nights yet again, when she was hot and tired, annoyed at her husband—this night, she decided after two hours in bed with him that there would be no binky.

Normally, she would have made up some elaborate scenario involving fairies, would have gone through a ceremony of wrapping the binky in a scarf and picking the perfect lilac bough outside on which to hang it as an offering to the fairies. But on this night, the blood of Nightbitch flowed through her veins, and she told the boy they would play a doggy game, and the only way to keep playing was to remain a doggy.

Doggy rules, she said sternly, and the boy nodded.

First of all, she said, doggies don't have binkies, do they? The boy looked at her seriously in the glow of the nightlight and handed over the yellow binky without so much as a small protestation. Jesus. She should have done this months ago.

Okay, she continued. And where do doggies sleep? The boy's brow wrinkled, and he held up his pudgy little hands in a puzzled gesture. Hold on, she said, groaning out of bed and down the steps to drag the oversized kennel from the living room, up the narrow stairs, and into her bedroom, where it fit perfectly in the corner. The boy watched in stunned amazement as his mother stuffed a down comforter into the enclosure, finally turned to the boy and gestured at the kennel with a Ta-da!

He pointed to the toddler-sized kennel and said, Eh?

Very good! Nightbitch said. What does doggy need to make his kennel cozy?

Without even a word, the boy collected his things—the soft blue blankie, the tattered teddy that had once been hers, his choo-choo pillow. She could tell he was excited about this new adventure, the novelty of it, the adventure, the game of being a doggy now at night. His mother was playing with him!? After denying him even fresh cold water!? She could tell the boy thought he had won that evening in their battle of wits, and this was what she wanted him to believe.

She helped him arrange his soft things in the kennel, and he curled inside without a sound, a perfect fit.

Door open or closed? she asked.

Open ickle bit, he said, and she closed it halfway, then reached in and patted his head.

She sat cross-legged on the floor and counted backward from one hundred to one, as she often did, swaying slightly in the darkness, and when she got to one she rose carefully and walked to the bedroom door, expecting to hear his little voice, his cry, but instead there was nothing.

She exhaled quietly, then began to laugh, just a chuckle that turned into an uncontrollable fit she had to continue out in the hallway, where she slid down to the floor to sit and cry and laugh, so tired and also so relieved, and she just wanted to go to sleep now, too, there on the floor. A sweet victory, but it was already ten o'clock, too late to watch something, so she washed her face and then spread out in her deliciously empty bed while her son dreamt in the kennel.

THE WORKING MOTHER WHO still worked, who had gone to grad school with her and then eased into marriage and motherhood and a successful work-life balance, wanted to get lunch.

How about lunch at the park? she texted. *You bring your son and I'll come over on my break and we'll just chat and catch up.* Sure, Nightbitch had thought. Of course. It had been so long since she'd seen the working mother—not since they had met up for coffee when the mother still directed the gallery, in fact—and of course it would be nice to reconnect. She would show her friend the working mom how she was really settling into her stay-at-home-momming, how she was happy and fulfilled, how she didn't even need art or a career at this point, no way, just some good, pure mothering time to devote herself purely to her son. And, honestly, it wasn't entirely an act now, for she had indeed, at least in some small way, convinced herself of this, of her happiness, and had bent her mind toward herbal remedies, toward Jen and that mommy scene, because what was the alternative? Grow so miserable and mad that the energy of these emotions generated a cellular change such that she became a she-wolf? Just run around the town as a dog and accept this as her lot in life!? This was not, could not be, the solution.

And so they had made plans and the working mother as well as the mother who did not work (but actually did, very much) showed up on the appointed day, at the appointed hour.

The working mother who was acknowledged for her work, since it fell outside the bounds of the home and thus was considered valuable and paid a salary, still taught art and made art and had all the things that modern women were supposed to effortlessly have, also had a perfectly packed lunch, housed in an eco-friendly insulated bag, her sandwich wrapped in eco-friendly beeswax paper that was washable and reusable, her compostable spork made from vegetable starch, and who could fault her for that? Certainly not the stay-at-home mother, with her individually packaged squeezies and bag of goldfish crackers and plastic baggies of off-brand cookies.

The women picked a nice bench in the shade of a tree right next to the playground.

You really have the life, the working mother said, watching the boy play.

I do, Nightbitch said proudly, for she did *have the life,* that stay-at-home life. And here, on this fine summer day, she for the first time felt true gratitude and sensed some sort of minuscule yet profound shifting of her deepest fears and dreams, these heavy rocks of need and yearning heaving around in her guts.

Ahhhh, she said, pertinent to nothing, and the working mother laughed.

Her friend went on, taking neat bites from her sandwich and launching into talk about her own artistic practice, her struggle to keep it up, her own children, but Nightbitch stopped listening nearly as soon as her friend started talking, instead rapt by a movement at the edge of the woods that bordered the park.

She froze with animal alertness. There, so close, so very tame, so very, very stupid, a bushy-tailed squirrel nibbled on a bit of trash.

Everything okay? the working mother asked, wrinkling her brow into a knotted little question.

Shhh! Nightbitch hissed, unmoving, then, in a whisper, Excuse me. Just one minute . . .

She inched from the bench, eyes locked on the squirrel, but it sensed in Nightbitch something threatening, and in an instant was off toward the tree line.

Squirrel! she yelled to her son over on the playground as she ran and pointed.

Squirrel! Squirrel! she yelled again, now to no one in particular. She barked the word out of sheer delight and sprinted after the little animal. Her son, not wanting to miss the fun, whooshed down a slide and ran, too.

The squirrel paused in the underbrush at the edge of the woods, and Nightbitch and son stopped together, yards away.

Get him, the boy murmured.

She had trained him well. He was a very good boy who knew not to move, not to scare it away. Instead, he waited for his mother's instruction.

You have to wait, she said quietly. Wait for just the right moment before you . . . and with the word *pounce,* that's what she did. She surged forward—launched herself, really—arms stretched forward, mouth open in a ferocious snarl, her son behind her saying *Raaaaar raaaaar raaaaaaaaaaaar.*

The squirrel focused into a pair of close-up terror-filled

eyes, a twitchy little nose, those small little hands, and Night-bitch was upon the animal—she would have it! it would be hers!—and she felt its fur in her very hands, but then the thing was gone with the *swish* of its tail, slipping from between her inept human fingers.

Arrrrrreeeeeeeee! Nightbitch hollered, now lying in the weeds, arms extended, flip-flops yards behind her.

Arrrooooooooo! the boy howled, throwing himself down beside her and laughing.

We almost got him! Nightbitch said conspiratorially to the boy, turning on her side to look at him. Grass prickled their cheeks, and the boy reached out to touch his mother's hair.

Is okay, Mama, he said. Squirrel!

We'll get him next time, she said, and he hugged her, and she stood with him in her arms and headed back to the play-ground, where the working mother waited.

Just a little game, Nightbitch said self-consciously, approaching the bench where the working mother waited.

That was . . . , the working mother said, searching for the word, . . . astonishing.

Just doing my job, Nightbitch answered as she rolled her eyes and smiled thinly, eager to change the subject.

Well! the working mother exclaimed. Motherhood really seems to suit you.

Sure! Nightbitch said, watching her son as he climbed up the slide. I guess it does. But I'm not *working* working, she said. Not like you. You know: money, art. Stuff like that.

Oh, come on, the working mother said, brushing non-existent crumbs from her lap. You're doing the hardest job.

I really hate it when people say that, Nightbitch said, even though it's true.

You should come to dinner this weekend, the working mother said, as though she'd had the most original thought in the universe. A videographer—someone they'd *also* gone to grad school with—was returning to guest-lecture that fall, at the program they had all attended, and for a moment, Nightbitch flared with envy, after which she promptly plummeted into a familiar self-loathing. What did she expect, after all? She spent her days chasing after squirrels with her son. She hadn't been working, not like them. Where was her newest project? Where was absolutely *anything* to show for the last three years?

Okay. Yes. She would go. But just for fun! It would be so great to hear about their work and be dazzled by all they had done. She would be a sister, a supporter, a feminist. She would relate her own triumphs as a full-time mom and celebrate their career successes while also providing heartfelt and active listening to the worries they no doubt had about their own mothering, their own children, whom they abandoned each day. Yes, all perspectives, all choices could be represented around the dinner table where they would break bread and work toward building a supportive community of women. So positive was Nightbitch, so thoroughly upbeat and might we say delusional, she could not even see how truly wrongminded she was being, for how could she *decide* to excise one of her most foundational urges: to create art? Yet, still, she thought, she hoped, she had decided she could.

THAT WEEKEND, WHEN HER husband was home, she wanted it from behind. She wanted him to bite the back of her neck. She wanted to fight and bite, and then she wanted to fuck him hard. She wanted it rough, and then, afterward, she wanted to be patted on the head, to have her hair stroked and straightened, her underneck rubbed, and then her belly rubbed, too.

The kind, good husband acquiesced, and as he did, she

told him he was a good boy, and he liked that. He liked all of it.

Afterward, he said, I don't know what's gotten into you, but please don't change.

If you say so, she replied, and lovingly bit his arm.

And it was after one of their many and uncharacteristic interludes on Saturday, as she lolled in their afternoon bed of rumpled, sullied sheets while their son napped miraculously in his doggy crate, which they'd moved into *his* bedroom, that a quiet feeling whispered in the clear, open space her marital harmony had created. This feeling was so quiet she might have missed it had she not had a moment to herself, still naked and in bed, listening to her husband while he roused their son from his nap. As she basked in this refreshing and rare postcoital child-free calm, she noticed, tickling the back of her throat, an insidious fear, which had been hovering in her periphery since that magical animal night. Had she let herself focus on this sensation, she knew she would quickly be overwhelmed and consumed by it. After all, what did it mean that she had turned into an animal not two weeks earlier? And who or what had been the source of such a transformation? What *force* had brought Nightbitch into being? She did not allow herself to consider fully these questions, to dwell on what darkness had called forth a monster, a beast, a creature from the deepest and bleakest crannies of her humanness. She did not let herself dwell on the tight ball of fear inside her, because this sort of indulgence was one she could not afford. She must rise from bed, tend to her child, her house, her own well-being. She must pull it together, to put it quite simply, for the sake of her family, because, otherwise, what? This entire thing they had going—this house and family and life—it would all fall to pieces if she fell to pieces, and so she simply could not. There must be a reasonable explanation, she reminded herself, and became determined to find just that: reason. Have someone explain things to her. And who other than Wanda White could do such a thing?

Spurred by the harmony within her house, and then by her fear of having it all crumble around her, she wrote another missive to Wanda White this same weekend, for she had not heard back since her first e-mail and wondered if she had the correct address (an academic one at the University of Sacramento), or if White was still alive (she no doubt was in her eighties or nineties, based on the publication date of her book and other odds and ends Nightbitch had been able to piece together), though Nightbitch had not been able to find any obituary for her. She had not, in fact, been able to find much of anything about White on the Internet, which was quite peculiar indeed, for she considered her online search-ing abilities fairly advanced, given her catholic approach to searching (that is, to search any and all possible words and combinations in the near and not-so-near vicinity to the tar-get subject). She wanted to tell her husband about White, but wasn't sure how even to begin explaining the woman, the icon, the looming and massive idea that White had become.

I'm obsessed with this book, she began, waving the *Field Guide* in his direction as he checked the settings on his work laptop at the kitchen table.

Oh, he said, not looking up. Tell me.

It's this weird field guide to mythical women around the world, but it's supposed to be true, she continued. This woman who wrote it is an academic. And the really strange thing is, whatever I read in it syncs up with what I've been feeling or thinking about, like magic. Or like the ads on your cell phone.

Her husband offered a sideways glance at the book.

Cool, he said. Can I look at it?

She unconsciously clutched the book to her chest, sud-denly protective of its wisdom; it did not feel correct to show

her husband its pages, which now felt so personal, even holy.
Through reading this book, she had been communing with
something greater than herself, with White and with the
women she invoked in her reportage. Suddenly the book felt
too sacred and tender a thing to parade about, especially to
her husband, who would most definitely not view it in the
right light, the way she had come to relate to it, for that is
what she now did: relate. She was in a relationship with the
book and with White, and she did not welcome her husband
into it.

Sure, she said, still clutching the book to her heart. Once
I'm done.

Just a look, he said, now turning to her and holding out
his hand. Having sensed that she did not want to show him,
he now wanted to look all the more. Come on, he encouraged.

But I need to write something first, she said, walking
toward the guest room, where her own laptop was located.

Hey! he hollered as she left.

She sat at her desk and placed the book in her lap. Why
had White not replied? she wondered, struck with the fervor
of a heartsick teen. And with such yearning right there, in her
throat, she began to write.

WW—
   Hello again. I have been awaiting your reply to my
last message, and since I've not yet heard from you,
thought I would write again. I hope I'm not a bother.
I hope you can see that I have been, one might say,
"spiritually compelled" to write. What I mean is
that your book and research have spoken deeply to
me, and I need to know the person who has written
a text so intimately in conversation with my most
private thoughts and desires.
   I'm wondering if you have, in all your travels,

ever found, say, a suburban American housewife or a mother in a small Midwestern town beset with, well, a sort of animalesque quality? Perhaps she was more hairy than usual? Somewhat aggressive? Prone to bouts of howling? Not actually mentally ill, mind you. Just willing to embrace a certain doglike playfulness, a whimsical approach to her motherhood, you could say.

Please, tell me: have you ever met her? And, if so, can you please put me in touch?

Further: might you be in the possession of a blueprint of sorts for how to be a magical woman in a small town in the heart of America? Might you have drafted some sort of instruction manual for how to exist between the world of ration and the world of imagination in a time when politics, public discourse, even the weather have turned ominous?

I have been unable to find any information online about you or your work beyond that of your Field Guide and am curious to know more about what must be your long and storied career and publication history.

I'm babbling. I'll stop. I wish you well.
MM

AND IT WAS JUST as things really seemed to be starting to come together—just as her son was now going to sleep on his own in the kennel, her sex life was reignited, she was making mommy friends, she was, dare she say it, *enjoying* mommy life a bit more, with her doggy games, and *not worrying* about her career, as so many Internet articles and well-meaning folks had suggested—it was just as her motherhood seemed to be coalescing, that she took the liberty of actually going out, of all things, on a weekend night with some old friends from grad school, the kind working mother she'd lunched with and their old pal the videographer.

What a novelty! What a delight! To join other accomplished women for a dinner cooked by someone else and a glass of white wine and stimulating conversation! A chance to share their respective trials and tribulations within a context of mutual respect and admiration!

The working mother who taught at the university started in about her work immediately, explaining even before they ordered that she had been *confronting and complicating the notion of appropriation, artistic ownership, and public persona* by recontextualizing Instagram posts within works of art. This woman—this working mother / working artist, who had it all without a hitch—simply printed out Instagram posts in large scale, and that was it; that was the art. Oh sure, there were claims of *curation* and the *power of juxtaposition,* but when it really came down to it, she had browsed Instagram and found some pics and gotten a large-scale printer and, voilà: art. Nightbitch had read about it on her website and then in the *Times,* where she saw that a recent piece had sold for half a million dollars.

The other grad-school friend—the videographer—had been *experimenting with the interplay between seer and seen* and the *ways in which we mediate reality,* as if that were a new thing, Nightbitch thought. As if there were actually any original thought that had even gone into such a project. This friend had just had a show in the Kelly Biennial featuring two literally unwatchable videos. In one, the video would cut in and out as the power surged and died, which was meant to inspire thought regarding our *relationship with information and power/Power,* though Nightbitch felt the installation would simply be annoying. It didn't even really *need* an installation, just an artist's statement. The other video, the videographer explained, was a real-time video of twenty-four hours of her day, alongside an actress acting out that very same day in that very same space. Her friend said something about performance: can we truly be ourselves while being watched blah blah blah. Nightbitch nodded and smiled. Sure. Okay.

And what are you working on? they asked her, and she stammered and chuckled, turned red, stared at the wall for a moment before saying something about the wildness of motherhood, the modern mother's impulse toward violence, the transformative powers of anger. Her friends squinted, then tilted their heads quizzically.

I'm just at the concept phase right now, Nightbitch added. But I think it will ultimately be a performance piece.

Ohhh, the working mother said, and then the videographer added, Your work has always been so dramatic, and though Nightbitch wanted to say, *What the fuck do you mean by that?* or *At least I'm not doing some bullshit social-media project that gives art a bad name,* or *If you're going for ultimate snoozefest with your work, then you're right on time,* instead she nodded calmly and didn't say anything.

It was meant to be a pleasant dinner, a reunion of sorts among grad-school friends, one of whom she hadn't seen now in, what, eight years? It began nicely enough—*how-are-you*s and family updates, chats about this old friend or that one—but soon enough, Nightbitch saw it, saw exactly what was happening.

You see, the old friends had been doing more work than she—gobs, in fact. They had all been colleagues and friendly competitors, neck and neck years ago, back in school, even back just before her son was born, but since then these friends had indeed moved forward, progressed in a reasonable and some might say even extraordinary fashion, given their talents and skills, whereas she had punched her artist card and checked in to stay-at-home-mommy land. She hadn't wanted her baby to be with the horrible women with rubber nipples all day. She had been desperate to hold him, to kiss his cheeks and smell his neck. And she hadn't wanted to cry as he nursed and then continue to cry some more as he fell asleep and she hadn't gotten to make him giggle and read his favorite books because he was so tired, exhausted, by his day at day care with the horrible women, where he would not—he refused—to sleep. And she simply couldn't work at the gallery and do her own work and then take care of the baby by herself, with her husband out of town. She couldn't, and so she had chosen the baby—*the baby, the baby*, his allure had been dreamlike and intoxicating—and had left the rest behind. And now. Now.

These other women—they were her friends!—had kids, but one had *sold a piece of art for half a million dollars* and also had a live-in nanny, while the other had the ability not to care about the horrible women and the day care, or at least not show it, not give in to it, and instead had enlisted her child in full-time day care, with before- and after-school programs, even before the child was in school. Nightbitch knew this because the videographer had said as much, in passing, with a laugh. A laugh! The videographer had no regrets—which she actually said after her third glass of wine—No regrets!—with a laugh and a clink of her wineglass against Nightbitch's—no ambivalence, a strong and clear vision of herself in the studio and her child elsewhere, wherever that may have been. So these other women, these successful women, of course they discussed their many successes, swapping the names of gallery curators and art-world agents with heightening excitement, screeching with joy as one announced a new show, the other a new grant, both of them comparing their residency schedules and teaching gigs for the coming year.

I just have too many opportunities being offered to me,

the working mother said. I'm going to have to let go of the ones that bore me, honestly. There's just not enough time in the day.

Nightbitch nodded, hoping that it appeared as though she completely understood. Not enough time for all those creative pursuits. Totally. Indeed.

Nightbitch had ordered a kale salad topped with a lovely piece of salmon, and the longer she ate, the more kale seemed to appear on her plate. She assiduously shoveled it into her smiling mouth, chewing and chewing and chewing. As the women talked, actually turned their chairs toward each other on the other side of the circular table and talked and talked and talked, Nightbitch chewed.

I am a cow, she meditated. I am a Zen cow in a soothing green field.

This meditation she needed to counteract the cud that rose from down in her guts, for it was there, she discovered with a startling pang of nausea, that she had pushed all the anger and sadness, all the disappointment about how her life had turned out. It was there she had buried the talented and plucky young woman with big ideas and an unusual point of view. That young woman was down in her intestines, biding her time, or perhaps dead, suffocated in all the shit. And up where Nightbitch still lived, up and out in the air and at the table in the lamplit restaurant tucked into a charming bricked strip of buildings in a quaint little college town, there sat a middle-aged mom, out of the art world for a significant amount of time, no longer a newcomer but also not yet emerged, not yet even introduced to the art world, really, save for some very minor regional shows, a few articles here and there, but otherwise decidedly unemergent, with no hopes of surfacing soon. And this was not how Nightbitch had viewed herself, not by a long shot, for she had been keeping this idea alive, that there was infinite time and potential and opportunity, that she wasn't *that* old, that her life wasn't over, but, sitting at that table, she saw quite starkly, through two glasses of white wine and an entire bale of kale, that she was none of these things and instead was, in a word, insignificant. She saw herself as these other women now saw her, a silent, flabby woman sipping wine without so much as a single exciting comment or opinion to offer to the conversation. She was so uninteresting that they didn't even need to acknowledge her for a good half-hour. It wasn't mean. It was just that she didn't figure into the conversation. (Surely it wasn't mean? She was talented. And she *would* have been as successful as they were, had she kept working. She assumed they had all understood this, had this as a shared understanding that put them all on an even playing field. Honestly, none of this had even been consciously considered until this very moment, when she was forced to see herself in this pathetic context, in this pathetic way.)

At first she thought she might cry, but then she saw she would do something far worse.

All of the rage and hopelessness of those long months before Nightbitch emerged tidal-waved back into her. Surely her friends had not meant a thing by all this, had meant no insult, had not even really been thinking of her at all, to be honest, but it was this lack of consideration that wounded her the most, that she could no longer even be a part of their conversation, not that she wanted to be part of such self-involved banter, but she would have liked to be invited to join and then reject it—she deserved that, at the very least. She returned to those horrible thoughts of her husband sipping coffee in a quiet shop while leisurely perusing a periodical, to her long days of trains and failed naps and encouraged poops in the potty and train tracks and more trains.

She swelled with self-indulgent anger, for indeed she saw she was on the verge of throwing a temper tantrum much in the same way her son tossed himself to the living-room floor, kicking and clawing, injuring himself in the process, and then crying even harder—and she could not, she would not, stop it. It was either blasting the anger out or turning the anger in, and she wasn't willing to keep it there any longer. She would not shred herself up inside, would not churn her guts to acid, would not grind her teeth in her sleep or cause her neck to go out, for the sake of being civil and mature and understanding and levelheaded.

And it was just as the videographer was making a joke, saying, Look, I realize I joke about being a narcissist, but I think I actually *am* a narcissist, that Nightbitch rose all at once from her chair—tipping the table and sending the silverware clattering to the floor, a glass onto its side, and the water therein onto the lap of the working mother, whose eyes widened and mouth formed a silent O—with a great roar, which halted chatter in the restaurant and plunged it into an eerie, stunned silence. There she stood, panting, so winded already was she from her rage.

She growled at the women, then barked and barked and barked, closing her eyes and forcing the animal sounds from herself, her ab muscles contracting violently, her pelvic floor heaving from years of diligent Kegel exercises.

I could crush a walnut with my vagina! she yelled at no one in particular, and it was then that the people around her came into sharp focus: her friends—The Artists—seated across from her at the table, one of them shielding her eyes as if she were looking directly at the sun, the other with a slight smile creeping across her lips. An old man at the booth behind them, mouth agape. A small girl in the next booth cowering into her mother's ribs, and her mother stroking her hair and shushing her and whispering comforting things as she glared at Nightbitch.

Instantly mortified, Nightbitch began to sweat profusely,

descended into an openmouthed pant, and had the fleeting thought that perhaps she was now in the throes of an early menopause. Then, despite her best attempts, she began to cry hot angry tears as she collected her bag and her coat.

The working mother tried to say something in a soothing, low tone. Nightbitch held up a hand.

Don't, she said, then monstered out of the restaurant in a lumbering walk, more tornado than human bipedal propulsion. She surged toward the door and disturbed everything in her wake, blowing napkins off tables and overturning cups and tripping and stumbling and snorting. It was her goal to get out of the place before the transformation really took hold, but she could not resist the smell of red meat after what seemed a lifetime spent chewing kale.

She stopped at a two-seater high-top by the door, a young couple, the woman with a sparkling ring on her left hand, bright with love. The young woman leaned back and stifled a scream as Nightbitch grabbed her half-eaten burger from her plate, ripped a bite from it, then dropped the bun, the lettuce and onion and tomato, to the floor as she exited the dining area. She shoved the meat patty into her maw and chewed and salivated as she surged away, down the street. She loped through puddle-strewn alleyways and, once out of downtown, crashed through shrubs, wanting not to be seen, to stay in the shadows, where she could pant and snort and sob.

She pointed herself toward the nature preserve, toward the dark and comforting woods tucked right into the middle of town, to cry and snarl in the darkness beneath the trees, cry and muck about in the tendril of stream that flowed toward her neighborhood eventually, if she followed it long enough, which is what she decided to do as she stood there letting the icy water numb her sore, bleeding feet. She had lost her sandals somewhere along the way, and the water felt so good she let out a little guttural howl. Snot dripped from her nose to intermingle with hot, dirty tears. She careened in the stream, pushing over fallen logs and pulling shrubs from the banks as she searched for something to steady her. It was her goal to make havoc, to leave a mess, to wrest from her form all of the rage and sadness and insanity of these years since her son was born. She had been storing it all in the puckered dough of her thighs, the sad little paunch hanging around her middle. In the dark-brown circles she could not seem to get rid of that framed her eyes day and night. In the joints of her fingers, which had now begun to hurt whenever she was tired or angry or sad, which was always.

Oh, those women! Those horrible women! She sobbed and splashed her way deeper into the woods, then came to sit on a fallen log and weep. She had not felt this way since, what, high school? Junior high? Less than and left out and lame, adolescent feelings that overcame her and made her feel stupid just for having them. She was a grown woman. She didn't want to feel this way. It was ridiculous. Yet still she sobbed quietly as she had not done in decades.

The Herculean effort of the last years, all the disappointments, the worry that she was not, despite everything she had sacrificed, a good mother, the anxiety that she would never return to her art and that this was now her lot in life, motherhood and nothing more, she felt all of it thudding through her and cried and cried, like a heartsick teen she cried. Hadn't she had a most wonderful domestic weekend full of refreshing sexual drive and normal, untroubled family life as a wife and mother and dog-mother who actually, totally had the dog-mother thing under control? So, so close to true and completely unconflicted contentment, thanks to her disavowal of art, her arduous psychological work of the past weeks to get a handle on her urges, to harness her desires. But then these mothers, these artists, who she considered with the bitterness of a hundred endless night-nights, a thousand artless afternoons.

She pushed a sound from herself she had not heard before, a long raspy growl made up of rage and breath, yearning and sorrow. There was a great and horrible power to the sound, as every muscle strained to expel it, her abs tightening and throat constricting. Her toes tensed, and her hands curled to claws. A blind animal-cry toward *something else*. An expulsion of all that had been inside her.

Beside her, from its hidden den, a raccoon answered her with its own ungodly talk, and without thought she dived headlong into the darkness at the bank, for she saw its two gleaming eyes. It had startled her, and she was furious. How dare it. How dare.

She took it in her hands and snapped its neck efficiently before it could bite her and threw its body with a splash into the creek. She tipped her head back and filled the sky with a howl as big as her entire life and, with that, was hell-bent on getting home, weeping now, as her adrenaline surged and her muscles overflowed with blood and she crashed through the night.

By the time she reached the place where she and the boy threw rocks into the water on sunny afternoons, the place just beyond the train tracks, and then, soon after, her very own backyard, she had slaughtered three small rodents and one helpless bunny that unluckily found themselves in her path.

In her backyard, she stretched out in the grass on her belly and smelled the earth and wiped her face against the soft green fronds. Her legs were scratched and her arms were scratched and her hands filthy and bloody.

She crashed into the house and did not yell a friendly *hello* to alert her husband she was home, as she usually did, but instead went straight to the bathroom and locked the door. There she stripped off her sullied clothing and pulled twigs from her matted hair. She turned the shower as hot as it would go, and stood beneath the water, to calm herself and wash the night away.

She cried herself to sleep in the guest bed and awoke earlier than her husband and son, then got up to cry some more. She saw she had twenty-six unread texts and turned off her phone altogether. She would never be able to face those friends again.

She was mad at herself for caring, mad at herself for feeling like a failure. In fact, wasn't viewing yourself as a failure the first step toward actually becoming one? She couldn't *think* that way. It wasn't productive. Yet, still, all she wanted to do was watch dumb movies and stay in her pajamas, and she could do that, because she didn't have to be anywhere in the world that day except with her son. She had nothing of import to do, no one depending on her expertise or excited to see a new piece from her. No, no one needed her but a two-year-old. She could do whatever she wanted—except for the crying, which she would do in limited increments while pretending to use the bathroom.

The obnoxious cat meowed and meowed and meowed brainlessly until she fed it a disgusting slime-sauced breakfast from a can, which it lapped up noisily. She deposited four frozen sausages into the tiny skillet on the stove, as she dropped frozen waffles into the toaster, as she sliced a banana and washed some strawberries. She wanted to pound through the walls with her fists as she moved the wet laundry from the washer to the dryer. She imagined herself ripping the head off a songbird with her hands as she wiped the kitchen table with a sponge, then turned to her son's tiny little plastic table and wiped that, too. She blew her nose and put on the coffee and listened to the news. She fed her family breakfast, helped her husband find things he needed to put in his suitcase since the poor guy couldn't keep track of his own stuff. He was never there, the silly goose! Of course he didn't know where anything was!

Her husband wanted to know what was wrong, and she told him it was just her monthly cycle, the erratic nature now of her midlife hormones, and he said, worried, Well, I've never seen you cry like this, and she just waved him off and began crying again.

I'm perimenopausal, she said, still sobbing, and was plunged even deeper into her hopelessness, yet in under ten minutes finally put a smile on her face, so as not to trouble her husband. He was a good man and didn't need the extra stress of worrying about her—not that he would even do that once he left. She didn't imagine he thought much at all about her emotional state when he was gone.

The next morning, she sent her husband on his way—after he had the little breakfast and cup of hot coffee she had prepared, which had been waiting for him upon his wakening, after he'd had a leisurely, restorative shit, after a nice long shower and an awaiting stack of clean clothes warm from the dryer, which she had folded neatly and left on the toilet for him after spritzing a little air freshener—and then descended further into her self-loathing, now sending hateful thoughts after her husband's car as it pulled away.

I'd like to take a leisurely shit one day, she thought bitterly.

Try as she might, she could not pull herself from it, and turned on cartoons and lay beside her son, watching as two bug things pounded each other over the head with mallets, laughing maniacally. This was too violent for him to watch, but he loved it, clapped and giggled. Yes, she *was* a bad mother, a horrible one. She felt another cry coming on, and rose to feed herself, for she had forgotten to do so while remembering to feed everyone else in the house; she again found the horrible cat, not even an hour after its breakfast, waiting on the corner of the rug in front of the sink, where it always lurked.

The rotting potatoes in the garbage smelled atrocious; the air was so dry, the clouds outside so thick, and the morning so gray. She realized with a yip, while hunched in front of the open fridge, that there was not a scrap of meat in the house, save for the horrible cat's horrible cans of food, for which she was again whining, meow after incessant meow. As Nightbitch scooped yet another can into the cat's dish, she sniffed at it, wondering, but it was too slimy and flaked, too altogether anonymous to excite her appetite. She watched with disgust as the cat sloppily gulped and smacked her way through the pile of unspeakable meat. The boy's cartoon dinged and beeped while Nightbitch seethed in the kitchen, glaring at the cat as she sipped a tepid cup of coffee, her bathrobe slung loosely around her.

She tried listening to the news, but it only incited her blood-thirst, so she shut it off and paced back and forth by the sink. She searched through a cupboard for something to stop the throbbing in her head and slammed the cupboard door without finding so much as an ibuprofen. She picked up a knife to cut . . . something, anything, turned to search for an apple or carrot or goddamn beef jerky, then stepped on the stupid cat, which had just finished its second breakfast and come to hover, weirdly and silently, just behind her feet. Nightbitch, of course, tripped, sprawled hard on the kitchen floor, and in doing so came down hard on the cat, which sent the cat skittering toward the living room, eyes wide and green, the ball of her body bobbing on spindly, cartoon-fast legs.

Nightbitch's knee pulsed with pain, as did her haunch. Her eyes flared with silent rage as she lunged after the cat, caught her by her back legs, pulled her across the hardwood floor, and plunged the knife into her chest. Though she did not think it possible, the cat's green eyes widened even more, not a hint of any intelligence behind them, just dull instinct, the smallest amount of instinct required to keep such a stupid animal alive.

She jerked the knife through the soft girth of its belly. The animal split open like a pair of tight pants. Nightbitch growled in her chest as she bent to wrap her teeth around the nape of the cat's neck. She rose in blind fury and shook the body back and forth, the cat deflating—squeak by small, breathy squeak—with each fling, blood splattering on the white cabinets and across the worn wood floor. A loop of purple intestine slipped from the wound and flipped back and forth like a wet scarf. A thick warmth spread down Nightbitch's chin and onto her chest, and in this ecstasy, she swung her head back and forth with even greater fervor, intestines and organs slapping her face and falling to the floor. She shook harder, furiously, blood flung to every corner of the kitchen, until a sharp *snap,* and the body relaxed into ultimate resignation. She stopped. Blood dripped onto her bare feet and in between her toes. She dropped the thing from her mouth into her hands and held it there, to sniff it and nudge it with her nose, examine it with an animal curiosity. To watch it and in this strange reverie stand still inside a gripping and extraordinary chaos.

And only now in her remembering did the events of the recent weeks begin to make sense. For of course she had known about it since she was a child, growing up as she had within the old German ways, with her old parents in the old Appalachian foothills, those thickly dark hills gripping in their valleys the secret of decades, of centuries. She watched her mother's hands, always in motion, crocheting intricate angels from thin thread, working in the herb garden and then binding the cuttings she had collected and hanging them to dry from the kitchen eaves, cleaning the meat from a chicken carcass, working her fingers between the ribs, holding the wishbone up in the window light to admire it, flicking a paring knife this way and that over a bowl of strawberries, folding together the freezer boxes, lining them with plastic bags, pouring and twist-tying and securing and stacking, searching through bushes taller than she for thousands of blueberries, in her curly hair, scratching her skull, her eyes tired and closed, working the knots from her husband's neck, kneading dough, searching beneath suds for dirty forks. She remembered the heavy navy-blue coat her mother wore year-round at the meat locker and its thick zipper, the force of her mother's hands as she wrenched the teeth closed and then touched each frozen side of meat, as if to comfort them. They swung in her wake, as if comforted. The single bulb within the locker cast a cold, hard light on the muscles and bones. The girl had known what blood smelled like from a young age, and knew the consequences of violence. Her parents, their religion, claimed pacifism, but there was violence in every day of their lives, the chicken heads and cracked eggs, the dead kitten in the little nest in the hay bales, a pig hung from a tripod to bleed, the slow bodies of deer turning in the trees.

Her mother had wanted to be a singer, an opera singer. She had the sort of voice that soared up above everything and took the air up there to transform it into something sharp and translucent and perfect. Instead, she collected her hair and covered it and went to church to sing four-part harmonies each Sunday. It was a virtue to blend in. It was a virtue to put the group above oneself, so she did, for her entire life. She had sung a solo long ago at a Wednesday-night service when she was still a girl, and who was in the audience but a cousin of someone or other, a big-city cousin there to absorb some local flavor. After the service, he approached her mother, wiping tears from his eyes with a crisp white handkerchief, to tell her he had never heard the likes of such a voice, that he worked in theater, that he himself would become her patron so she could go study at the best vocal school in Europe, and he handed to her a little white card. She kept this hidden in the base of a music box on her dresser, for her family thought the dream to sing in Europe was the height of stupidity, the height of vanity. She promised herself she would do it when she grew up, but little did she know. This is how she told the story, and then how she ended it, *little did I know,* and her daughter would always ask, *Know what? Know what?*— was desperate to know—at which her mother laughed longer and harder than seemed called for and told the girl to go to bed, it was late.

For a time, even after her mother had birthed a perfect baby girl, there was talk toward Europe, so much talk it almost turned evil, threatened to tip over into the terrain of the self-involved—the individual, her husband reminded her, was of little import to the church—and so. Her father was a fine man, but her mother was extraordinary. She remembered warm summer nights, her mother sitting barefoot on the lawn, a record player spilling opera all over the now black grass, the now black air and unmoving trees. That's how the girl fell asleep each night, with opera unspooling through the open windows and her barefoot mother in a flowered skirt, lying there staring up at the stars. One night, she had a dream of her mother, outside in the grass, set upon by foxes and raccoons and wolves. Her mother meowed like a kitten, and each time one of the animals attacked her, she petted it lovingly and meowed as it pulled her apart. The girl watched from her dream window with a great despair growing in her. *I knew it,* she said to herself. *I always knew it.* She woke heaving and went down to find her mother, to make sure she was safe, the dream still alive though she was awake, the whole thing a confusion: Her mother was out there with the kittens? But her mother didn't even *like* the kittens. No, wait. She was singing. . . . And she saw, by the light of the moon, that her mother was still there on the lawn, unmoving. The girl feared her dead and called her name, at which her mother sat up with a start and wiped her face. Why are you crying? the girl asked, and her mother said, I'm not crying. I'm tired. Go to bed.

It's just that the kittens would not stop following her, had followed her on the long walk to the bus each morning. She sobbed and threw rocks at them, scolded them for following her, and told them to go back home, but they knew her fingers tasted like milk and wanted to lick them and have her tuck them away in her warm jacket. She begged her parents to take the animals inside so that they wouldn't follow her, wandering so far from home and certainly becoming lost for good once she boarded the bus. She imagined them crying all day in the rocky lane, hungry and cold, then wandering off into the woods to be eaten by a fox. She sobbed and begged her parents, and they were wide-eyed at her despair. They'll be fine, they claimed, perplexed by this small sobbing girl. You're going to miss your bus, they said, pushing her out the door. They could not be bothered to watch over the kittens, for they were *just animals,* and the girl ran as fast as she could the half-mile to the bus stop, crying and running, her legs hot with it, her lungs full of gravel, for she loved these little kittens as if they were her own children, she cherished them, and her parents could not be bothered to care, and in this way she knew there was some horrible chasm between them that would never fully be spanned. She felt very alone as she waited for the bus, her face wet and shoes muddy, and always the air of that era was cold, colder than she had expected, in the forever shade of the dark woods under a no-sun sky.

She went to her grandmother for a solution, a wrinkled near-blind woman who lived in a little house on their property and only ever wore plain dresses and plain shoes and smiled as she sat in the sunlight. Her mother's mother, she barely spoke English, instead muttered in convoluted German, but still the girl went to ask for a spell, for she knew her grammy had them in her little book, whose worn cover featured hex signs and unfamiliar symbols, the text all in German. I need a spell to keep the kittens safe, she said to the old woman, who sat silently in a straight-backed chair on her little porch. The woman smiled, her whole face lighting, and bade the child enter her little shack, which smelled of garlic and dirt and candle wax. She pulled the little book from her nightstand and thumbed the soft pages. The girl was wondering how she could read the faded words when the old woman pulled a magnifying glass from the stand to examine the book more closely. She studied it for a time, looking for just the right page, and then took the book to the kitchen table, where she left it open to consult intermittently while pulling jars from her shelves and putting a heavy metal pot on the open fire. As the girl watched, she dumped into the pot dried herbs and fresh ones, an amount of carefully measured water drawn from the hand pump at the crude sink. She told the girl to collect three dandelion heads from the lawn, which she did obediently, and as she came back into the shadowy house, she saw her grandmother slipping the body of a small rodent into the brew. When all ingredients had been collected and concocted, they drank chamomile tea until the pot reached a boil, at which point her grandmother took it from the fire with a towel wrapped round its handle and to the fence line at the edge of the pasture, where she dumped the boiling mixture under and along the fence while mumbling quietly in German.

Okay, her grammy said, and the girl hugged her waist, smelling the life of her. She loved no one more. The next day, all the weeds were dead where they had poured the concoction, the rodent body was gone, and the kittens were asleep in their nest as she left for school.

Her mother was *good* and *responsible* and *holy* and always somewhere far away in her own head, or with a headache, or napping, or just, please, leave me alone. Forget your grammy and her book. Be serious. Do something sensible. And always the girl had thought her mother was pushing her out the door, away and away, go fast. She thought this had been a sort of abandonment, but now she saw it for what it was: her mother's best love. How many generations of women had delayed their greatness only to have time extinguish it completely? How many women had run out of time while the men didn't know what to do with theirs? And what a mean trick to call such things holy or selfless. How evil to praise women for giving up each and every dream.

It had been so long since she had remembered all this,

so long since she'd even thought of it, for there had been a great forgetting when she left home—a purposeful forgetting, because to forget her childhood meant she had survived it.

Her own wood-and-bone projects, her sewing with the playground installation, had all called on the skills she'd gathered during her quiet Appalachian upbringing. She knew how to keep bees, dip candles, brush wool, use a spinning wheel and make yarn, dry onions and garlic, develop photographs with vegetable juices, bake absolutely anything, make every single sort of braid, sing every single sort of song, track an animal through the woods. She knew her cardinal directions, how to tell a fast pony from a slow one just from the look of its face. She knew enough to live inside an entire life all on her own, and yet her husband—with his electronics skills, his engineering—he was the one who made all the money, even though she could make a world, and then, too, make a person to live in that world.

And what of that person, her most beautiful boy? He opened his eyes each morning, and the first word from his mouth was *Mama*. He needed to be lifted from bed, for he was so tiny and so sleepy, then dressed, fed, bathed, played with, sung to, tickled, swung high in the air, chased. He needed her to *watch me, Mama*, nearly every second of his waking life. Sometimes he took his soft little hand and put it on her face, moved her head to where he wanted her to look. And it was in this gesture she saw an entire impending future, one in which all things of this world revolved around this boy: when she woke and when she slept, where they went and what they bought, the very direction of his mother's gaze. If she was not careful, he would come to know the world as a place that bent to his every whim, for she did indeed want to bend, because she loved him, but in the hardest moments—moments in which, for instance, she held the limp body of the cat in her bloody hands—she grew resentful of this innocent little soul, whose life would be one of ease, one of knowing that he was taken care of and could have whatever he wanted, that the world was in a very real way *his*. She didn't want to deny him things, to make his life harder, but already she felt this pull inside her, to make him *responsible* in a fundamental way, to tell him *no* and *no* and *no*, and, sure, she was trying to train him against what the entire world told him, was trying to say, Look, I am not all yours, I am not only here for you, but of course, ultimately, she was his, all of her.

three

———

Oh dear.

Her kitty.

The fluff.

The stupid-sweet little fluffenwaffer. The smoosh. The rug. Fluffy paws and jingle meow. She had once wanted to decorate her with tiny ornaments, because, while sitting, she took on a perfectly conical shape and resembled a Christmas tree. Her ballerina. Her baby. Oh dear, indeed.

How long had she stood there within the bloody mess she had created? Two cartoons' worth of time? Five? The boy entered the kitchen to find his mother's face covered in blood, her hands, too, a bloodstained robe sliding from her shoulder as she picked tufts of black fur from her mouth, a pile of black fur at her feet, motionless. Blood on the cabinets. Blood on the floor. Blood on the ceiling.

The boy froze, eyes wide, looking from the pile to his mother, then back again.

Oh no. The boy! What had she done? She stood stock still, watching the boy as he tentatively edged toward her, sniffed her robe, then sniffed the dead cat. He nudged the body with his nose, lifted the cat's paw, and watched as it fell.

He looked again at his mother, then let out a small, joyful howl, then nudged the cat's bloody body with his tiny foot.

Oh, honey, Nightbitch said, jolting back to the dry air of the gray day, back to the realities of a mother in her robe and a boy in his pajamas rejoicing over a cat's dead body in the kitchen, the boy howling and poking the dead animal, bloodying his perfect little toes, how this looked and what this might mean. She did not want blood on his perfect skin, did not want him to involve himself in this insanity. It all must be shut down, must be cooled off, the doggy games and whatnot. Oh Jesus. What had she been thinking?

She hadn't been thinking. That was it. She had been pure emotion, pure yearning and rage. No thought could have possibly gone into such a thing.

Poor kitty, she said, stroking the animal, now a pile on the floor. She looked into its fixed, dead eyes. She looked at the horrible wound down its belly, purple guts spilling out. She tried to push it all back in. She grabbed a towel from beneath the sink to wrap the creature, to try and dignify this undignified situation.

Oh dear, she said.

Get kitty! the boy screeched, his blood rising from the scent of death, and Nightbitch sank even deeper into worry. Worry that the doggy games had gone too far, that she herself was out of control and had crossed some line, that her son might be permanently damaged from such a childhood, that some might even construe this as abuse, bad parenting, mental illness, if given the opportunity to. Why, there was blood *all over the kitchen*. Who did this? She needed to do a thorough cleaning immediately.

Poor, poor kitty, she repeated. It was an accident. I tripped over her and must have . . . Here she stopped for want of what to say. I must have lost control of my human faculties and gone dog-bananas on this poor cat? I did hate her, but she didn't deserve to die? She was very beautiful yet very, very dumb?

They both looked at the animal.

Eat it? he asked after a lengthy consideration.

Oh no, Nightbitch said, touching the top of his head.

Kitty isn't for eating. We must bury her in the backyard. Say goodbye, kitty. We loved you. Kitty was our friend.

So that's what the pair spent their afternoon doing, digging in the backyard, first with shovels and then with their hands, spraying dirt behind them as they tunneled into the earth, deeper and deeper. It was, in a word, a delight. The smell of the loam, the wriggle of worms, thick tree roots in which to sink one's teeth and pull and pull and pull.

When they finally had a hole deep enough for kitty, both mother and son were blackened with their work, faces muddy, with tender fingers, but still—it had been worth it, for the fun of it.

They wrapped the cat in an old baby blanket and laid her in the ground. The boy looked on solemnly.

We should say some nice things to send her off, she said.

Oh, cat. You were quite beautiful, and your meow used to be so sweet, like a bell. Thank you for being our kitty.

Kitty soft, the boy said, then scampered into the hole to place the last remaining unopened can of cat food beside her.

She was scared now, really *really* scared, even more scared than after that first transformation and nighttime romp, and she did not turn from this emotion but instead fell all the way into it. It was the same scared she'd felt back in her twenties when she drank too much and, in the morning, was left with a vague sensation of dread. What had she done? Where had she been? She needed to Change. She must, she must, she must *Get It Together*. She frantically decided (yet again) that it was, in fact, high time, that she could not go on like this, with the unhappiness and this now uncontrollable rage, especially not around her son, her poor sweet little angel of a son, whom she would never harm, not ever, but, still, look what she had done to the cat, it was terrifying and she was terrified, brought nearly to tears of ultimate terror when the thought of gripping the back of her son's neck in her teeth passed by her like a driverless school bus packed with hysterical children careening toward a cliff. She would really lean into *setting goals* and *achieving outcomes.* She would get *back on track* in a real way, no matter what. She would now take a deep, cleansing breath and set her sights on *being sensible,* as her mother had once, had always, commanded.

She must maintain a placid disposition of motherly care even while the panic of the world whizzed around inside her. No coffee. More vegetables. Cook the meat. Clean the house. Go for walks. A consistent bedtime each night, and consistent getting-up time, too. Plenty of socialization . . . But she could not bring herself to leave the house, and instead committed to a quiet week of crafts and trains and cooking and lawn care.

FIRST, SHE CLEANED THE kitchen, top to bottom, wiping down everything with water and vinegar, giving the boy a bucket and a rag to slop all over the floor.

Make a mess! she commanded, pointing at the bucket of sudsy water. His eyes grew large, and he set about his work seriously, and messily. After the water, she gave the boy the vacuum hose and put him to work sucking up every bit of twig or leaf or dirt, and this he did with unmatched zeal, bidding his mother scooch the oven away from the wall ever so little so he could suck up the cobwebs behind, tearing a piece of construction paper apart piece by piece and placing each one into the end of the hose to have it sucked efficiently and satisfyingly into the clear plastic receptacle.

After the kitchen, she set about deep-cleaning the bedroom. She pulled up and smoothed the rumpled bedcovers while the boy dived beneath them, canceling her work. She and her son dug from the sheets two old tennis balls and a rawhide bone, the boy's leash—which he held above his head in celebration, for he had already forgotten about this treasure—and, finally, a short length of rope knotted at each end, good for chewing or pulling or fetching. She wiped the thick coating of dust from the ceiling-fan blades. She wiped water from the floor around the dog dish. She collected the piles of clothes and threw them all on the freshly made bed to fold.

Beneath the sweatpants and sports bras and T-shirts piled by the bed she found a stack of the boy's bedtime books and, at the bottom of that, her *Field Guide*. She must read this again, tonight! But as soon as she had made such a resolution, she doubled back on it, for could this book be trusted? Was this book really an original source? Could she in any way realistically attribute scientific authority to an expert in mythical ethnography? And why had Wanda ignored her e-mails?

Well, what else are you going to do? she asked herself. In these times, under these circumstances, what will you do? Even if she was Getting It Together, it was clear that her answers were not going to reside in the land of logic, the land of doctors and prescriptions, the land of peer-reviewed journals, the land of the goddamn sun rising in the east and setting in the west. Yes, answers to her questions resided in the land of the backward sun, the land of counterclockwise rotation, in the land populated only by artists and fortune-tellers and people on stilts. And wasn't Wanda White, mythical ethnographer, indeed a native of such a land? Whether scientist or something else, she was on a similar journey. And so Nightbitch would read *Magical Women* and take it to heart, because there was very little else her heart could realistically handle these days.

It was one thing to kill a wild bunny, but quite another to kill the family cat, especially so gruesomely, and while her young son was in the house. She thought about this at naptime, as the boy snored ever so quietly beside her in bed. Sure, they had had fun burying it, but, no matter how resilient the boy's psyche, that indelible image of his mother in the kitchen remained: hands slick with bright blood, tufts of black fur still stirring in the air, the dark-blue-and-purple guts of the animal slipping onto the worn wood floor, a floor that needed to be refinished. The blood had stained the spots where the varnish had worn off the boards and abided no matter how much she scrubbed.

Fuck, she muttered to herself.

Then *Fuck* again.

Her husband would be home on Friday and would, of course, inquire about the cat, as he always did. And what would she say?

She meditated at length on this, the best approach, how to present the situation so that it would have the least impact, so that it would land as gently as a feather on his forehead, so very, very lightly that he would barely feel it at all.

He was not one to overreact or jump to wild conclusions, but he also wasn't one to take risks or overlook things that needed a good looking.

Should she lie? Bend the truth toward a less grisly scenario?

And would the boy even remember today? He was two, after all. She didn't remember anything from being two, not a smidge, and so perhaps any permanent memories and/or damage would be avoided?

She would simply have to frame the whole thing as a horrible accident. Perhaps she dropped one of the cast-iron cooking pots on the cat accidentally while ferrying it from stovetop to counter? Or perhaps she found the poor creature flattened in the street, an anonymous driver already far off on the other side of town. A hit and run! she would declare.

But of course there was the matter of the boy, what he had seen and what he now knew and remembered. Surely he would want to volunteer the information of his mother's bloody hands or the cat's most curious innards. She could not bend the truth too far, and so she thought and thought and finally came to a totally reasonable explanation and thought some more as she fell into sleep next to her napping son.

That night, given her afternoon nap and gruesome events of the morning, she could not sleep and she could not sleep and she could not sleep, and finally opened her *Field Guide* to find Wanda discussing predatory women, those "truly rare breeds" who, though terrifying, "would never injure their own young, even to their own detriment." (God bless, Wanda, she thought, with relief.) "Take, for instance, the highly poisonous Apothecarian tribe, who, on the brink of starvation in the mid-seventeenth century, ensured that their young were not only fed, but fattened, while all the matured adults of the species died off one by one."

White continued:

> *Even greater proof of the magical woman's fierce devotion to the furtherance of her species, we find the WereMothers of Siberia . . . a particularly evasive species. It is unclear from where they originated or how they mother cubs without males nearby. (It should be noted that males perhaps do not even exist, for there has been no empirical confirmation of their habitation in Siberia. It should also be noted, males are not necessary, since the WereMothers appear to be self-fertilizing. More on this later in the text.) Yet there have been sporadic sightings of this truly regal species.*
>
> *The Siberian WereMothers are one of the few species I've had the pleasure of seeing firsthand. On a personal excursion for reasons unrelated to research, I found myself in the far-*

thest reaches of the region in the deepest part of winter. Daytime lasted but a mere six hours, and though my provisions were well stocked, I still feared for my safety and warmth.

A Soviet military helicopter had dropped me near the center of the Eastern Siberia taiga, an eco-region spanning over twenty degrees of latitude and fifty degrees of longitude. Despite their suggestions that I not undertake such a remote trip during such a harsh seasonal period (temperatures dropped to sixty degrees Fahrenheit below zero at times), I was still able to convince them of my aptitude, hardiness, and resolve, and they acquiesced to my request.

Once in the larch forest, I hiked through the shallow snow covering the permafrost with a forty-pound pack. Adept at winter camping, I was prepared to spend three weeks in this terrain. However, that first night, I was overcome by an intense fear I had never before experienced. I would categorize this as a sort of psychic malaise, irrational and disorienting.

I found myself wandering through the snow in my sock feet and many thermal layers in the early-morning moonlight. I was both sweating and hypothermic. I was unaware of who I was and why I was in such a locale. As you might surmise, this was rather out of character for me, a person who considers herself to be highly rational and levelheaded.

Ahead, in a moonlit clearing, what appeared to be two heavily furred women beckoned me. They appeared to be pregnant, with distended torsos, and gathered around them were anywhere from twenty to forty cubs in all phases of maturation. The WereMothers walked on all fours, though they had opposable thumbs on their front "paws," if I could even call them that. Rather, they appeared to be modified hands, incredibly similar to those of Homo sapiens. Their faces I found to be quite beautiful, a mix of human and canine features, with a protruding snout and large, soulful *eyes. Though I cannot be entirely certain of the accuracy of my memory at this particular moment, I recall that these creatures told me of their origins in Pripyat, Ukraine, some forty years earlier and three thousand miles to the west, though they did not speak in the customary way. Rather, it seemed they used some sort of telepathy to dispatch this information directly into my mind.*

I approached the WereMothers, barely aware of my actions and the astonishing appearance of these creatures, though later these indelible images would return to me in hypnotic, waking dreams.

The pack of cubs formed a sort of platform—one single mass working in unison—onto which one of the mothers pushed me. I stretched out atop the pack, and they moved as one body, transporting me beneath the trees to a cozy den in a well-protected cave. "What good children," I repeated again and again within my spinning dementia. Inside the cave, a low fire burned. Eyes flickered in the dark recesses of the habitat. I estimate that a dozen WereMothers were nestled within, along with countless cubs.

In the cave, in the firelight, I was better able to study the WereMothers, even in my much-depleted state. Their pelts were truly glorious, as thick as bear fur and sparkling with hairs that appeared to be made of pure silver. One Were-Mother wrapped me in a thick flannel tick stuffed with down. Where such a linen had been procured was mysterious, but I could not and did not question its warmth and comfort.

The cubs snuggled beneath the blanket, and their warm little bodies served to raise my core temperature quite quickly and efficiently. One WereMother provided me with a wooden bowl of something very close to chicken broth. The cubs barked in such a way that I thought I was able to distinguish language, in an obscure Russian dialect that approximated words such as "ball" and "play." Another WereMother licked my face, and it felt like a warm cloth, reminiscent of my own, human childhood.

Did I imagine the smell of freshly baked bread? Might I have hallucinated the lullabies I heard that evening as I drifted in and out of sleep? The WereMothers were the gentlest of creatures, though their large canine teeth were terrifying. I had no doubt they were masterful hunters and protectors of their young. I also wondered, had I been a man, what fate I might have met that night, wandering crazed in the forest. Perhaps—ironically—my womanhood was what saved me that day, rather than dooming me.

I spent the remainder of my trip with the WereMothers. I witnessed the birth of many cubs and also spontaneous reimpregnation just days after cubs were born. If I had had more time to spend in my investigation of this most lovely species, I would have been curious to see how such life cycles were sustainable over long periods of time.

Just a year ago, I returned to this region in search of the WereMothers and, though I am certain my geographical calculations were correct, was not able to find a single trace of their existence.

SHE WATCHED HER SON closely that week to see if there would be any residual trauma from what he had seen. She searched the Internet for *kids who have seen violence,* and the boy did not appear to have any of the symptoms—no odd aches, no bad dreams, no separation anxiety (not that they were ever separated) or moments of aggression (other than the ordinary doggy snarls), just giggles and cartoons and crashing his cars together in the living room, dumping buckets of sand from the sandbox on the lawn and then raking the sand into the grass with his little-boy-sized rake. No, he seemed fine, but, still, she took him twice that week to get ice cream at the stand down by the river, and they threw rocks into the flat, muddy ripples. They went to the park with the old amusement rides, and they rode the toy train eight times, each time in the caboose, the boy never tiring of it, and crying when she told him she was out of tickets and it was time to go.

Yes, she would go to Jen's herb party. And, yes, she would invest in herbs. She needed all she could get at this point. Was there a Rage-Be-Gone variety? Something to ward off magical transformations into a rabid canine? No-Dog, perhaps?

The next day, in a continuing effort to *make headway* and *turn over a new leaf,* Nightbitch sat at her son's tiny plastic table in the kitchen and wrote TEN THINGS I WANT TO DO BEFORE I DIE, in all caps, on the back of a piece of construction paper covered in crayon scribbles. It was an excruciating self-help exercise, one she would never, ever reveal to another soul, but still. Her son sat in a large casserole dish full of unpopped popcorn, plastic trowel in hand. He wiggled his bare feet in the kernels and laughed. There was a baking sheet beside him, various spoons, plastic bowls, and many, many kernels strewn nearly to the living room.

Nightbitch stared at the sinkful of dishes without seeing them. Ten things, ten things. Good god, she couldn't even think of one. "Lose ten pounds," she wrote lamely, then stopped.

Did she really have no desires anymore? No deep passions? Where had the vitriolic emotions and sweeping gestures of her twenties disappeared to?

Oh god, what did she want to do? There had to be something.

She forced herself to jot down anything—blindly, just go—

and so she scrawled "I want to run naked through a meadow and catch a rabbit and snap its neck and then rip its throat open and drink the warm blood from the wound" and

I want to tell the truth

I want to hump legs

I want to chase horses around a barnyard and make them whinny and kick up dust

I want to be in a church choir and wear a robe but instead of singing I just howl all my hymn notes loud as I can

I want to never brush my hair ever again

I want to wear the same linen dress for a year

I want to stink!

I want to run and run and run into the cornfields all the way to a stream and then follow it to the ocean—I'm sorry, but I'm not coming back—and I want to have very, very passionate sex with a stranger and I want to sit on a fully decorated cake without underwear and I want to perform a large anonymous act of extreme vandalism and I want to be an artist and a woman and a mother I mean a monster I want to be a monster

And certainly her wishes had been affected by what she had read of the WereMothers earlier, for she found the passage so enchanting that she had been transported from her stuffy bedroom and into the cold, clean woods of the WereMothers where they lived together and helped each other and were in a constant state of babies. She loved babies! And she loved the thought of having twenty other wives to live with. Imagine the efficiency! Imagine the friendship! Sure, perhaps you were part wolf, but still. For Nightbitch, there truly was something so enticing and exhilarating at the thought of rejecting all established society for something remote and magical, for a community suited particularly and only to the community's needs. Was being free to do what you needed and be who you wanted—truly free—*monstrous?* If so, it was not a wrong kind of monstrous, but a beautiful one. A way of being to celebrate rather than run from.

In an uncharacteristic move, she collected her son then and took him to the mall, which delighted him, for there was an ornate, full-sized merry-go-round inside, and carts shaped like choo-choo trains in which he could ride, and she indulged him that day in his every desire, and then indulged herself as well. Even though, in theory, she hated the mall, with a child to take care of all day long the shopping center became a wonderland of endless coffee and toddler-friendly activities, which, when visited only once every three months, was an absolute joy. When she allowed herself and the boy a trip, she indulged entirely in its basic, perfume-sample-scented delights. At the fast-fashion store made for customers decades beneath her own age, she bought a cheap pair of black faux-leather pants as her son sucked on an enormous grape lolly, the likes of which he had never been allowed. She bought a faux-fur vest and a coat with "real coyote-like fur trim." She bought leather boots in caramel and midnight and ivory. She found earrings dangling with purple crystals, a necklace made of desiccated seeds. She bought the boy French fries and a *hangurger,* as he called it, and allowed him to attend to it himself, slathering ketchup down his shirt and smearing cheese in his hair, as she devoured her own burger with her collection of bags at her feet. Once home, she left the boy to nap in his car seat, for he had fallen hard into it on the way home, warmed by the late-afternoon sun, everything about him dirty and content. Inside, she changed from her holey T-shirt and shorts too short for her age to her favorite ripped linen caftan and soft fringed moccasins. She wore a red feather boa she had bought for her son. That entire week, in fact, she wore whatever she cared to, day and night, ripped or stained or leather or linen. She became more powerful and more terrifying. She saw it in the eyes of other mothers, in their sidelong glances and stares and quick turns askance. She saw it in the eyes of men, men both hungry and horrified.

I dare you to talk to me, she told them with her mind, and they never dared.

That same night, her husband—rather uncharacteristically, as if he could sense something was amiss, even from his hotel room in Omaha—wanted to video-chat, but she simply couldn't in her current state—unwashed, hair spiraling to the greatest of heights, an all-over furring of her body, a wild, wild look in her eyes—and so she pressed cancel, but then he tried again.

He had a way of doing this, knowing the perfectly wrong time to insist on being connected.

You never call me anymore, he said later, when he called a third time that evening.

Normally, it was her texting and texting and texting him throughout the day, bored and lonely and just wanting some human contact, *Hi,* and later *What are you up to?,* and then, even later, *Must be busy today,* and, finally, *Hi* a second time. He more often than not did not reply to her texts and then, in the evenings, would answer her calls with a clipped *Hello.*

Are you working? she would ask.

Just doing some paperwork. What's up? he would say with an air of efficiency and business, this conversation another thing to check off the list.

Ah, well, just call when you can, she would say, and he would respond with a few words of exhaled relief, and she would wonder, How hard is it to talk to me? To just ask me about my day? To inquire about the child? How goddamn hard is that?

But now it was him calling. And it was delicious.

We've just been so busy today, Nightbitch said.

It was late, and the boy was sleeping in the kennel, curled up on a stack of pillows. He had fallen asleep in there all on his own for the first time in his life. Before, it was those long hours of books and stories and songs and water and hugs and crying and on and on, but now she simply licked his face, tilted her head back and let out a little howl, and then scurried downstairs. The boy cuddled up in a little pile and pulled the wire door closed, not latching it but simply creating a sense of safety, a barrier between him and the monsters in the closet and the monsters in the hallway and the terrifying darkness all around.

He went to sleep completely on his own, she added.

Seriously? her husband said, astonished.

When I left, I told him I'd be back to check on him in five minutes, and he was out cold in the kennel when I went back up, no stories, no nothing. She said all this in a torrent of words, not leaving room for him to interject. She wanted to explain it fully and positively, to show what a good idea it had been. I know you don't like the kennel stuff, she continued, but he's *asleep.*

Her husband laughed.

I guess he'll have some good stories, you know, as an adult, he said.

You don't even know, she said.

Let's hope it sticks, he added.

Oh, it will, she said. You should see him. He just loves being a good doggy.

THE NEXT DAY, AS she pushed her son on a swing and he squawked with joy, as they tunneled in the sandbox in the backyard with their hands, their paws, as she boiled yet another pot of macaroni noodles at dinnertime, as they went on their evening walk through the neighborhood, marveling at the texture of tree bark, chasing a bee from one flower to another, listening for the song from a bird and then singing back, she thought about animals and escape, about freedom and desire, about wanting to be a monster.

It was now, she realized, that she would need to grow focused and quiet, to narrow her eyes and look into the future and see there her success and then work toward making that success happen. No more pouting. No more aimless doggy games. She must be single-minded in her pursuit and effective in her approach. And she would get her son to help her, somehow.

On Thursday, she and the boy spent the day watching online videos of wolves and foxes and dogs, mothers with litters and lone wolves tracking prey, foxes pouncing and playfully plunging their heads into deep snow in search of warm, blood-beating mice far below. They went to the library and checked out all the nonfiction books with the subject of "Dog" from the children's section, and took three trips to lug them out to the car. When they arrived home, they spread the books on the living-room floor and lay there, looking at pictures, reading, discussing, play-acting, trying out a hunt, a pounce, a chase, a hide, a confrontation, sniffing and circling and fighting and snuggling.

She stood in the bathroom and teased her hair until it

was as wide as it was long. She whitened her teeth and took special care to polish her canines. She had stopped shaving her armpits, her legs, the tender folds of skin at the top of her legs and the mound of hair that grew at her center. A true furring was indeed taking place. She rubbed her fingertips over the stubble in her armpit, so comforting was this new part of herself. So, too, she had stopped waxing her lip and plucking her eyebrows, and that week practiced not looking in the mirror altogether. No need was there for makeup any longer, for expensive bleaching creams or sunblock, for tinctures designed to erase fine lines or inhibit aging or protect from environmental pollution. She threw pelts she had bought and pelts she had found over the bathroom mirror and the full-length in the bedroom. That night, she licked her son's face clean, and he licked her cheek *good night* and then curled in his kennel, as simple as that.

NIGHTBITCH ARRIVED AT Book Babies in her ripped linen caftan, the frayed edges unraveling dangerously, her hair unwashed now for a week and protruding hugely from her head in a frenetic net of curls and knots. Her freckles had been drawn out by the late-summer sun, and her shoulders were burned red from her daily sessions of fetch with the boy. Her toenails were unpolished, the bottoms of her feet dry and cracked. They were in need of serious exfoliation, yet she made up for this grooming oversight by accessorizing exquisitely with purple crystals dangling on thin golden hoops in her ears, a length of pliant leather around her neck, a load of golden bracelets weighting her arm made from leaf-shaped links, slim bangles, turquoise beading. She smelled of lavender. It was Friday, and the week had danced by so smoothly, so quickly. A focused and slicing one-person waltz, she thought.

Oh my god! Jen exclaimed upon seeing her, and the rest

of the Book Mommies turned to see. You are so boho! she said. I love what you've done with yourself.

The others looked on less enthusiastically—disapprovingly, one might even say.

You guys, Jen said, turning to Babs and Poppy and the other dubious Book Mommies. She is so . . . Joshua Tree.

Thanks for your enthusiasm, Nightbitch said, taking a seat beside her and letting the boy loose to run around the room, barking.

What inspires you? Jen prodded, the Book Mommies already on to talking about Kindergarten Roundup.

Oh, you know, Nightbitch said. I guess you could say it's a sort of art project I'm developing.

Oooooh! Jen said, eyes widening. You're an artist!?

Used to be, Nightbitch said.

What's the project? Jen asked, only to be set upon by her twins, screaming over a piggy puppet they both wanted but neither could peacefully have.

Nightbitch dug through her bag, looking for nothing, just to have a task with which to be occupied, for how could she say what her project was? Something to do with dogs? Magic? Or not magic, exactly, but power? Feminine power, finally wielded, for wasn't that what all those witches in Colonial America had been burned for, all the folk-medicine practitioners, the midwives? Too much power makes a woman dangerous, and that was her project: creation and power.

After settling the piggy war, Jen turned again to Nightbitch, her last question already forgotten.

I've always been a secret hippie, Jen whispered, following her confession with a wink.

And oh! she continued with a start. I'm so excited you're coming to the party! I saw you RSVP-ed yes.

Yes, Nightbitch said, then yes again, for there was no add-on comment available to her, like *Looking forward to it* or

I can't wait, for these were not exactly true, and these days she could not bring herself to utter such quotidian niceties.

We'll have so much fun, Jen said with a clap and a squeal.

TELL ME AGAIN, HER husband said, after arriving home later that day, throwing the boy high in the air to make him laugh, taking his shoes off, unpacking his suitcase, drinking a beer as he leaned against the kitchen counter and then, off-handedly, inquiring as to where in the world the stupid cat was. He ran his hand through his hair and focused intently on his wife.

Explain again, he said.

Okay, she said, inhaling as she looked at the boy on the floor who was busy loading a garbage truck with marbles. Honey, she said to him, go pick up garbage in the living room, babe.

Ho-o-o-o-o-o-o-o-o-nk, the boy said happily and drove away.

Well, like I said, Nightbitch began, it was a hectic morning. I was horribly tired. Hormones or something. She paused to laugh nervously. And I was cutting up apples for applesauce, and had that heavy pot full of water and apples, right up to the brim. You know how heavy those are?

Yeah, he said.

And so I turned with the pot in my hands, and for some reason also still holding the knife—just trying to do too much all at once—and she was right there—you know how she lurks—and I dropped the pot right on her poor little head, and then the knife, which went right into her.

You dropped a knife on her?

I dropped a knife on her.

A *knife*?

It was *so* sharp.

But I don't think she felt anything, Nightbitch continued in a rush, because the pot had definitely killed her, or at least knocked her out? She wasn't breathing, is what I'm saying. I checked very closely. And I tried to, well, push everything back in, but, oh god, it was just a mess.

She began to cry very gently at this point, and the tears were not fake. She did indeed feel genuine remorse, a low, mean ache about what had happened and what she had done.

What a disaster, she said, and her good, kind husband wrapped his arms around her.

What did the kiddo think? the husband asked, holding his wife at arm's length and smiling wryly.

He asked if we should eat her, Nightbitch said through tears, and they both started laughing.

Oh Jesus, he said.

He liked burying her, she added.

I'm sure he did. Well . . . at least we don't have to put up with her pooping her furry pants anymore.

Or with her whining for food.

Poor kitty, the husband said.

Poor thing, Nightbitch added. Poor, poor thing . . .

NIGHTBITCH ARRIVED LATE TO the party on Saturday afternoon. Jen's house was in a development called Prairie Breeze on the east side of town, a place to which Nightbitch had never had reason to venture before and did not, to be honest, even know existed. The houses asserted their dominance as she crawled past, each one more misshapen and sprawling the deeper she drove. Vinyl-sided garages and faux-stone dormers, screened-in decks and front porches bearing curated flowerpots and smiling frog figurines and signs that commanded LOVE or BE GRATEFUL—the houses seemed as if they had built themselves, had fulfilled their own destinies for materials and square footage by raising themselves up in much the same manner as rapidly dividing cells, spewing out an entire abundance of inelegantly modeled houses, two stories tall and then three, grotesque in their expanse and yet, to the same degree, horribly ordinary. Vinyl siding, faux brick, faux stone, faux-cedar shingles—these were the finishes of choice, in a color palette ranging from puce to beige to dark cream.

Nightbitch found Jen's house at the farthest reach of the development, fashioned with not one but two vinyl-sided turrets, each with its own widow's walk and antiquated parapets. The sky was a dying violet as she parked nearly two blocks away, for SUVs and minivans and station wagons lined the street.

Each house in this part of the development had a wide skirt of grass spreading all around it, finely cut, uniform in color, weedless and without feature, save for what appeared to be a small moat that circled Jen's house, a curved little bridge leading over to her front door, medieval in appearance, with black wrought-iron hardware.

Before Nightbitch had even knocked, Jen flung the door wide.

Hiiiiiiiiiiieeee! she screamed, then grabbed Nightbitch's arm. You guys, it's my fashion idol! she spurted, and indeed, Jen's demeanor had transformed, her formerly silky-smooth blond hair teased to nearly the same lengths as Nightbitch's, no fewer than four golden necklaces dangling an array of gems around her neck, a loose-fitting pair of soft gray linen pants and a hemp tank with unfinished seams above her bare and dirty feet.

I'm boho! she said, dragging Nightbitch into the living room. Do you love it?

I do, Nightbitch said. I really do.

Jen's house, she explained as she led Nightbitch to the

sofa, was *castle-inspired,* for she had *really wanted to assert her personality in the turrets and moat* and had always *had a dream* of living in a castle.

When I saw it was within reach, I insisted, she finished. I told Alex I would settle for nothing less.

Wow, Nightbitch said, impressed and delighted by how utterly bizarre Jen was turning out to be.

So—this is Jen, Jen said, turning to her right and gesturing at a mother who offered a little wave.

Also Jen, she added, touching the next mother's shoulder.

Jen! she said again, putting her arm around yet another mommy. She laughed, and the other Jens laughed, too.

What are the chances? Nightbitch said, smiling and trying to appear friendly and nonjudgmental of the name Jen.

I mean, is everyone here named Jen? Nightbitch asked.

Ha ha, the second Jen said in lieu of actual laughter.

Let's have a drink, the original Jen replied, wandering off toward the refreshment table.

Let's have five! another Jen yelled, her words swallowed up by laughter and chatter, by the boppy notes of eighties hits wafting in the background.

Nightbitch, a bit reluctant to be fully assimilated into the multi-Jen universe yet nevertheless fascinated by it, followed Jen to the refreshment table.

Let's see, we have white, white, white, and rosé, Jen said, examining each bottle of wine and turning to Nightbitch.

White is great, she said, accepting a glass that Jen had filled nearly to the rim.

Time to mingle! Jen said brightly, pulling her back into the center of the room, where Nightbitch was quickly overtaken.

Jen's husband was president of a local bank. Jen's husband was an ER doctor. Jen's husband ran a local outdoor-gear store or taught at the university or was an administrator at the university or worked out of town each and every week doing mysterious things to capillary electrophoresis machines.

But what about Jen, the *original* Jen, the Big Blonde and possible golden retriever?

Jen, what did you go to school for? Nightbitch inquired, a bit tipsy now, having talked to some half-dozen Jens, whom she found for the most part indistinguishable from one another.

Jen, drunk, snorted with laughter, then stopped abruptly.

No one has asked me that in a long time, she said thoughtfully. I was a communications major.

Ah, Nightbitch said. What did you do with that?

Oh, well, I started working for this PR agency, Jen began, then took off, telling her tale of That First Job and The Excitement of It, her new office-ready clothes that made her feel so grown-up, the working lunches, the thrill of a promotion, that sense of being a vital part of a system, the paycheck every two weeks, which, while not quite enough to live on comfortably, still felt lavish.

Even a budget back then was, like, sexy, she said. I felt like a goddamn oil magnate.

Nightbitch laughed kindly. Yes, she understood.

But then I met Alex, and before you knew it we had the twins, and wasn't *that* a surprise, and, I mean, going back to work was preposterous, and I just, well, gave up—I mean, gave *in*, I guess, to the direction that things were going, because who really wants to work anyway, and also it's not like I really had a choice . . . she said, trailing off.

Sure, sure, Nightbitch said, sensing that Jen was done talking and now wanted to wander off somewhere inside herself, which is what she definitely seemed to do then, staring that blank mommy-stare for a time from a corner of the living room as she distractedly chewed a carrot stick.

She was now, yes, worried about Jen, because she had

asked her questions that should not have been asked and stirred up something that didn't need to be stirred. She would never wish Nightbitch on another mother, certainly not, for while feral-mommy-time had its fun, its vitality and power and brazenness, at its core it was something very private and sad, those deeply held dreams that a mother had tucked into a cold, dark corner of herself. It was no good to go in and start checking on them, turning on the lights, and throwing back the sheets, because then you didn't have sleep-dead dreams anymore. You had a raving, roaming bitch who wanted to kill animals with its mouth.

After eating no less than ten carrot sticks in quick succession there in the corner, Jen disappeared for a half-hour with the excuse of refreshing the snacks, only to return freshly made up, with an air of tropical fruit, a too-bright smile stuck to her face.

Time for herb presentation! Jen hollered aggressively. Get your vino refills, ladies! Fill 'em up and find a place in the living room!

Jen took her post at a table positioned in front of the towering fireplace made of rough stones—gorgeous, really, as it rose from the living room and up to the gables on the house, a truly astonishing feature that made Nightbitch long for a sizable turkey leg on which to gnaw and a goblet of mead.

On the table, bottles and containers were arranged handsomely, as one expected at these kinds of events.

Okay, you guys, Jen began. I know lots of you have been to so many of these before, but I'm really excited to introduce the line to our new recruits, and also let you know about some new autumn-themed products!

Who's ready to have more energy and be happy? she yelled, after which all the mothers yelled in unison, I am!

Who came here today to live the life you deserve? Jen

shouted, the *deserve* hanging there like some sort of indelible verdict or threat.

The life I *deserve*? Nightbitch thought. What was that? Some sort of curse?

I did, came the harmonious response.

Oh my god, Nightbitch thought. Holy fuck.

And it was here, despite her best efforts, that she began the old ways of thinking, spiraling down, down, down, into a grim churning. For to maintain a critical stance toward the world at large meant that she was not a fool, had not been duped, that she would not be taken in by the accepted thinking of the day simply because that was *how things were* or because of *fun* or *simplicity* or *being a good sport*. No. To be Nightbitch meant always to be on guard, to doubt and confront, to critique and question, her husband, her motherhood, her career, these women, capitalism, careerism, politics and religion, all of it, especially herb-marketing plans. But— and she truly couldn't believe she now felt this way—she *needed* this, needed other women, other mothers, and even if these weren't the exact right ones, they were a start. The cold terror of the cat murder left her desperate for some kind of equilibrium, to return to her self, or at least to a transformed self that owned her dreams and desires, but wielded her power with even determination.

She looked around the well-lit living room, at the medieval candelabras, the royal dining table, the cannon inexplicably positioned at the front window, the thirty-some expectant faces emanating hope and teamwork and a can-do attitude.

Jen talked, an expression of desperate positivity squeezed onto her face, of the *flagship regimens,* then touched bottles, one by one.

Calm now, she said.

Alive, she insisted.

She passed a small white bowl to the right, one to the left, and the women obediently participated in their strange communion, touching the medicine to their lips, swallowing, eyes widening or closing, depending on the blend.

The doctors have equipped us to compete in the mental-wellness market, Jen said, and all the women nodded, and one began to cry.

The crier stood to testify, weeping ecstatic tears, a single ray of light piercing the high, stained-glass window and coming to light her face like the Virgin's in a Renaissance painting.

Jen saved my life, the crying mother said, looking to Jen. I have been saved, and I believe in this product. It has changed my life. I am living my best life, she said with an enormous sob as she sat. The woman beside her rubbed her back and murmured in her ear.

We each have our own profound why, Jen said, hands now positioned as if in prayer. A silence settled over them, and many cried quietly. Jen passed around a bowl of Happiness, of which all partook.

My why is vitality and fulfillment. My why is financial agency, Jen said, then continued, explaining the deep history of the company, its sacred beginnings, how these formulas were hundreds, probably thousands, of years old. How they weren't created just to sell and make money. How they had first been concocted for ancient dynasties by holy men with finely honed knowledge.

They would have been killed if they'd given a king something toxic! Jen exclaimed, at which an affirmative murmur rippled around the room. These have been refined for hundreds of years. They carry within them sacred knowledge. They were once meant for royalty, and now they are meant for you.

Children burst from a door on the other side of the room and galloped, screaming, through the middle of the living room, spilling two glasses of wine, then sprinted up the stairs, followed by a teenaged sitter, who offered an embarrassed *Sorry*, then followed the children up the stairs and slammed a door. Jen closed her eyes and inhaled deeply.

Okay, she said. These tried-and-true products, when combined with our work-at-home opportunity and supportive marketing strategies, create a winning situation for all of us in which we can realize our dreams and live our best lives.

There were more testimonials, more crying, a chart projected on the wall that outlined the earnings that quarter from their chapter. Next, the projection of an elaborate flow-chart that demonstrated the *earning potential* of each mother and how they were *weaving a powerful web of financial support* for each other. They all needed to *project success*. They all needed to *use the products so that they could better speak to their restorative qualities* when selling. They had to *be outgoing* and *strike up conversations on airplanes, in the line at the grocery store,* wherever they might find an unsuspecting, captive audience of one to whom they might spread the gospel of herbs.

Who's ready to join the team? Jen asked, raising her hands in the air and closing her eyes in evangelical ecstasy.

I am, one mother said, standing.

Me, too, another mother added.

Silence overtook the room, and Jen opened her eyes to look directly at Nightbitch.

Okay, Nightbitch said. Jen ran to her for a too-tight hug, then to each of the other women. She squeezed their hands and murmured happiness at them, asked for six hundred dollars, which they each handed over, in cash.

It truly was the perfect selling storm: wine, herbs, peer pressure, devout glee. It was like floating in a warm pool, as easy as falling asleep, and just as comforting.

They all ceremoniously received their new herb kits, large

cardboard suitcases of sorts which one could open to present an arrangement of herb bottles displayed in a carefully crafted foam bed, each one labeled with a name like Hope and Wow! and then a tagline: "For those mornings when nothing seems clear" or "Centers energy at the pudendum for otherworldly orgasms."

The mothers began to wander off then, toward the refreshments or the backyard, where Nightbitch glanced at one mother, wineglass in hand, entering the cornfield that bordered the vast expanse of lawn. The sun was setting far beyond as the field swallowed her. Nightbitch wondered if she should say something to someone, but didn't, for wasn't it that mother's right to disappear? Perhaps she had taken a dose of Into the Wild and just needed time to get away? Nightbitch would allow her whatever it was she needed, and instead turned to the living room, the floor now littered with mommies in all states of consciousness.

A Jen, silk blouse askew, her flirty mules strewn on the plush cream carpeting, asked Nightbitch what her deal was.

What is your *why* for joining? she demanded drunkenly. And don't give me some bullshit answer.

Well . . . Nightbitch weighed her answer, the words swimming in her head, for the white wine had indeed gone straight there. The wine, combined with the truly what-the-fuck cultic ceremony in which she had just participated, the peculiar stress of the week, the dead cat, the peculiar stress of the summer and her transformations, not to mention the handful of twiggy balls she'd swallowed in the hope of boosting her vitality in the past hour—all propelled her toward her confession, perhaps too familiar, for she barely knew these women at all, but who actually cared?

Well, Nightbitch repeated. This is really horrible and embarrassing, and I hesitate even to say it. . . .

Go on, drunk Jen commanded.

I accidentally killed our cat this week, she said, and it was a breaking point for me, I guess you could say. I just need some balance. Some structure. I'm looking for some stability.

The room settled into a deeper silence, whether because some of the mothers had passed out in day-drunk swoons there in the ever-soft carpeting, or because some were appalled by her admonition, it was hard to say.

I let our pet parakeet go accidentally, the drunken floor Jen said, putting air quotes around "accidentally" and making a face.

I let the fish die, Babs, on the couch, admitted, gesturing with a glass of white wine. Benign neglect. But I didn't want to take care of them, clean their bowl. The kids didn't care. It was their job to take care of the things.

I stepped on Percy, Poppy admitted quietly, only loudly enough for Nightbitch to hear.

What was Percy? Nightbitch asked.

A gerbil, she whispered.

Later that evening, she recounted the events of the party to her husband with great excitement—Jen's castle house and the presentation, the fervor with which they all endorsed the herbs, the depths of their feelings exhibited by tears and the raising of hands, the women at the end on the floor, the sheer spectacle of it all, the absurd delight—and they laughed together. She showed him her herbs, presenting each one on her hand like a game-show hostess, reading him taglines, delighting in the novelty of it, how they were not the sort of people to buy into such things, but she had, and wasn't that a hoot?

So—wait—you did have to buy into it? the husband asked.

Well, yeah, she said. But it's a small price to pay for access to these women who are just . . . beyond. And, anyway, I consider it research.

For what?

An art project maybe, she said. But I don't want to talk about it.

He hugged her then and smiled.

Okay, he said. Okay.

THAT WEEK, HER NOTES to White turned philosophical, contemplative, poetic, cryptic. She had not kept a diary in many years, and now this was her diary of sorts, a chronicle of her thoughts in the deepest part of the night, or when her son was napping, or in the long, slow hours of late-summer afternoons, when the sun walked across the sky and time itself started and stopped, the temperature rose, the naked boy splashed in a kiddie pool in the driveway, Nightbitch in a floppy hat and cutoff jean shorts, a sports bra, dipping her toes into the ice-cold water, and them together inside this infinity, forever.

She would always have that moment, and many others, locked inside her, a perfect little glitter globe to shake whenever she needed. It lived there, as if another new, tiny organ pumped into her blood the power of ultimate creator. I made you, and I destroy you as well. I am your entire world, and then, also, I am the person you leave behind. I will always be with you. You will never understand me.

At times she terrified herself, wondering if she was a god, if being a mother was one way of being a god. Of course, she couldn't strike anyone down with a lightning bolt, but she could bring a person into being using little more than a handful of clay. Way less, in fact. How were mothers even a thing? How had they not been outlawed? They were divine, beyond horrifying.

WW—

I am interested in longing, in longing so deep it threatens to splinter a person apart. I am interested in a profound longing for an unknown existence, or for a better life, without any idea of what the specifics of that life would look like. I'm not getting this right—I'm interested in knowing about the longing that unites all women, all mothers. What is that longing? How could we possibly long for something beyond our offspring?

It's almost as if having a child allows a woman to see how much infinite potential there is, allows her to see infinity itself. (Am I making any sense?)

It's almost as if having a child does not sate a deep yearning but instead compounds it.

Look, the mother says, look at what I am capable of. I make life. I am life.

But how can I become a god?

Yours,

MM

IN HER BEDROOM: A beige plastic dog-kennel lined with a fuzzy blanket and a thin cushion dragged by her son to her bedside, a healthy ficus in the corner with a small bit of digging in the dirt, a trail of soil spilled onto the floor, a stainless-steel doggy bowl full of fresh water, a stainless-steel doggy bowl full of bone-shaped cookies, many faux-fur throw rugs—white, off-white, white tipped with gray, black—thrown around the room, on the floor, on a chair, one on the bed, a dreamcatcher dangling by the window, its white feathers fluttering softly in the breeze, piles of clothes here and there tamped down into perfect places on which to rest; an overly expensive linen caftan, the seam up the back torn, tiny holes, frayed edges, stained with something brown; a black satin eye mask, serums, a wooden box full of jerky, an unlabeled spray bottle full of a lavender concoction, a bit of rope, balled-up socks that were once wet but now are dried and almost crusty, two dirty tennis balls in a corner, a dozen large feathers on the chest of drawers, a picture on the wall of a bunny nestled in green grass with dandelions growing all around, a bed pillow with no case, the corners gnawed at and off, a stack of children's books—Grimm's fairy tales, a book of French illustrations, bear book, bee book, trains—piled on the floor by the bed, a light catcher suctioned to the window that created rainbows on the walls when the sun caught it just right, many vases of fresh and unfresh wildflowers, a real raccoon pelt slung over the mirror, a pile of sticks good for chewing. Of course, it needed to be picked up by the time her husband returned home. Of course, there would be need for just enough tidying so that an extended explanation was not in order.

It's a game, she rehearsed under her breath, as she took the sticks and arranged them in a vase with the feathers, as she collected the stuffing from the pillow, and she heaved piles of clothes into the washing machine. It's just an experiment, she said, refilling the water bowl. It's . . . It's what I need, she concluded, stripping the bed of its soiled linens. She tossed a dirty shirt to the boy, who followed her on all fours and, as he had been taught, collected the cloth in his mouth and bounded down the stairs—he had been practicing all day— and galumphed around a corner and toward the hamper.

When he returned, he obediently sat at her feet and turned his perfect face to hers to let out the smallest little *ruff*, not like a child saying the word *ruff* but like a child who was actually part dog communicating via his language of choice, a guttural, quiet little animal sound that Nightbitch adored so intensely it made her insides hurt.

What a good boy, she said, touching his head and then squatting down to nuzzle his neck. She held his bright, soft face in hers and could have cried. What a very good boy.

SENSING THAT SOMETHING WAS changing, transpiring, evolving, though unsure precisely what it was, her husband called each night from a sad hotel room somewhere in South Dakota.

How's the work? he asked.

The work, she repeated. A long pause. The work is the life. There isn't a distinction.

Okaaaay, he said.

I've felt for so long alienated from my work, from myself, but I see now that the work and the life are of a piece and it's simply my job to find the connections.

You're speaking in riddles, he said. Or at least like some sort of cult leader.

I feel I'm being quite clear.

Did you eat one of those weed gummies? he asked, but then realized he was speaking into the space where his wife used to be. She had hung up. She was gone.

WW—

I have been meditating recently on what exactly an artist is and what art itself possibly could be. Consider: an animal who takes colors and smears them on woven fibers just to make an appealing arrangement of said colors, "appealing" defined in any number of ways and enjoyed by a self-selecting group of other animals, then, too, despised by others of the same breed, who do not enjoy looking at it, do not find the arrangement of colors interesting or surprising, sometimes even grow enraged by the colors there on the fibers, at times becoming so enraged they gather together outside the habitats created to house the colors and do not allow other animals to venture in, so troubling or dangerous or morally depraved do they find these colors. Imagine.

Or: an animal who finds all the best rocks, beautiful for their symmetry and smoothness, and then arranges them within a metal framework she has created through a process that involves fire and a great expression of energy from the animal, a raising of the arm and striking of the hot ore time and time again, until it is formed into a rod.

One animal howls beautifully while another hits wires with mallets.

An animal moves across a flat expanse in a darkened space in ways that suggest longing or elation or a vast and an unrelenting desire to transcend her animalness and ascend to another level of being, whatever that is.

To shape sensory experience and in doing so communicate . . . what? Does it even matter?

MM

Why, it was sort of like talking to God, wasn't it? These letters closer to prayer than correspondence. You just wrote them and then pressed send and they floated away into the electronic ether, off into the mystery of the Internet, because who really, truly understood how it actually worked anyway? And we might say that Nightbitch, during this time in her life, became quite religious, each morning rising to see if there was a response, and each night sitting down at her cluttered desk—moving the sewing machine to the side for a time—to write another missive to Wanda White, a person

whom she believed in yet had no evidence of, save for the tattered book on her nightstand and single contact page on a
university website.

CONSIDER THE GUEST ROOM, which she now called
her studio. The bed, unmade, with wrinkled covers that contained many books: the *Field Guide,* of course; a book on herb
craft and the poison path; the book her grandmother had
used to make her concoctions, but in English, found online
at a rare-books site; a history of disruptive performance art;
a book about textiles and costuming; an instructional sell-
er's manual for herbs. Dig deeper and you would find a pair
of forgotten underwear, a single forgotten vibrator, a dusty
book about taxidermy. In the corners: a dirty orange yoga
mat, foam blocks, a strong cloth strap, a pile of nice rocks.
On the walls: pictures of dancers contorted in the most won-
drous of ways; photos of women who dressed as her grandmother had, plain dresses and long braided hair; many pencil
sketches that studied animals in motion—horse, dog, cheetah, bear; hex signs she'd made from her childhood memories
of such signs hung high on barns; an interior shot of a meat
locker; stills from extreme acts of art, including a woman
giving birth in a storefront (for, yes, she had found such a
happening, a happening she herself had once dreamt), an
artist holding his arm with a face in agony because he had
just shot himself with a gun for the sake of art, a woman's
face operated on so as to approximate that of the Madonna
in a famous Renaissance painting, a naked woman sleeping
on a pile of straw with two large hogs. Closet door ajar, and,
spilling from it, spools of thread and beads and buttons and
skeins of cloth, more books, earth-tone paints, leatherwork
tools, a trash bag of wool ready to be brushed and spun, a tub
of beeswax. On the desk: a sewing machine, an entire galaxy

of pins and needles and snips of thread, a jar nearly full of dead bees. Hanging from the shelf above the desk, a dozen rabbits' feet, nearly cured, which had now been there for two weeks.

She showed her son the closed, white door to the guest room and said seriously to him, Never go in here. You understand? This is where Mommy works, and her work is very important and not for little boys or doggies. I'm serious. Do you understand? she demanded.

The boy, never before having seen his mother in such a state, stern and with a seriousness that bordered on violence, twisted his face to tears.

No go, Mama. I no go. And she took him in her arms to whisper *Shhhh* in his ear.

ARE YOU OKAY? HER husband asked later that week, over the phone.

I am better than okay, Nightbitch said.

Okay, he said.

A pause extended between them. Nightbitch heard nothing in that silence, not cable news playing in the background, or the chewing of food or clinking of silverware.

That all? he said, to which she responded by tipping her head away from the phone and singing one clear note of the prettiest howl she could muster, a howl she had been practicing that week. When she was done, the silence puddle pooled again until her husband offered a Wow and Okay and Whatever you're up to . . . sure.

THE WEEK HAD PASSED as weeks did, with The Schedule, the doggy games, and then the mundane chores, groceries and dishes and dinner and bath time. By Friday, she was tired, bone-tired, tired down to her bones and then inside them.

She had awoken that morning with the urge to go and run through a tall meadow and battle with a groundhog, and so had taken a double dose of Calm Now, but then the boy wanted her to pull him in a wagon, endlessly, through the neighborhood, and, after, to watch him ride his pedal-less bike around and around and around the cul-de-sac. Perhaps it was the circular route his bike ride took, or the ways the leaves fluttered in the breeze and dappled the sidewalk in butterfly shadows, or the double dose of Calm Now, but she felt her life force drain from her as she watched, then sat, then lay down in a bit of grass, then fell asleep.

MAMA! the boy yelled, inches from her face, and she woke with a start.

Good god, she said, sitting up. Jesus. She rubbed her eyes, disoriented.

She took a triple dose of Mombie and tried a little bottle that said *Alive,* and by lunch her heart was thudding in her chest and she was twirling the boy around the kitchen and they were mixing together cookie dough, which somehow wound up in every corner of the kitchen, at which they both laughed blithely, sliding pans into the oven and out, feasting on cookies, crumbling them all over the floor, pretending to be a monster and *num-num-num-m*ing them to smithereens, then laughing and laughing and laughing hysterically until they were both exhausted and crashing from too much sugar and no lunch. They both sat on the worn wood floor of the kitchen, and the boy said, Doggy?, and Nightbitch said, No doggy, and then they both lay down right where they were and went to sleep, just like that.

So it had been *a day.* A weird, long day. And as she waited for her husband to return home that afternoon, and the boy spooned buttons from a casserole dish into a metal bowl on the wooden floor, that old night-night rage ballooned inside her, but instead of erupting into a great show of bluster and heat, instead she grew calm, clear. It was plain she was now owed years of night-nights. And it was also now clear her husband would make it his job to attend to night-nights each night he was home. It was as simple as that.

They had been switching off on the weekends, her husband Friday and Nightbitch Saturday and so on, but, truly, every night he was home he should do them. She thought about this as she sipped a glass of white wine on the kitchen floor, cross-legged beside her son. Yes, night-nights were significantly easier now, given that the boy slept in his kennel, but still. There were books and stories and sometimes a great waiting before she could sneak from the room.

She was exhausted by the time her husband arrived home at 6:00 p.m. and she handed the boy to him and said, I'm done. You're doing night-nights every weekend night from now on. Thank you.

Her husband tipped his head quizzically and tickled the boy beneath the chin to make him laugh.

Sure, he said. Seems fair.

He walked inside with the boy, asking him about his day and tickling him and kissing him all over his face, and Nightbitch remained there in the warm early evening, beneath the wide arms of the trees, in the sweet air.

Why, she had only ever had to ask! It was so easy. She grew irate, not exactly with her husband but definitely generally with him. If it was this easy to get him to do things, then why had he not been doing them from the start? He should have offered. Moreover, why had she not been demanding more? Why had she not claimed the power and authority that were hers? Where had she learned to push it all down to the pit of her stomach, all her sadness and rage and annoyance, to fill up the space above with white wine, to carry on to the best of her ability and pretend toward contentment when all the while she could have been saying things, saying *Fuck this!* and *Could you please?* and *I need.* She returned to her mother lying in the dark grass in the middle of warm summer nights and wanted to pull her up, take her by the shoulders, shake her with both love and great, great anger. Look at you! she would say. You're amazing! You're my mother! Why are you acting like this? Go to Europe. Insist on your joy. Time is short, and you must make great haste, not only for yourself but for me as well. Please. I'm begging you.

She wanted to save her mother. She saw now she had always wanted this.

Nightbitch resolved to demand things—all sorts of things. To ask. To not assume that she had to cook the dinner and do the night-nights and clean the house and pay the bills and buy the presents and send the cards and schedule the appointments and keep track of every last thing all by herself. This was, after all, a partnership, wasn't it? This was, after all, the modern era, empowerment and feminism and all that, and she had not been taking advantage of any of it because, she discovered as she thought further, she did not have a job. Or, rather, she did not have a job that paid any money whatsoever; in fact, it was a drain on money, represented negative money, this mothering job. Because her husband paid for their lives, paid for the privilege she had of staying home each and every day and devoting herself completely to motherhood and nothing else, she had felt, ever since she stepped down from her position at the gallery, that she was in no place to demand anything. He worked all week, and she felt it was too much to ask him to lift a finger on the weekend, because she had automatically devalued her work from the start. She had been, she saw now, inculcated by a culture that told her, Look, it's cute you're a mom, and go do your thing, but, honestly, it's not that hard; you're probably not all that smart or interesting, but good for you for feeling fulfilled by mothering.

That night, her husband put their son to bed, and the night after, and the next. There was no debate. Sure, perhaps in the future he would ask for a night off, but she was filled with such magnanimity, such brotherly love for this man who without objection did as she asked, that she would always take over a night for him, no problem, because he was lovely and she loved him, and Thank you, she said that evening as he came down the steps. She opened her arms and took him in and kissed his neck and then smelled him deeply.

Thank you so much, she said.

THAT MONTH, SHE BEGAN to sleep in the guest room, her studio, whenever her husband was home. The room devoured her, in fact, as soon as her husband returned from work, and she disappeared until her husband and son ran out of things to do and then puzzled over where Mama could be.

I need alone time, she explained that first weekend. Time . . . to myself.

At night, after her family was fast asleep, she wandered the night-inked streets, through tidy garden beds on the corner lot, through a thicket of lilac bushes where she stripped herself of her clothes and grew her hair long, tested the strength of her elongating muscles, stretched and scratched and then burrowed deeper into the thicket and out into side lawns and back lawns, under a swing set, between two loose boards hanging crooked in a fence. She sniffed at suspicious holes in the ground, stuck her head into the big ones, and came out with grass hanging in her hair and dirt marking her face. She found a leaky faucet dripping at the back of one house and lapped from the puddle beneath it. She spot-

ted a tabby cat in another yard, crouched on a step near the
screened-in porch door, and with lightning speed took off in
its direction. The tabby paused, hissed, then scampered just
as quickly beneath the porch, and Nightbitch stuck what she
could of her body beneath and growled low and hard.

Come here, she snarled. You fucking cat, get over here.

The tabby would not budge and only pushed itself deeper
into the darkness, its eyes visible and flashing yellow-green
when they caught the moonlight.

The weekends of rehearsal—for that was indeed how she
viewed it, as a vital part of her artistic practice, a development
of her work—she moved through the neighborhood following
the dark constellations of shadow that tatted the yards and
streets. She visited the soft patch of moss she liked to roll in,
with the feel of its velvet softness on her naked back, her chest,
her thighs. She traipsed through flower gardens and sniffed
each bud, then tasted the green twists of leaves and stems
that seemed most promising. She sprinted to the elementary
school ten blocks down to smell the playground equipment
as she panted and huffed, to sniff the ground for stray pieces
of chewed gum, candy wrappers, a bit of sandwich or candy
bar, or to find a good ball for chewing. She continued on to
the soccer field behind the school, where bunnies liked to nibble on dandelion greens, and watched the small, twitching
bodies in the moonlight, plotting her attack. Then, the next
weekend, she set out in the opposite direction, to the train
tracks and creek where she had gone that first night, to find
sleeping men on benches whom she passed by without fear,
despite her nakedness, her vulnerability, because she did not
feel vulnerable, not a bit. She ruled this neighborhood. She
presided over it. She was its monster, its mistress. She trusted
the strength of her body and depth of her rage, the rage now
tempered by her vision, her singular direction deeper into the
mystery and creation itself.

Try me, she thought at those sleeping men. Just try me. She waded into the creek to wet her fur and muddy her underbelly, to drink the cold, clear water, to push her nose into the soggyrottensweet of the muddy banks.

It became habit, after her weekend traipses during that enchanted month, for her to return to their quiet home in the cul-de-sac in the late-night or early-morning hours, stand at the back French doors to watch her husband splashed in the blue glow of his computer. She would tap lightly on the window, and he would let her in, then lead her to the bathroom as he would a child, to turn on the hot water, light a candle, peel off his clothes, and then wordlessly help her into the shower. He washed her body with soap and a cloth, cleaning her face, her breasts, in between her legs. He washed her hair, massaging the mud from her scalp, then slowly working a comb through the tangles with conditioner.

You are a prince, she told him, and he said *Shhh, shhh,* and kissed her back, her shoulders, her eyelids, her mouth. They made love each night after she returned, after he cleaned her, after she had wandered so long and far that her muscles ached and her bare feet were raw and riddled with splinters and she was all over covered with dirt and sweat and the sweet midnight dew of deep summer. What a husband, to love her through such a thing.

AND IT WAS ON a Monday at the end of this month, as summer made her final overtures on fine September days with a heat that still inspired trips to the ice cream stand by the river, that she and the boy went to the dog park, although they didn't have a dog. It would be one of the last perfect days to run beneath a blue sky and taste the sun-sweetened wind.

We love dogs! Nightbitch declared to anyone who glanced their way—kindly or unkindly, it didn't matter.

May we pet your dog? she said, petting a dog as her son touched its cold, wet nose.

May we chase him? she asked another owner, who barely looked up from his cell phone, only grunted an affirmation, after which she and the boy took off, and the dog, too, off across the green expanse inside that dewdrop of a day.

It was only then she saw them: a golden retriever, a basset hound, and a collie, clustered over by the pond, all of their front paws in the cool water, mouths agog and tongues lolling as they panted in the heat.

Oh my god, Nightbitch said. She moved toward them hesitantly, over the trampled grass, the boy trailing behind her.

Hello, she said to them, approaching hesitantly, and they each quickly twisted their heads to look at her.

The golden retriever offered a bright *Ruff!* and the boy barked back. They walked to the animals, who sprang from the pond, all wet fur and muddy paws, to have their damp heads scratched and sopping backs patted, to lick the boy's hands enthusiastically to make him laugh and then nose into Nightbitch's legs.

She took the retriever's head in her hands and looked into its eyes.

Jen? she whispered, and the dog blinked, playing it cool. They eyed each other for a time, until Nightbitch said, Okay, fine. Go on, and slapped the dog's haunch.

She searched the edges of the park for anyone calling after these dogs, walking toward them, tossing them a ball, or offering them a treat, but each figure was engaged with some other animal, in the process of chasing or being chased, hollering, whistling, throwing something or picking up poop. No one there seemed to be in any way attached to the doggy trio, save for a lone figure at the farthest reach of the dog park, standing quite still, notebook in hand, watching the scene unfold.

It was Wanda, exactly as she imagined Wanda to be, slim and lithe, with a cloak of silver hair. There was a wonderful ease about her, wearing a smart shirtdress and sensible shoes, a straw hat. Nightbitch squinted to bring her more into focus, but she was so far away.

Nightbitch walked in her direction, excitement rising, for this *must* be Wanda White. She took deep breaths to calm herself but could not, was overcome with pure jubilation, a force so strong she began to run, arms outstretched toward the woman. She knew it was her. She just knew.

Excuse me, she shouted, sprinting toward the solitary figure at the edge of the park. Are those your dogs? I'm trying to find the owner.

The woman—still so far away Nightbitch could not make out the particulars of her face, could not read her expression or deduce from her demeanor her response to the question—cocked her head toward Nightbitch, paused, and then shouted No! She walked briskly in the opposite direction, toward the woods that bordered the park.

Stop! Nightbitch screamed in panic, which had the opposite effect she had hoped for. The mysterious woman was now also running, hat in hand, her hair streaming behind her, headlong into the woods.

Wanda! Nightbitch yelled again, an edge of desperation in her voice that she could not control. She began to hyperventilate and shake from the exertion and sheer emotion of it all, still running, her heart thudding and legs hot with their effort.

The woman disappeared into the woods as Nightbitch stood panting, hands on her knees.

Please, come back! Nightbitch pleaded to the woods. Please. She stood at the edge of the woods and listened as the woman crashed through the weeds and fallen branches and brambles. Already Nightbitch could not see her through the thick, late-summer growth, nor could she leave her child behind to follow, for he was already in a panic, himself chasing after his mother, who was running away from *him*.

Wanda! she yelled, into the brush. Wanda! But no response came.

WAS THAT YOU I SAW at the dog park this afternoon? she texted Jen that evening, followed by a puppy emoji and a tree emoji and a sunshine emoji and then an upside-down smiley-face emoji, as if to say, *What a dumb-dumb I am if that was in fact you!* A bold move on her part, she thought, yet safe. Not asking her directly if she was actually a dog sometimes, but allowing her safe passage into such a conversation. Plus, she hadn't really been in touch with Jen since the party, just a Book Babies here and there. She waited and waited while the three little dots blinked at her as Jen typed.

Ha ha no, Jen wrote back, *but I've been meaning to text you.*

Just what someone trying to hide their true identity as a dog would text, Nightbitch thought.

Jen went on, after the pauses and hesitations of a million *lol*s and *omg*s and a nervous *not to be totally weird* and disclaimer that this could be *TMI,* but it was just that Nightbitch seemed *so open-minded and into art* that she felt she could express to her *totally bonkers changes* of late that she had been experiencing, that she didn't *feel like myself lately it's hard to explain,* that she just kept *having these like stoner thoughts lol,* and maybe it was just aging *or whatever,* but she felt things were out of control and she didn't have anyone to talk to and might she, this new mother in their circle of friends, be interested in getting together one to one, *no herb talk, just hearts in conversation.* She just really wanted to talk because of Nightbitch's own recent transformation—*bold* and *trendsetting,* she called it, then added, *I love how you don't care what anyone thinks!* She added jokingly, again, that she didn't want to come off as totally weird, and she hoped her new friend would be able to hold what she had to tell her in confidence, because having this sort of thing get around could really *creep everyone out.*

Sometimes I'm up all night roaming the neighborhood, that's how bad it is, Jen wrote, and hope swelled within Nightbitch, a hope she had not known she had been harboring, a brilliant magnanimity and feeling of goodwill toward all women, all mothers, for how she had longed to have just one person in whom to confide all her most private urges and thoughts! And who would have thought it would be this mommy, this Jen, with her herbs and strawberry shampoo and suburban McMansion? Nightbitch could have cried with delight and relief at the prospect of another mother like her, with similar struggles and puzzling propensities. *I would love to meet!* she texted earnestly. *Can't wait.*

She raised the phone above her head and did a little dance in the kitchen, then whizzed around in circles, chasing what once had been a tail.

THEY MET AT THE university's museum of natural history the next day, a wonderful little place Nightbitch had enjoyed visiting as a grad student. She hadn't yet been there with the boy and was tickled by the idea. Besides, weekdays at the museum were as quiet as a tomb, which, in a sense, it was, because it contained the oldest collection of taxidermy west of the Mississippi, so old, in fact, that the mothers and their wards could see straw filling through a hole in the rhinoceros, a bit of cloth where fur should have been on a cheetah.

Jen had never been, and expressed her great wonder that

such a place existed in their little town, reiterated how creative Nightbitch was.

I wish I were artsy, she said wistfully as her two girls chaperoned Nightbitch's boy around the room, each one taking a hand and pulling him this way and that, mothering him, if you will, in a way that made Nightbitch want to tell them to stop, inform them that it wasn't their job to take care of him, that they should be enjoying the displays and not worrying about caring for this little boy, that their aspirations should be toward, say, taxidermy rather than caregiving. Instead, she laughed dryly at Jen's comment.

Jen had arrived in a most uncustomary state. Though her children were indeed washed and dressed in coordinating outfits, their silken hair collected into pigtails that protruded like horns from the tops of their heads, Jen herself appeared haggard, uncharacteristic bags beneath her eyes, her eyeliner uneven and too far from the edge of her eyelids. Her tank top was on inside out; sure, it was one of the kind that was hard to tell right side from wrong, but these sorts of details seemed to be Jen's forte.

I was inspired by you, so I'm experimenting with teasing, she said as they considered a giant sloth. She gesturing to her own blond tresses, which, even in the low light of the museum, appeared oily and matted. Nightbitch, of course, liked the aesthetic very much, and with each small thing she found askew, her joy only rose. She must not force Jen into saying anything, she reminded herself. She must remain reserved and thoughtful, a listener, in no way trying to manipulate the situation. She looked on Jen as she might her prey on a dark night—gently, cautiously.

The little crew made their way to the bird room, Jen chugging coffee and popping herbs stored in a stroller compartment. The bird room was circular, with skylights high above and a circular kiosk lit from within that showed the flight paths of many North American species. Around the outer edge, an array of taxidermized songbirds was mounted on the wall, some on twigs, but most in a way that reminded Nightbitch of her junior-high bug collections, a pin stuck through each insect and into a block of Styrofoam with neatly typed labels underneath.

There were so many buttons to push in the bird room, and the children busied themselves with the task, layers of birdsong enveloping the room as the two mothers stood in the soft glow of the displays.

Okay, Jen said, holding her coffee cup and looking very tired indeed as the birds sang. You're so creative, Jen began. And a really good mom. I just . . . Jen began to cry.

It's okay, Nightbitch said. Let it out.

She panted in anticipation, clear and ice-cold.

Say it, she willed Jen. *Say you're a dog.*

Look, I have my own . . . stuff, things I don't tell anyone, Nightbitch said, to put Jen at ease. I mean, everyone has problems.

Though Nightbitch had hoped her own admonition would soothe Jen, instead it seemed only to heighten her anxiety.

I'm in such a pile of *shit*! Jen said, whisper-hissing the word *shit* so that the children wouldn't hear, not that they were listening anyway. I'm *fucked*. Not even my husband knows. Especially not him.

We all struggle, Nightbitch said. They were so close to a moment of true communion!

I just . . . Jen buried her face in her hands, then dragged her fingers from her forehead, around her eyes, and over her cheeks. I've lost so much money on the herbs, Jen confessed. Like over ten thousand, she whispered, and everyone thinks I'm so successful, but really it's just me buying my own products. And Alex doesn't know any of it—I mean, it didn't really take that much doing, since I manage the finances—but I don't know how to get out. The local market is saturated! No one needs herbs! We all already have them! We're just trying to sell them to each other.

She looked mournfully at her children, who were now holding the small boy on the floor and tickling him, to all of their great delights.

Nightbitch said nothing, for this was not what she had expected, not at all.

I need to project an attitude of success, Jen continued. All the girls are looking to me to make this work, but I just can't, she said, then pushed a button in front of her to make an owl hoot long and low.

And of course. Of course Jen was in deep. Of course she had sunk too much money in the herbs.

Of course she wasn't a dog.

Why, Nightbitch had been so *silly* to think such a thing. What a *riot* to imagine this mother roaming through back lawns, naked and haired. Nightbitch needed to really reel it in, to—and how many times must she say this to herself?—*pull it together,* but no.

No.

She would not. She would not pull it together.

Oh my god, you don't even know what to say, Jen said, looking desperately at Nightbitch for an encouraging word, an *It's all going to be okay.* The trio of children now clamored around them, orbiting the center console in a spirited game of tag, shrieking and pausing to push buttons and then run and shriek some more, but the mothers paid them no mind whatsoever, in that way mothers are able to do, Jen there, ashen and desperate, her hair a goddamn mess, and Nightbitch glowing with something, as though she had absorbed each and every one of their worries into herself, like nutrients, and had used these worries to grow stronger, clearer, more sure of her purpose, for there was really no turning back at this point.

Look, you don't need to pull it together, Nightbitch said to Jen, clutching her biceps for emphasis. She looked her square in the eyes.

Fuck the herbs and fuck the money, she continued, and went on to unreel a diatribe against multilevel marketing, for she had just listened to an entire podcast about these things, and explained to Jen how they prey on women who feel disempowered, who are stuck and at home and are taken in by promises of financial agency, and that she shouldn't feel ashamed. That she could get out, and that Nightbitch would help her get out. That she should tell her husband, apologize, but assure him she would fix it. (No tears, Nightbitch commanded. You're strong as fuck.) That they would get all the other girls, as Jen called them, out, too. That she had been thinking long and hard about womanhood and motherhood, about herself and all of them, really, and that it was time.

Time for what? Jen asked, moved by Nightbitch's effort, yet still visibly exhausted, her eyes, her skin, the way her mouth pulled at the corners.

Look, Nightbitch said. You worked in PR, right?

A million years ago, Jen said.

I need a publicist, Nightbitch said. And I'll pay you, at least eventually.

What the fuck? Jen said, laughing a little, and the children all ran to them, their disheveled mothers standing in the bird room.

Nightbitch now was the one to link her arm in Jen's.

Let's walk. Let's talk, Nightbitch said. There's so much we need to do.

Later, at home, she would open her *Field Guide* to read:

I want you to know: never before in the history of women, magical or not, have they been more empowered, more in touch with profound universal forces, more capable of summoning by whatever means necessary that which is essential to their evolution and fulfillment.

FIRST, READ THIS BOOK. Now look: This is how I run. This is how I appear at night. Here are my skins. Here are some props. Here my ideas and dreams. See this dance? This gesture? This animal? This spell? Learn them all. Good. Take off your clothes. Run. Pounce. Roll in this mud. Smell your way through. Here a mouse. There a chewed wad of gum, good to lick. Lap from the puddle, then jump into the stream. Follow it to the dark alley. Crouch. Growl. Pace. Pause. Here is the prey. Here is your power. Here is how I kill an animal. Don't flinch. Don't turn away. Look more closely, look at it, the heart of violence, the heart of need. Meditate. Sleep, or don't. Here is how to grow your hair, and here is how to lose it. Listen. More. Be still, then move. Examine your teeth. Pet your own soft hairs. Demand more and do less. Tell, don't ask. Howl, howl, howl at the moon.

Wanda White says the mysteries of the universe are revealed in the mundane, the body, this day, the grasses and the sky. Forget civilization. This is just woman and nature, her very own nature.

My god, Jen murmured then, in the moonlight, face streaked with mud. Oh my god. You. It's you.

PERHAPS, HONESTLY AND TRULY, it was that Nightbitch had wanted her husband to discover her secret. Perhaps, since she had already recruited Jen into her art, her project, her plan, it now felt even more underhanded to be working outside of the knowledge of her husband—her husband, who had been the one to first show her the Japanese ladies peeing on the octopus and other such delights, and wouldn't he, actually, be amazed at his wife rather than repulsed should she reveal to him her true nature? Additionally, Nightbitch— the project of Nightbitch—was edging closer and closer to a public airing, and it felt right to introduce this personage to more and more people. And hadn't her husband proved, in the past, even with her most bizarre projects, to be her biggest proponent? Despite all her rage over the past months, despite the countless ways in which she might have indicted him in her mind, could it be that he might be her ally, perhaps even her greatest supporter? Surely these sorts of thoughts had been working on Nightbitch as she developed her performance, as she read Wanda White and prepared to show herself in one way or another.

On an ordinary Saturday night, Nightbitch innocently went outside to take the trash to the can, but while she was there, a particularly sinister stream of air brought the smell of the decomposing bunny she had buried some weeks earlier, for certainly it was not the cat, which they had given a proper burial, four feet deep. No, the bunny had been laid to rest in a shallow grave, and, ah, that smell! So thick and black and pungent, redolent of blood and dirt and shit and rot. She had been avoiding that smell because she found it irresistible, and this night, with her husband upstairs doing night-nights, she certainly had at least a bit of time to go take a little look-see, right? No harm in toeing about the still-loose soil beneath the crab-apple tree, beneath the wide leaves of the hostas. Not a big deal to kneel down in the wet earth and sink her hands down even farther, searching for a bit of fur or bone or sinew. And entirely reasonable for her to remove all her clothes, since she wouldn't want them getting dirtied beyond repair or infused with the stench of the carrion. Certainly not!

She just wanted to . . . see the bunny. To smell it. Perhaps to roll around a bit in it and then, of course, to take a long hot shower with lots of soap and other things people used to maintain their domesticity.

She unearthed a bit of muscle that had been marinating in the mud. Was that a touch of fermentation she smelled? A mineral tang of the dirt and old blood? The almost sweet rot of the flesh itself? Just a small bite, she considered. Not even a mouthful, more like a nibble. It would be almost a jerky of sorts, she reasoned, dried and chewy. Succulent. She closed her eyes and inhaled deeply, holding the scraps of carrion in her hands.

Then her husband was there, beside her. Silent in the twilight.

Where she assumed panic would have been, a vast vista of sublime calm extended instead. He knew. He was seeing what she was. Well, this was it, then, wasn't it? Might as well get it over with. She had once been a girl, then a woman, a bride, expectant, a mother, and now she would be this, whatever this was. A wild, complicated woman with strange yearnings. Stubborn and angry—soft and sweet, though, too. She was creator and then also the dark force that roamed the night. She was part high-minded intention and part instinct, raw flight.

Hello, she wanted to say to him. I am your wife. I am a woman. I am this animal. I have become everything. I am new and also ancient. I have been ashamed but will be no more.

Your new project, he said, then laughed. This dog stuff. The midnight excursions. I get it.

Yes, she said, then plummeted down deep into a blank, open space inside her, where she stared at the long and forever sky. She was trying to remember something. It was so far away. Her husband waited. The dark wound around them. It shifted and clicked. Above them, animals jumped between branches and the leaves bounced heavily.

Yes, she said a moment later. She looked at her husband as if she had only just met him. Yes, with dogs. A project.

She left the bunny scraps in the dirt and crawled to him, then crouched and growled and pawed at the ground. She lunged to his right and took off, raced the perimeter of the lawn to feel the power of her body, to feel the cooling night air against her skin and in her hair. She leapt over the short fence and rolled in the overgrown grass of their neighbor's lawn, scratching every last spot on her back and haunches, her legs, before meandering over to a fringe of wildflowers, to pee on them.

She was aware of her husband as a dark spot in the dark lawn and ran back to him, hopping the fence again in one elegant movement, then jumping onto him, placing her hands on his shoulders and nuzzling the dirt and dank and dog of herself into his neck, and knocking him down to lick his face, his neck, his tummy, sniff his crotch deeply, then take the hem of his boxer shorts in her teeth and pull.

He laughed. He laughed and laughed and laughed, and soon they were both dogs and they were in love.

Later, in the shower, her husband placed his hands on her scratched shoulders, looked into her eyes.

Your best work, he said, something in his face softer and broken. An astonishment, maybe. A person he hadn't yet shown her, though they'd been together over a decade. In that face she could see that he loved her and was in awe of her, of what she had made. That he had never meant for her career to be quashed. That he had always wanted for her happiness, and art, and that now he saw all she had become and saw it was hers, saw that she existed as a creative force independent of him or their son but also in control of them. That he would do for her whatever he could, because of his love and devotion, his near-childlike adoration of her, which had gotten lost in the ho-hum of every day after day for years and years.

The mothers came in groups of twos and threes. They were dressed in clothes reserved for nights away from small sticky hands: a flowy silk blouse, their most expensive handbag, an off-the-shoulder sexy thing, white white pants. They each looked lovely, these mothers, and had about them an air of ease.

It was the end of a season, with a universe of cicadas in full voice, inspiring in each mother that long, sad pull that arrives when the air touches their arms warmly, then departs with a chill, when disheveled schoolchildren wander the sidewalks each mid-afternoon and the melancholic, hazy weight of all the years past arrives at once, the *what ifs* and *should have beens,* the memories of beautiful, shirtless boys at the lake and a wet beach towel against the cheek, the high white sun, a cold, green grape bursting sweet in the mouth. Yes, it was the perfect time, the perfect night, for feeling and for drinking and for forgetting.

They came to the house of Nightbitch not knowing precisely why, only that there would be wine. Jen was the *event ambassador,* as she dubbed herself, authoring the Evite they all received and talking incessantly about how *groundbreaking* and *totally avant-garde* the event would be. These were the Book Mommies—every last one of them—the herbal-remedy crew, those committed to leggings and essential oils. Yes, perhaps it was nearly all the most ardent mommies in town, for a great horde of women arrived that night, much to Jen's great pleasure. She stood by the rickety archway overgrown with honeysuckle that led to the backyard, clipboard in hand, wearing a form-fitting suit from her old PR days. How easily the silky lining slid over her curves! How efficient and capable she felt within its beautifully tailored confines!

Hi. Hello. Welcome, she said as each mother filed past. Help yourself to refreshments, please, she directed with a newfound solemnity, a professionalism that had been absent from her unrestrained herb presentations, for this was hers, hers and Nightbitch's, whom she would not let down. In this she had a deep investment, a desire to build something all her own, so they could both succeed and flourish.

Jen took special note when Nightbitch's old grad-school friends arrived, the working mother and the videographer, for she knew that Nightbitch would want them to have the very best seats.

All the mothers were tickled to find that music lofted from the open French doors on the back of the house, and that a table set up on the back patio, covered in a white cotton cloth embroidered with the sweetest of little blossoms, held bottles of chilled rosé and Pinot Grigio and little plastic cups stacked in straight towers.

There were crystal bowls heaped with nuts, and entire chocolate bars nested in a basket, freshly cut vegetables for those who were so inclined, sparkling waters. There was an irresistible bowl of fat, glistening blueberries that seemed to replenish itself magically, no matter how many handfuls the mothers took. Another basket held still-warm baked goods, all the carb-rich indulgences the good mothers refrained from, trying to get that post-baby weight off, trying to slim those thighs and calm that muffin top, but perhaps tonight, just one.

They all sat in the backyard, in three rows of white folding chairs arranged in lines with an aisle running down the center. Why, it almost looked matrimonial, these chairs and

the hors d'oeuvre table and the little wooden stage arranged
at front. Yet the tiny stage would not host a wedding, No,
indeed. The mothers whispered in hushed tones, hands over
mouths: Look at that, what *is* it? It couldn't be. But it was,
at the center of the platform, a thick red steak, raw, covered with a glass bell jar. The mothers sat and tittered and
drank and laughed and whispered. They looked for Jen, to
inquire as to the details of the performance, yet she was no
longer by the gate and had, it seemed, dematerialized into
the growing dusk. How odd, they murmured, sipping wine.
They theorized this or that about what was or wasn't going
on. And isn't it rude that the performance hasn't yet begun,
whatever it is? How odd—I mean, do you even know who the
performer is? I can't really place her, but I don't care. At least
there's wine. And then laughing and sighing, and I'm tired,
and I got a sitter for this? Seriously, what the fuck? But then
a syncopated thud wafted through the open French doors—
I hear the drums echoing tonight, the man sang—and the mood
changed entirely to one of ultimate relaxation. One of the
mothers closed her eyes and sang along quietly, and another
mom leaned back too far in her chair and toppled over, and
they all started laughing—cackling, really—as they righted
the drunken mother, telling her, Don't worry, and It's your
night, and Of course I'll give you a ride home, and if not
there's always Uber, Do not worry about a thing, How many
nights has Kevin gone out and not given a second thought to
you at home with the kids. *I bless the raaaaaaains,* they all sang
in unison, dancing now in the sparkling dusk, one mother
holding her glass of Pinot aloft and singing off key, another
duo swaying cheek to cheek, like lovebirds.

After the song, they talked and talked and talked until it
was late, later than they had planned to stay, and the moon
was up. They had lost track even of their hostess, where
she was and why she hadn't yet appeared to greet them;

perhaps she was among them right now, one particularly drunken mother suggested.

Perhaps *you* are the hostess, she said, jabbing at one woman's chest, and you're just playing some sort of trick! By then the music had evolved to something low and throbbing, jazz but not jazz, darker and heavier than that.

It was then the creature appeared, what some would describe as a *dog-type thing* or *kind of a small bear* or *a werewolf? I don't know what the fuck it was.*

It moved through the aisles carefully, slowly, and none of the mothers cringed or pulled back as you might expect. No, none of them reacted as we might surmise an ordinary mother would react. The working mother and the videographer leaned in, straining to see it as it came toward the stage.

They all watched. They were drunk and brazen and horny and rude, but they were also all quiet—reverent, even. They were perhaps the best mothers they had ever been.

Queen, one of the mothers murmured as the beast strode past her.

Another, deeply moved, fell to her knees, then crawled behind the animal. Another. Another. A few of the less hale mothers grew frightened and uncomfortable and worried whether their rabies boosters were up-to-date and had to leave.

Good riddance, the other mothers said.

This is some sort of cult, one said, and another replied, I just listened to a podcast about stuff like this. And another one: I am so drunk, oh my god. But still they stayed.

The ones who stayed . . . they stayed because they understood, understood the movement of Nightbitch, the hair riding the peak of her spine, her teeth bared against the moonlight, each movement made of power and darkness and anger and survival.

This mother, this dog, will *fuck you up,* and the moms knew this and they loved it.

One mother tipped her head back and howled at the moon. Another curled next to a rotting stump and slept.

The others rent their vestments from their bodies, and in the cool splash of moonlight watched as the dog, this Nightbitch, slunk onto the wooden stage. A spotlight that had been shining since they arrived, originating from an upstairs window, lit the platform, and the creature snarled and snapped. She pushed the bell jar from its place, smashing it, then hungrily devoured the steak laid out for her. It took quite some time for her to eat, but they all sat patiently, transfixed, and watched and watched.

Silence. She turned her eyes to the mothers, blood smeared over her face, her cheeks and chin, her eyes alight with what? With madness? Power? Ecstatic knowing? Feral femininity?

One mother screamed and broke the spell, and then another mother yelped, and it was done: whatever balance had been reached was now horribly off kilter. The animal lunged from the stage into the fray of drunk and naked mothers, and they screamed and ran from the backyard to their dark cars lining the street. Only the working mother and the videographer remained in their seats, speechless, awestruck, crying softly from the sheer drama of it—the sheer, magnificent artistic drama—and holding one another's soft hands.

My clothes! one mother said.

My keys! another lamented.

Fuck! yet another mother spat.

Nightbitch chased each and every last one until they were gone, off to catch Ubers en masse and try to joke away their nakedness, and then grabbed in her maw a cupcake from the dainty table, devoured it, disappeared into the underbrush of the neighbor's overgrown backyard to find a small, beating heart and stop it.

―――

WHEN NIGHTBITCH'S SON HAD been born, what most surprised her was that she had not recognized him. She had thought for sure that the boy would look like someone she knew by heart, but he had an angry red face and a wide nose and a mouth like an old man's. It had taken years for him to age into her son, the one she now knew. When she looked at him now, she often thought, Oh, there you are. Yes, I recognize you, for he looked like her and like her husband as well, but then again, in certain moments he was precisely her father, and then, in turn, precisely her father-in-law.

In the very deepest moments of it, she could not tell herself apart from her son who was so evidently a part of her, physically, that she could not shake the vertigo that overcame her at times, this feeling of sameness paired.

She considered how one day she might be called upon to care for her parents, who, still in wonderful health in their seventies, would certainly at some point make a turn for the worse. She imagined them living in the guest room and, each morning, emerging skinny and rumple-haired, still sleepy, sitting down for breakfast next to her son for pancakes and vitamins. They would nap like infants in the morning and afternoon. Perhaps, near the end, she would need to bathe and change them. And though this would certainly be a burden, there was, it seemed, a place of great love that had opened in her heart, which looked on such tasks with gratitude and reverence when done by choice rather than by inertia. To cleanse her mother's back lovingly with a warm cloth. To suds her father's thin hair. It would be an honor to nurse them, for they were parts of her.

This must be what it means to be an animal, to look at another and say, I am so much that other thing that we are part of one another. Here is my skin. Here yours. Beneath the moon, we pile inside the warm cave, becoming one creature to save our warmth. We breathe together and dream together. This is how it has always been and how it will continue to be. We keep each other alive through an unbroken lineage of togetherness.

WANDA WHITE IS NOT a person. Wanda White is a place at which a person finally arrives.

Nightbitch, this mother, stands behind the heavy velvet curtain, in darkness, smelling her own rosy musk. Yes, she is here, at Wanda White, in anticipatory ecstasy, just before she ascends to whatever is beyond that darkness and that stage—invincibility or air, something.

The squeak and pull of the curtain ropes. A darkness, and then a small light. She smells every single person in the room.

There, on a stage, in the dark. A pelt of hair bristles down her back. She turns her closed eyes toward the ceiling and inhales deeply. The hairs on her face move gently within an unseen draft.

Here she stands, naked. Her hair hangs in her eyes and over her face. Her open palms face the audience.

She begins this performance as she has begun every performance, by opening the space within her chest, then opening her mouth, opening a single perfect channel between heart and voice and letting out a long, high howl that echoes throughout the room.

Someone gasps as the lights rise a bit more. She opens her eyes but sees no one. She falls to her hands, then lopes across the stage. She turns to snarl at the audience. Someone laughs. Someone stifles a scream.

Music begins to soar in the background, as if from a long-forgotten childhood dream, or nightmare. Violins swell. The trumpets herald the beginning of something, though what precisely the audience cannot yet be sure. A tympani thuds, *ba-bum, ba-bum, ba-bum.* On a stage somewhere far away, a soprano presses her palms to her chest and opens her mouth to release a long river of song, winding and glorious, full of grief, full of love. She sings in German, or a language that sounds like German, it's hard to tell, what is that she's saying? The audience imagines this singing woman, her heaving breast, her ropes of braided hair. They imagine her, most peculiarly, on a dark lawn, unspooling her song in the night. She is barefoot and the supple grass threads her toes. She sings beneath a tree with wide branches in which hens roost. She wears a simple cotton farm dress. Each and every person sees this same woman in their mind's eye, and each and every person wonders who she is, what her song means, marvels at the chickens in the trees. This is just the first of many tricks of Nightbitch's performance.

Nightbitch paces on the stage, the music surges in the background, the audience grows uneasy. But of course what makes them the most uneasy is the artist herself. She is what they have come to see. She is why they have handed over their hard-earned dollars, to witness such a spectacle, because, well, what *is* it, exactly? Is this real? Or is it all a ruse? And what exactly is even in question? Surely this woman exists, but what about her hair? One could imagine reasonably that the hair on her head is her very own, but what of the hair on her back? Her arms? Her feet?

Most unsettling is the way that Nightbitch moves, on all fours, with animal fluidity. It is the sort of thing they have only ever seen before in horror movies or, if they are not horror fans, in their most distant nightmares. How does a person move the way this woman does? Surely she must be trained in dance or some pioneering modern movement practice? Certainly she must have practiced for hours to get the movement just right, this carnal pacing, this instinctual awareness, the way she tips her head to smell the air, the way she lopes forward toward the audience, then spins with lightness and bounds back into the shadows?

After the performance, the audience convenes around the front doors of the theater, some saying that the bunnies that arrived onstage soon after the music began had most certainly hopped from the ink-black shadows of the wings, easing their way into the light to stare and twitch softly. They all agree that certainly this had not been some enchantment, that there must be a reasonable explanation for such bunnies, since none of them are yet ready to embrace what, deep down, they feel was very true: that the bunnies had *arrived* onstage, and not in any customary way. Even more terrifying is what the audience would ponder later, each one of them tucked in their beds: but from where had the animals *come*? This is what bothered them so. Were they real creatures, the same kind one might come upon on a safe and leisurely hike in the woods? And were there now bunnies missing from the woods somewhere, bunnies that had just been nibbling on flowers but then popped out of existence in the woods and into existence there on the stage? And if they hadn't been transported *from* a place, then what *were* they? What were they made of? And who had made them? These questions made each and every audience member want to weep, but instead they wandered off into uneasy sleeps, where they stayed all night.

Yes, the bunnies were the inciting incident in Night-bitch's performance. All of the reviews had reported as much, though none had mentioned the barefooted soprano beneath the tree, the *collective vision,* we might call it, the entire audience had. This was considered a spoiler, something the audience had to experience in the moment.

And so, the bunnies arrive onstage, first one, then a hand-ful, then a dozen. Some cower near the woodsy backdrop.

Others threaten to jump right into the audience, so close are they to the front edge. Nightbitch, meanwhile, waits, as still as the darkness around her. You can see each muscle as it moves, see her tenseness, see her waiting inscribed on her body.

Small piles of bones, glinting with gold, dot the dark stage. Nightbitch stands in the center and raises her open hands at her sides. Slowly, as the music fades and a dull, low note throbs into the theater, she raises her palms as if conducting the slowest and most silent orchestra ever imagined. As her hands float up, up, and then a bit higher still, the piles of bones shift and glimmer, and the gold plating catches the spotlight and reflects it back in a million brilliant shards. The bunnies hop offstage in fear as the bones rise, as if on strings, as if they are some sort of otherworldly zombie marionettes, though the audience can see no strings or other trickery, no matter how intently they squint, no matter how carefully they search. The bones take on the shapes of small animals, though not an ordinary sort. This one, a type of coyote with long ear bones reminiscent of prairie rabbits. Another, what seems a deer, but with a tiny catlike head. Yet another, with the hind legs of a rabbit and a set of the tiniest antlers, antlers that in no way could have been found in nature. Yet there is still a natural quality to the bone animals, the audience will report. A logical quality, even. They make sense within the world of Nightbitch, their small, delicate movements, their heads that twitch back and forth, the small careful steps they take, the ways in which they tumble to the black floor and then move back into alignment, reconstituting themselves as if through the power of a god.

It is then that Nightbitch and the bone animals perform an uncanny choreography—"an enchanted hunt," the critics call it—as Nightbitch by turns moves in time with and then in hunt of the gilded skeletons, all to the throb of the low, dark music. The audience will report they could have watched the performance endlessly, so rapt were they by the animal movements of the woman and the bones—*which seem to float effortlessly about the stage all on their own, how did she do it?*—so stupefied were they by the spectacle, so perplexed by what they were seeing, unable to separate reality from artistry.

Yet they all, that night, waited for what came next, for of course they had heard what was to happen by that point. The show had now been written about and reported on, critiqued and analyzed and condemned and looked at from every angle possible by critics and writers and animal-rights activists and the public at large. And though it was indeed a bit gauche to identify Nightbitch simply for her real-time slaughter of bunnies onstage, that is indeed what she was best known for, though it should be noted that there were so many other aspects of the performance far more interesting and peculiar.

And so, after her dance with the bones, she stalks the bunnies, now hidden in the shadows, the hunt itself strangely lovely, intoxicating, even the moment she pounces and takes a creature in her mouth and shakes and shakes it until it hangs limp in her mouth. The theater now is quiet, dead quiet, and she lays the unmoving animal on the stage and then looks at the audience. She growls, and they grow uneasy. It seems she is now stalking them. A few folks at the back rise slowly and edge from the room. A moment of stillness, and then pandemonium breaks out as Nightbitch springs from the stage and the audience members burst from their seats to scream and scatter.

Some audience members will report that it was then that they were chased into an inexplicable forest area, so thick with leaves and vines that it was hard to decipher whether this was something the artist herself had constructed or in fact a space-time anomaly that had emerged just for the performance, only to disappear after that night. During the unspecified event, as it came to be known, they came upon a den of WereMothers, who took them in and gave them delicious soup. Others will report that, during the unspecified event, they encountered marvelous bird women with extravagantly feathered wings who taught them how to fly, and it was in this way that they exited the theater. Still others will speak of women who appeared and disappeared at will during their unspecified event, goddess-type apparitions who conjured in viewers the most profound feeling of goodwill and unity, to the point where they wept in their presence and fell at their feet.

The collective mania and alleged hallucinations commonly experienced at the show were studied at length by psychiatrists, who concluded there must have been a large-scale drugging—after all, each audience member was given a small packet of pills, labeled Howl, upon entering the theater, as well as a little paper cup of water, and *encouraged strongly* to quickly swallow them down so as to *challenge notions of wellness and perception* in addition to experiencing *the most immersive effects of the performance.* Or perhaps the drugs had been administered surreptitiously, pumped through the vents via the heating and cooling systems at each venue. Who could really say? If not drugged, the audience must, then, have been hypnotized, the psychiatrists reasoned, and led into an imagining by the artist, though Nightbitch reported she had not studied hypnosis, nor was she a licensed practitioner. If they had been hypnotized, she said, it was inadvertent, and a testament to the mesmerizing nature of the art itself.

"The intoxicating effect of the show only underscores Nightbitch's artistry," Jen offered in an official statement to the media to counter the doubters and naysayers, to respond to those who would say of the show that it was nothing more than "druggie left-wing poppycock," not "real art," nor "serious art," but, rather, a "common sideshow" meant to titillate and wow the dumb masses. "The effects experienced at the end of the show represent the culmination of over two decades of rigorous artistic practice. The sometimes extreme experiences that audience members have at Nightbitch's show only underscore the heightened level at which this artist is working and the transformative capacities of art."

And in response to those who called her show "needlessly brutal" and "the worst of performance art" and "an abomination that conjures the basest element of humanity and puts it on exhibit for all to see," Nightbitch herself explained that her work was meant to underscore the brutality of motherhood, how a child's first act is violence against the woman who created it. Yet the mother loves the child with the most powerful love known in this universe.

This thing comes from us, she would explain in interviews. It rips its way out of us, literally tears us in two, in a wash of great pain and blood and shit and piss. If the child does not enter into the world this way, then it is cut from us with a knife. The child is removed, and our organs are taken out as well, before being sewn back inside. It is perhaps the most violent experience a human can have aside from death itself. And this performance is meant to underscore the brutality and power and darkness of motherhood, for modern motherhood has been neutered and sanitized. We are at base animals, and to deny us either our animal nature or our dignity as humans is a crime against existence. Womanhood and motherhood are perhaps the most potent forces in human society, which of course men have been hasty to quash, for they are right to fear these forces.

Her most devout fans wear pins that ask WHERE DO YOU GO AT NIGHT? with the image of a ferocious dog, mouth open, about to attack. The pins and other merchandise are the work of Jen, who has proved herself to be a PR genius, creating the most dazzling of campaigns, with bunnies showing up in high-profile and peculiar locales, mysterious social-media blitzes, a masterfully concocted and exquisitely executed "mystery" her crowning professional achievement. Sales of the once-out-of-print *A Field Guide to Magical Women* skyrocket, though no one, absolutely no one, can track down Wanda White. When researched by reporters, the University of Sacramento proves to be a short-lived institution no longer in operation and White herself a persona which exists only as an online profile at a defunct school.

Those few audience members at the theater who manage neither to panic nor to flee, who harbor a most resilient and imperturbable disposition—an *engineer's evenness*, one might say—these folks bear witness to the very end of the show, Nightbitch there onstage, with a small boy—her son—to whom she delivers the limp body of the bunny, for him to sniff and then caress. As the curtains creep closed, this is what those few brave folks see: a feral woman and her offspring with the still-warm body of a rabbit in his hands. They will report that the duo emanated a beauty they had not seen before, despite the protestations of some that exposing a child to such a thing was abuse.

No, those who had seen it would argue.

Here was a woman who now knew that life unfolded through mystery and metaphor, without explanation, who looked upon her perfect son in front of her, a person she had made with her strongest magic, standing right there in a blinding spotlight as if he weren't a miracle, as if he weren't the most impossible thing in the entire world.

ACKNOWLEDGMENTS

Thank you to my agent, Monika Woods, for your stead-
fast guidance, as well as to Margo Shickmanter for your
superb editorial stewardship. Thank you to the entire team
at Doubleday—Tricia Cave, Lauren Weber, Lorraine Hyland,
Victoria Pearson, Maria Carella, and Emily Mahon—for all
the care and work you put into this book. Thank you to my
smart and generous friends and readers, in particular Sarah
Shrader, Kerry Howley, Nina Lohman, Alisha Jeddeloh, Jenny
Colville, Helen Rubinstein, Sarah Viren, Ariel Lewiton, Kris-
ten Radtke, Zaina Arafat, Lauren Haldeman, and Ingrid
Yoder. Thank you to the Iowa Arts Council for financial and
professional support. Thank you to Jami Attenberg for your
#1000wordsofsummer, which is how this book got drafted.
Thank you to Lee Running for your artistic genius and inspiration for this book. Thank you to Melanie Bishop, whose
mentorship is the reason I'm a writer. Thank you to Mark
Polanzak for your decades-long camaraderie and collabora-
tion. Thank you to Paula and Tom Michel for all the hours of
child-care. Thank you to Linda and Wayne Yoder for encouraging me to follow my own path. Thank you to Seth for being
my biggest fan even on my worst days. And thank you to my
one and only Coco, who transformed me. I love you.